LYNN MONTAGANO

I'm a former TV news writer who took the plunge and finally wrote a novel. I know, right? Insanity. Prior to jumping into novel writing, I spent the majority of my career working in radio and television as a promotions director, writer and associate producer. I love any job that is challenging and creative. I grew up in a small town in Rhode Island before spreading my wings to discover this great, big world. Traveling, like writing, has become a necessary part of my life. My favorite place is and always will be London. It's my home away from home. For now, I'm a displaced New Englander hanging my hat in Northern California. If you can see me through the fog, wave hello.

Unravel Me

LYNN MONTAGANO

A division of HarperCollins*Publishers*
www.harpercollins.co.uk

HarperImpulse an imprint of
HarperCollins*Publishers* Ltd
77–85 Fulham Palace Road
Hammersmith, London W6 8JB

www.harpercollins.co.uk

A Paperback Original 2014

First published in Great Britain in ebook format by HarperImpulse 2014

A catalogue record for this book is
available from the British Library

ISBN: 978-0-00-810500-6

Automatically produced by Atomik ePublisher from Easypress

*For the girls who are my real life Lia and Stephanie;
Bethany, Crissy, Deana, Kelly, Jenny, Renee and
Tamara.*

*Deana and Renee - thanks for always knowing what
group we're in and where my comb is. I hope you
make it off the island soon.*

*Kelly, Jenny and Tamara - even though we're scat-
tered around the country, I couldn't have asked for
a better, more fabulous group of ladies to be lucky
enough to call my longtime friends. Heart you guys!
Can we all be in one state at the same time someday
soon?!*

*Crissy - thanks for being my partner in crime and
joining me on many, many adventures through
Orlando, Scotland and England.*

*Bethany - My sister from another mister. Thanks for
all the pep talks, laughter and crazy poses on roller
coasters.*

CHAPTER ONE

The newsroom was in a frenzy. A meth lab had exploded in one of the motels along US 192 westbound. Nobody was hurt but most of the rooms had to be evacuated. I was in the middle of typing the reporter's package intro, ignoring the steady beeping of my cell phone. It was Stephanie. She'd been texting me all day, presumably to continue her barrage of insults.

"Did the keyboard do something to piss you off?"

I stopped pounding my fingers against the keys and looked up, meeting the bright, almond eyes of my co-worker and cubemate, Sydney Makeeda.

"Didn't even realize I was doing it, Syd."

She laughed. "I can tell. I thought your hand was going to smash through the desk. Everything okay?"

"For a Tuesday? Mostly."

"How's that delicious British boyfriend of yours?"

I couldn't help but smile. Alastair Holden always had that effect on me. "He's good. He flew back to Glasgow though. I guess they needed him at headquarters."

She let out a low whistle. "Hot, English and the head of a media company. Can you and I trade lives for, like, ten minutes? Don't tell Ray."

"Sydney!" I laughed.

"Will he be back soon? I can tell you miss him like crazy."

"I hope so."

Mindful not to abuse the keys anymore, I finished typing the intro and sent a message to my executive producer, Jeanie, so she could take a look. An alert from the Associated Press dinged on everyone's computer like a warped version of Carole of the Bells. Amid the chaos, my desk phone rang.

"Lia Meyers," I answered a little more haughtily than normal.

"I want to offer you an exclusive interview."

The low voice with a slight rasp made me sit up straight.

Jesus.

"I'm not interested, Nathan," I grumbled, pissed off that my ex-boyfriend had the balls to call me at work. Or at all.

"You should be." His smugness seeped through the phone. "I've considered every station in Orlando but want to give it to you."

Stretching back in my seat, I took a deep breath. Securing an interview with him would rank highly with my news director. *Bruce loves this exclusive shit, especially when it involves a U.S. senator's son who also happens to be an influential businessman.*

"What's it about?"

"Still as inquisitive as ever," he chuckled.

If I could have reached through the phone and torn out his vocal cords I would have done.

"It's a perfectly normal question to ask. What is it?"

"Some damaging information has come to light about a prominent figure. That's all I can say right now without giving too much away."

I squirmed in the chair. His pompous attitude irked me.

"Alright," I said. "How do you want to do this?"

"Have dinner with me tonight and we'll discuss the details."

I drummed my fingers on the desk. "There's always an underlying scheme with you, isn't there?"

He laughed. "Come on, Sparkle. It's a business meeting. My treat, of course."

"We don't need to have dinner to finalize an interview. We can hash it out right now on the phone."

"No, we can't." His tone was clipped. "I have a conference call that started five minutes ago. Felicia will email you with the restaurant information. I'll see you at eight."

He killed the call before I had a chance to react. Dinner with him? My skin crawled. I didn't want to be in the same city as him, let alone share a table at a restaurant. A notification appeared in my inbox. Grimacing, I read the message from his assistant. He'd made reservations at Norman's in the Ritz. *Our restaurant.* Rubbing my temples I stood up and walked to Bruce Singleton's office.

"Lia. I was just going to call you." My news director hunched over his computer, squinting at the screen. All the frizzy mad scientist hair on his head bobbed as he nodded at an invisible request. "Sit, sit."

"I've heard from Nathan Greyson." I didn't wait for Bruce to initiate whatever it was he wanted. "He says he'll give us an exclusive interview about something. Did you reach out to his public relations team recently?"

"No. Did he tell you what it was about?" Bruce eyed me curiously.

My mind raced. *What does he want?*

"Something about information coming to light involving a prominent figure. I'm going to meet, um, call him back later. As soon as I know anything more, I'll fill you in."

We chatted for a few minutes about the evening show before I went back to my desk. I had some down time before the broadcast went live and decided to call Stephanie.

"Hey," she answered after the first ring.

"Hi."

The awkward pause between us made me cringe.

"What are you doing tonight?" She broke the silence first. I slumped in my chair.

"I'm supposed to have dinner with Nathan, believe it or not."

"Are you shitting me? Why?"

"He wants to give us some exclusive interview about something," I sighed.

"So where does the dinner come in all this?"

"You know him. There's always an ulterior motive."

"Are you going?"

"I don't know."

"What do you mean you don't know? You're not going. Simple as that."

I tapped my fingernails on the desk. "If it were just him asking me to dinner, obviously I wouldn't go. But this is—"

"Lia, he's an asshole. If he wants to give you guys an interview you can talk to him on the phone about it. He knows that. You know that. Come on."

I'd just about had it with Stephanie's attitude in recent days so her proclamations, although correct, pissed me off. *I'm not a helpless animal.*

"Look, I appreciate your concern or whatever but I'm going. End of story."

"Do you need me to book a table at the same restaurant in case he tries something?"

"No. Your covert operations aren't necessary but thanks."

Silence. Again. My eye twitched.

"Did Alastair go back to Glasgow?"

"Yeah. He left this morning."

"That was quick," she muttered. "How long was he here? Two weeks?"

"Yep."

"Well, be careful," she said, sounding grim. "I still don't trust him."

"Let's not start this again, okay?"

"I can't help it, Lia. It's like you're ignoring everything that happened at the estate."

"We're working through all that," I said, my jaw tight.

"Right. I forgot. He collared you with a diamond necklace and all of a sudden he's Prince Charming."

"He didn't collar me."

"Whatever. He's manipulating you. He's using your feelings for him to control you."

I played with the diamond-encrusted 'A' hanging from my neck. "And you know this how? You barely acknowledged him when he was here."

"I hear things. His reputation isn't the greatest when it comes to women."

"You hear things. From who? Darren?"

"No." She paused. "Cassie."

I rolled my eyes. Cassie Zanor was the graphic design manager at the company that recently hired my best friend, Stephanie. They happened to be located in Glasgow and did most of the marketing campaigns for Alastair's company. For some reason, Stephanie had been taking everything this girl said as gospel.

"She doesn't know him," I replied smoothly. "Neither do you."

"How well *do* you know him, Lia?" she shot back. "From what I've heard, he's a master at concealing his motives. He takes what he wants and disposes of it when he's had enough. Look how easily he pushed you aside in England. You think he won't do that again?"

My heart rate increased making the blood pound in my ears. Stephanie always knew how to play on my deepest fears with precision. Taking a few cleansing breaths, I stamped down my burgeoning anger.

"I appreciate your concern but you have to stop. I'm not doing this while I'm at work."

The message line on the rundown beeped. *One body found at the scene. Not explosion related.* Cradling the phone against my shoulder, I typed a quick reply to Tyler's message asking him to send more information when he talked to the police.

"You sound busy. Give me a call later."

"Yeah. There's a breaking story. Bye." Annoyed, I slammed the phone down and tried to focus on the rest of the show.

* * *

I sat at the impeccably set table in the restaurant, dreading Nathan's arrival. I hadn't seen him since he thought letting himself into my apartment was a smart way to win back my affections. I shivered. Not even the soothing shades of ivory and yellows calmed me. Of course he'd arranged it so we were sitting at *our* table by the picture window. Glancing around the cozy, circular dining room I watched other patrons enjoy their meals, drinking with ease and engaging in relaxed conversation. I sipped my Prosecco, hoping it would take the edge off.

A low hum of chatter vibrated through the room. Looking up, I saw Nathan striding toward the table. All eyes were on him. His tall, powerful body was complimented by a stunning double-breasted gray suit which had been paired with a sapphire tie to match his eyes. He looked every bit the privileged son of a U.S. Senator. *Too bad he's such a possessive, controlling asshole.*

"Lia." His smile spread easily. Unbuttoning his jacket, he sat across from me. "Thank you for agreeing to see me."

"Like I had a choice," I muttered.

"You always have a choice," he said softly. I shot him a skeptical glance. I knew this act far too well.

"What do you want? I'd rather not spend my entire night here."

"Relax. Have some more wine. This won't take long but I'd prefer not to jump right into business." Something in his tone made my hair stand on end.

He waved the server over and ordered a bottle of champagne, along with oysters and shrimp ceviche. My guard sprang up, rigid and unyielding. He'd ordered my favorite appetizers. *What's going on?*

"How's married life treating your sister?" He ran a hand through his short, sandy blond hair.

6

"Dayna's fine," I snapped. "What do you want?"

Smoothing down his tie, he leaned forward. The unflinching gaze he locked on me froze my blood. I sipped my sparkling wine, waiting for his response.

"I want to apologize. For everything. The fight when you thought you were pregnant. The Black and White Ball. Waiting in your apartment. I realize that I wasn't the best version of myself when we were together. You deserved better from me."

Dumbfounded, I stared at him. This wasn't the first time he'd apologized. I had a mental rolodex of remorseful statements he'd professed over the past two years. Something about this one unnerved me. Sincerity reflected deeply in his eyes. Clutching the cloth napkin on my lap, I wet my lips. My instincts remained on high alert.

"I'm going to take that at face value and say thank you," I said slowly. "Why are you saying this now?"

Settling back into his chair, he shrugged. His eyes coasted over the diamond necklace resting on my neck.

"Holden give you that?"

I stiffened. "Yes."

He smirked. "A bit understated for a media mogul, no?"

"Some people don't have a need to flaunt their wealth. You should try it."

"Don't underestimate him, Lia. He's worth billions and controls Britain's top media enterprise. Now that they're buying up stations here, he's going to be more conscious of who he allows into his inner circle. He may not be flashing his cash with cars and jewelry but he is in other ways. If you don't believe it, you're not paying close enough attention."

The palms of my hands ached from my nails digging into the skin.

"I'm not telling you this to hurt you or start a fight," he continued. "I know his type. The Holden family name rests upon his decisions now. It's a huge burden. One false step and the empire goes down the drain."

Nausea rolled through my stomach as the server arrived and placed our appetizers on the table. Nathan leisurely reached for an oyster, enjoying it without a care in the world. I refused to let myself become consumed with his words.

"You don't know anything about him."

"Did you tell him where I worked and where I'd be on the day he showed up unannounced?"

A harsh breath pushed out of my mouth.

"Exactly," he stated. "That Brit has just as many, if not more, resources than I do."

The annoying, self-gratifying grin on his face drove me mad. *Bastard.*

"Stalking is your territory, not his. Don't lump him into the same low-life category as you just because he sucker punched you."

I'd defend Alastair until I took my last breath. An overwhelming emptiness filled me. I missed him. I wanted him here, not thousands of miles away.

"He's lucky I'm not a petty man. I could have reported him for aggravated assault."

Nathan's voice clung to me like barbed wire. His dark blue irises slid over my face. Reaching across the table, he lifted my hand. His touch made me cringe but I couldn't make a move. Too many eyes casually watched us and if I made it look like there was about to be an 'event' they'd whip out their smartphones without hesitation.

"You know how this works, Sparkle. I vetted you long before asking you on our first date. I didn't do it because I got off on having that kind of power. I did it to protect my family name."

"So, the stalking and the jealousy and the possessiveness were an added bonus?"

Narrowing his eyes slightly, Nathan squeezed my hand. "Do you have any idea how rare and special you are? A woman like you doesn't come around more than once in a man's life. I did what I had to do to keep you in mine."

"And look how that ended," I snickered.

Pain and regret ravaged his face. I was so used to Alastair's stony façade I'd forgotten how expressive Nathan could be. A twinge of guilt spread through me conflicting wildly with the general feeling of disgust I'd had since he called me. This whole dinner meeting felt strange, more like an act of contrition than business. But why? What did Nathan have to gain by being so forthcoming with me? An image of him punching the wall inches away from my head hijacked my mind. A sliver of terror streaked through me. I pulled my hand away from him. Contrite or not, he could be dangerous when he wanted. Reaching for the ceviche, I pushed aside my anxiety.

"So what's this exclusive story you have?"

He grinned. "Business already? We haven't ordered our main dishes yet. Patience. I'll tell you."

"You'll tell me now or this dinner ends. I've spent more than enough time listening to your bullshit."

"I realize you're angry," he murmured. "I thought this could be the beginning of a healing process. For both of us."

"What's in it for you?" My brain was fried. I knocked back the rest of the Prosecco in one gulp.

"Your trust." He grasped my hand again.

His admission left me speechless. I couldn't wrap my mind around this version of the man who'd made my life a living hell for two years. Well, not two whole years. He was rather charming and fun in the beginning. *Oh my God, STOP IT.* I was so confused. I wanted to believe he was truly sorry. I didn't know why, exactly. Sitting with him, studying his expressions and demeanor, I had no reason to doubt the validity of anything he'd said. I wished I knew his motive. He always had one.

"Excuse me, Mr. Greyson?"

A petite, brunette woman stood next to our table. Nathan eyed her with mild interest. I snapped my hand away, aware our uninvited guest had seen it.

"Sorry to interrupt your dinner. I'm Rachel Jameson with—"

"I know who you are," he cut her off. "Feel free to call my public relations department if you're looking for an interview."

"Oh, actually, that's not why I'm here." Rachel smiled widely, unaffected by Nathan's curt manner. "I wanted to talk to your date." She fixed an inquisitive stare on me, her chocolate eyes gleaming.

I knew who she was, too; a blogger for Orlando's society pages. Dressed to kill in a fitted orchid maxi dress, she exuded the unflustered confidence a tabloid reporter needed to possess. Rachel was well known around the city and had stirred the pot on numerous occasions with her exposés. More succinctly put, she'd base most of her writings on assumption rather than fact.

"What do you want to talk to me about?" I tried to employ an impassive expression. Not sure if I succeeded. She'd referred to me as Nathan's 'date' for a reaction. I wasn't about to give her the satisfaction.

"I don't want to intrude on your evening, Miss Meyers. Give me a call when you're not busy." Passing me her business card, she flashed a cunning smile. "Enjoy the rest of your date."

I was beyond suspicious. She'd referred to this dinner as a 'date' twice. I broke out into a cold sweat. Nathan's cell phone rang loudly, rattling my already shaky nerves. Excusing himself, he left the table to take the call.

Reaching for my own phone, an unsettled feeling crept into my bones. I scrolled through a few emails. There wasn't anything from Alastair. It was late in Glasgow. He was probably asleep, although he'd been known to work well into the night. I sent him a quick text.

8:50pm Miss you xx

8:51pm Ditto, love x

My heart ached to be near him. What I wouldn't give to go

home and find him sprawled across my mattress.

8:53pm Remember, don't pack anything when you fly here.

8:54pm Nothing?

8:55pm No. I'll have everything you need. And maybe a surprise or two. x

Smiling, I put the phone away. The server came by to take our order but Nathan was still off on his phone call. I ordered yellowtail snapper for myself and a rib-eye steak for him. It was his favorite and I assumed he'd want it anyway. He didn't return to the table until our entrées arrived.

"I'm afraid I have to cut this short. Sorry we didn't get to talk much business." Nathan paid for the meal as promised and escorted me to the valet. "Thanks for dinner, Lia. I'll give you a call next week."

His brusque manner surprised me a bit. *What is it with these guys and their mysterious phone calls?*

"Sure. Whenever you want to tell me what this big exclusive thing is, I'll be waiting." I cast him a cool glance, wondering if there even was a story.

* * *

A large white envelope rested against my door. I eyed it suspiciously before picking it up. My name was written clearly in block letters across the front but there was no address. I turned it to see if there was anything written on the back. Nothing. I turned it over again, noticing how light it was. A cold chill ran down my spine. I unlocked the door and walked inside my apartment.

I couldn't stop my hands from shaking as I opened it. *Oh my God.*

A stack of eight-by-ten photos fell to the floor. Dropping to my knees, I sifted through them. There were photos of me at the grocery store, walking into work and going to the gym. The last one made me shudder. The perfectly framed photo of me standing with Alastair in the private lot at the beach sent me over the edge. I clasped my hands to my mouth and screamed. Trembling, I threw the photos, scattering them across the living room. Yanking my phone out of my bag I dialed the first number that popped into my mind.

"Hello?"

"You son of a bitch. How dare you."

"Lia? What are you tal—"

"Fuck you, Nathan. Don't play innocent with me. Whatever your plan was for tonight just blew up in your face."

Tremors shook every nerve in my body. I paced the room like a caged lion.

"You're upset. What happened?"

"If you think for one minute I'm going to allow this to continue, you are sorely mistaken. I don't care who your father is, I'm getting a restraining order."

Muffled voices filled the background. I strained to hear what they were saying.

"I swear to you. I have no idea what you're talking about. I'm at my parents' house. Let me come over—"

"The photos, Nathan," I shouted. "The envelope of photos that was waiting for me at my door. Who do you have following me this time?"

"Nobody," he answered quietly.

Rage shook me to the core. I hated him. I hated his lies.

"I don't believe you."

A long, exasperated sigh cascaded through the phone. "You're going to have to trust me on this one. I don't have anyone following you. All the things I told you at dinner were true. I want this to be a time for us to heal. Why would I do something like this? I have my faults but I'm not that arrogant."

Tears bullied their way out of my eyes, rolling fast down my cheeks. He sounded so goddam sincere. I couldn't think straight.

"Lia, let me come over. Let me help you."

"No." I ended the call.

CHAPTER TWO

I navigated the streets of downtown Orlando in a fog. The loud blast of a truck's horn jolted my attention. I swerved sharply, avoiding a collision. Sitting at the red light, I shook from fear and anger. By the time I arrived at Stephanie's condo I needed a stiff drink.

She opened the front door as I trudged up the walkway.

"Jesus Christ, Lia." She ran out, grabbing the overnight bag from my hands. "Were you followed here? Are you alright?"

"I don't know."

"Come inside. I already have wine poured."

Smiling a bit, I followed her into the kitchen. The table was set for a romantic dinner for two. Raising my brows, I glanced at my best friend. Her jet-black hair, which she was letting grow out, sat perfectly arranged in a low bun. She looked fresh off the pages of Vogue in her lime green tank dress.

"Am I interrupting something?"

"Um, well." She blushed. "Sorta. But don't worry about it. This is more important."

"You had a date?" I sat down and took a sip of wine. "Stephanie Ann Tempe, are you keeping secrets from me?"

She rolled her eyes, sitting down. "Not really. He's just some guy I met last week. We've gone out a couple times. Nothing to get all excited about."

"Last week? Why didn't you tell me?"

"You were busy with Alastair. I didn't want to intrude."

"For crying out loud. Telling me about a date isn't intruding. Stop being ridiculous."

"It's not important." She waved her hand. "What are you going to do about Nathan?"

I took a long sip from the glass. Dealing with Nathan wasn't my main concern. Telling Alastair about this weighed heavily on my mind.

"I think— I'm not sure if he's the one behind it."

"Are you nuts? This is his dirty work. I have no doubt." Her ice blue eyes flashed with determination and anger. She despised him almost as much as I did.

"That's the thing. It does reek of him but it's too perfectly arranged. I mean, really. Is he cocky enough to invite me to dinner under the false pretense that he has some big juicy gossip about someone only to scare the shit out of me by leaving an envelope filled with pictures at my doorstep? He's an asshole but he's not that twisted."

While Stephanie droned on about Nathan's ability to manipulate various situations, I thought back to the birthday party I went to at Sydney's. I thought I'd seen something flash in the sunlight. *A car windshield? A camera lens?* My head pounded.

"Have you told Alastair yet?"

I snapped out of my reverie and looked up.

"No. It's, like, three in the morning over there. I'm not waking him up."

"You have to tell him."

I bristled at her tone. Honestly, one minute she's warning me about him and the next she's pushing me to run to him for help.

"I will, I will. Relax."

"Before you go see him this weekend."

"What are you, my mother?"

"I'm only trying to help."

"Really? Then mind your own business for once, please. I'm not a defenseless animal who needs rescuing."

We stared at one another for a minute, tension billowing through the kitchen. Sometimes being her friend tested my patience. I knew her concern came from a good place and I appreciated it, my only problem was she didn't know when to back off.

"Fine." She sighed. "You can stay here as long as you want. Have you thought about going to the police?"

"Yeah. I just don't know what they can do. There wasn't a threatening note or anything. A pile of pictures in an unmarked envelope doesn't exactly scream mortal danger."

Stephanie pursed her lips. "You were followed. I think you should at least file a complaint or something. That way it's on record and if something else happens they'll know this is a recurring problem."

Rubbing my temples, I nodded. Working in the news enabled me to establish good contacts at the police department. I knew who to call if I decided to go down that road. Exhaustion creaked through my body.

"I'm beat. Thanks for letting me stay here."

Stephanie circled the table and hugged me. Even though I had a flesh and blood sister, she was as close to me as Dayna. We could fight like cats and dogs or have disagreements but our bond remained unbreakable. I could always turn to her, no matter the circumstance.

"The guest bedroom is all made up," she said, squeezing me tight. "Seriously. You can stay here as long as you need."

That was as close to an apology as I was going to get for the time being.

Once I snuggled under the blankets, I reached for my phone. I wanted to call Alastair but I didn't want to worry him. He'd probably flip out and fly back here. His little quirk about always needing to know if I was safe was no joke. Telling him wasn't an option until I knew all the facts. He didn't need added pressure, especially with everything he was dealing with at work.

And then there was Nathan. *What am I going to do about him?* Anxiety churned through my body. I tossed and turned forever before finally falling asleep.

The next day was uncomfortable to say the least. I was jumpy and paranoid. I nearly suffered a panic attack in the afternoon walking to the bathroom at work when I heard footsteps behind me.

"Hey, Lia."

I spun around, my heart beating a mile a minute. Katie Vitale, our morning show reporter, stood next to Edit Bay One. Her eyes widened at my blatant display of fear.

"Didn't mean to startle you. Sorry."

"It's okay. My mind is just littered with a zillion things."

She grinned, tossing her strawberry-blonde hair over her left shoulder. "Ugh, I know the feeling. They're having me cover the Malone trial starting tomorrow. I'd rather stay on the motel explosion."

"I think we've milked that one for all it's worth."

"Well," she huffed, "I guess. Hey, are you going to be around this weekend?"

"Nope. I'll be out of town."

Folding her arms, Katie sized me up with a shrewd glance. "Visiting the competition?"

Her slightly sarcastic tone irked me. Not everyone at my station was dazzled by that fact I was dating our biggest rival's newly minted CEO. A smile tugged at the corners of my mouth. "I'm visiting my boyfriend, yes."

"Must be nice to get all this time off. I asked to use a vacation day next Monday so I could go to Panama City for the weekend. I was told I'm needed in the area just in case something new breaks in the motel story, which you so succinctly described as being 'milked.' Obviously, Bruce sees it differently. But you get to flitter off to Scotland. You have Singleton wrapped around your finger, don't you?"

Funny how a few snotty words from someone could turn me from being paranoid to exasperated in less than ten seconds. I clenched my fists in an effort to control whatever response was about to be unleashed.

"I'm not taking any time off, not that it's any of your business. I switched my schedule with Louise."

Giving me her best *whatever* stare, Katie turned on her heel and sauntered down the hallway. This wasn't the first time she'd voiced her opinions on my love life. When I dated Nathan she'd made it clear I'd landed the biggest catch since Kate nabbed Will and I should marry him immediately. Sometimes working in a newsroom was like being in high school.

I spent the remainder of the afternoon reordering stories in the rundown and editing scripts. Sydney and I chatted about her upcoming cookout bash at the lake house. She and her husband, Ray, have been throwing this late summer party for as long as I'd lived in Orlando. Aside from the massive fireworks display at Lake Eola on the Fourth of July, the Makeeda family soirée was the biggest event of the season.

By the time I settled into the control room for the broadcast, I'd managed to push aside my annoyance over Katie and my trepidations over the photos.

I decided to stay with Stephanie one more night and headed home on Thursday. Everything looked exactly as I'd left it. Pictures were still scattered across the living room floor. I shoved them back in the envelope and tossed it on the kitchen table.

I peeked out the window. There were still another couple hours of good sunlight. A long, hard jog would be beneficial. I changed and drove out to Cranes Roost Park. Drowning out the world with music, I ran around the lake until my legs begged for mercy and the July humidity saturated my lungs. Running in this sweltering heat drained me but I loved the escape. At no other time did I feel more alive than when I ran. Once I arrived back home, I filled the tub and soaked my sore muscles. Exhausted, I collapsed into bed.

* * *

"Hello?" I mumbled into the pillow. I think the phone was at my ear. The ringing finally stopped. Squinting at the clock on my nightstand I learned it was barely five in the morning.

"Did I wake you, kitten?"

Blood sang through my veins as I heard Alastair's velvety English accent through the phone. I smiled. "You're five hours ahead of me. You know you did."

His low, throaty laugh curled my toes. I half expected to turn and see him lying next to me.

"Sorry. I wanted to hear your voice. I don't like waking up alone."

"I know the feeling," I said, sliding my hand along the cool sheets where his body should have been. "Are you working from home today?"

"No. The office. I'm in between meetings. I have about seven minutes to give you my undivided attention."

I laughed, stretching my legs. "Well, well Mr. CEO. A whole seven minutes? How do you plan to spend this time?"

"Enjoying the sound of your voice," he answered, lowering his tone. "I like hearing you first thing in the morning."

I closed my eyes, amazed at how quickly my heart was beating. Goose bumps rippled across my skin. The effect he had on me transcended an ocean and several time zones.

"Are you trying to seduce me over the phone?"

"Only if you want me to. Although I'd need more than," he paused, "six minutes."

"I doubt that," I muttered, kicking off the blankets. My internal body temperature was off the charts. Another one of his deep, sexy laughs quickened my pulse.

"Patience, love."

"I'm barely awake. You're a tease with a gorgeous accent who knows how to push my buttons. Thin ice, Holden, thin ice."

"I should wake you up early more often. Which buttons am I pushing, exactly?"

Christ. I could almost see the smile on his lips. Shifting on the mattress, I curled up on my side. The pillow he'd used still smelled like him. I inhaled deeply, wishing I could wrap myself around him.

"Patience, chief."

"Fair enough."

I squeezed the phone. Hearing his voice unhinged me a bit. I wanted to tell him what happened this week. More than anything I wanted to feel him next to me. Steeling myself against the unwelcome onslaught of emotion, I took a deep breath.

"You're awfully quiet. What's wrong?"

"Nothing. I'm just a little tired seeing as someone thought it would be funny to wake me up at the crack of dawn."

There was a long pause.

"You're sure there's nothing else bothering you?"

I hated lying to him.

"Only that I miss you like crazy."

He sighed heavily. "I can't wait until you get here. I have a few things planned for you."

"Oh?" I sat up, leaning against the headboard. "What things?"

"A lesson, of sorts."

My erratic pulse skipped a few beats. "What type of lesson?"

"Something I've been wanting to teach you. A curiosity of mine, really. I'll ease you into it, until you get a feel for what you're doing. Then, I want to see you take control and show me what you can do."

I squeezed the pillow to within an inch of its life. In all honesty, whatever he just described made my ovaries move. I swallowed hard. "I think it's safe to say I'm intrigued."

"Good. I have to go, love. Think of me today."

"Obviously."

He laughed good and loud. "Have a safe flight. I'll see you tomorrow morning."

A smile remained plastered to my face all day. That early morning phone call was the perfect remedy for my weeklong jitters. Not even a barrage of breaking stories derailed my good mood.

"Are you humming?"

I looked up from the computer screen and was greeted by Sydney's smiling face.

"Uh, maybe?"

She laughed. "Don't be embarrassed. I'd hum too if I were heading for a weekend of naughtiness with a hot Brit."

I grinned, feeling my cheeks heat up.

"Seriously, Lia. That man is too gorgeous to just cuddle. The illegal things I would do to him," she smiled.

"Sydney!"

"Hypothetically speaking, of course." She winked. "I only have eyes for Ray."

My desk phone rang, mercifully ending the over-sharing session.

"Lia Meyers."

"Do you have a minute?"

I clenched the receiver, wishing I hadn't answered. "What do you want, Nathan?"

"Rachel Jameson is behind the pictures."

"What? How do you know?"

The length of the pause was torture.

"I don't want to get into that right now."

My stomach rolled. I swallowed, trying to keep a serene tone. Sydney might be working but her ears had sharpened.

"I'd appreciate it if you could go into a little more detail."

"Not over the phone while you're at work. I debated whether or not to call but felt you should at least know that. Let me come by when you're home and we can talk."

"I can't. I'm going straight to the airport from the station."

"Shit," he hissed. "Don't go visit him."

Any shred of the good mood I'd enjoyed all day disappeared. I glanced over the partition separating my cubicle from Sydney's. She had headphones on to listen to a press conference. Turning my chair so it faced the back of the newsroom, I lowered my voice.

"I don't know what little scheme you've cooked up with Rachel but it needs to stop. I should have known she was in on it when she showed up at dinner. You're a piece of work, Nathan. How many times do I have to say it? This is over. We're done. Don't call me again."

I pulled the phone away from my ear only to hear him yell for me to stop. I didn't know what possessed me to listen.

"You're not giving me any choice here, Lia. This isn't how I wanted to tell you." He almost sounded apologetic. "Rachel was hired to follow you. She's being paid to dig up dirt from your past and to keep an eye on you."

Panic seized my heart. "Who hired her?"

"I don't want to do this over the phone."

"Who hired her?" I asked through clenched teeth.

Nathan sighed. "Money was wired to her from an account in the United Kingdom."

My body went cold. All the lively sounds of the newsroom faded into oblivion. Immense pressure squeezed between my ears. I couldn't believe what I was hearing.

"Lia." He paused. "The authorizing signature was from Jason Holden."

Dropping the phone into its cradle, I stood up abruptly and somehow walked to the restroom. One of the editors was washing her hands. She smiled as I brushed by and locked myself in a stall. The cool stainless steel door did nothing to soothe the heated skin on my forehead. For the most part, I was numb. So much had been thrown at me over the past few months and this new revelation didn't deliver the massive blow I would have expected. Partly because I didn't believe a word coming out Nathan's mouth and partly because I refused to accept what I was told.

Alastair's uncle isn't financing a tabloid reporter to dig up dirt on me. That's ridiculous.

I leaned against the door. My heart pounded so quickly that the inside of my ears hurt. We were barely three weeks removed from the biggest breakthrough in our relationship. He had opened up. He told me everything. *Or did he?*

No. I wouldn't allow my insecurities to run rampant. This was all part of Nathan's sick, twisted plan to win me back. Anger roiled my stomach. Straightening, I walked out of the stall, did a quick check in the mirror and went back to my desk. I zeroed in on nothing but the rundown and various scripts that needed tweaking. The broadcast flew by in a nanosecond. The next thing I knew, I was in the sanctuary of my car.

Gripping the steering wheel, I forced myself to breathe. I had a nine-hour flight to endure. The last thing I wanted was to spend it pissed off. I drove more aggressively than usual through the traffic. My only goal was to get to the airport lounge and try to unwind. Since I didn't have any luggage, I zipped through security.

Once I was settled in the lounge with a glass of chardonnay I felt better. Not great, but better. Of course I flirted with the idea of getting back in my car and going home. If his uncle really was behind all this nonsense, visiting Alastair was the last thing I should do. It hurt my heart to even consider the possibility. All of this could be cleared up quickly if I asked him. *Oh yeah. That will go over well. Hi, Alastair. Is your uncle stalking me? Oh, he is? Amazing.*

The ridiculousness of that scenario made me laugh. A couple of passengers looked at me funnily. I smiled at them and sipped the wine. By my third glass, a nice fuzzy calm settled my nerves. The Holden family wasn't investigating me. They had no reason to.

CHAPTER THREE

A sizable group of family and friends were gathered near the arrivals entrance at Glasgow International Airport to welcome weary travelers home. I assumed Alastair's driver, Paxton, would be picking me up. I scanned the crowd for a tall broad-shouldered man in his forties with salt and pepper hair. All I saw was a young guy in jeans, black t-shirt and backwards baseball cap with his back to me.

Shuffling past him and another group of people I wondered if I'd have to take a taxi. The thought annoyed me. Plus, I was cranky because my period decided to show up early thanks to the high altitude while flying.

"There you are."

I turned toward the familiar rich voice and wound up staring directly at the guy in the ball cap. Seeing Alastair always hit all my hot buttons. The casual look didn't mask his aura of powerful elegance at all.

"What the hell is on your head?"

Alastair laughed. "You don't like it?" He turned the hat so it faced the proper direction. It made him look slightly younger than his thirty-one years. The letters HWM were embroidered on the front.

"It's cute."

"I was trying to be incognito."

"I'll let you in on a secret. Don't wear a Holden World Media hat if you don't want to be recognized." I grinned, wrapping my arms around him. Feeling his athletic body pressed to mine set everything straight. His energy really had become an extension of my own. When we shared the same space, I felt more alive, more aware. Just…more.

"I need to get you out of here and back to my house so I can welcome you properly," he said, draping an arm across my shoulders.

He whisked me off to the parking lot and drove back to his neighborhood in Bearsden like a man on a mission. The tree-lined street was quiet and pretty. His light gray sandstone house sat on a pristine lot with a manicured lawn and vibrant patches of shrubbery and flowers.

Still so perfect on the outside, like him.

Most of the world only saw the stoic, successful young businessman who'd recently been named CEO of his grandfather's media empire. He handled his business dealings with the cool precision of a surgeon. As much as I craved him when he was in CEO-mode, peeling away the hard exterior to expose the vulnerable man who only showed himself to me was a drug I would never quit.

I'd barely walked through the front door when he lunged, pinning me against the wall. At the mercy of his lips and tongue, I gasped, inhaling sharply. The rim of his hat knocked into my forehead. I ripped it off his head, throwing it across the hallway. He kissed me with such ferocity I thought he might bruise my lips. Circling each of my wrists with his hands, he held them firmly against the wall and pushed the weight of his six-foot frame into me. I liked it when he was untamed. His passion for me was a turn on.

"I missed you," he said, biting my bottom lip.

"It's only been four days."

"Felt like an eternity." Gripping my wrists tighter, he flexed his hips into mine. The friction sent a pleasurable wave through me.

"I want you. Now. Against this wall." He kissed me again, this time slower and deeper. Each stroke of his tongue was matched with a tantalizing thrust of his hips. He knew exactly how to get me firing on all cylinders. Heat blossomed and spread through my body. Maybe he was right. Four days did feel like an eternity.

He grazed his teeth down the side of my neck, setting off a barrage of goose bumps. Releasing my wrists, he slid his hands down my body and started unbuttoning my jeans.

Shit.

"Alastair."

He looked at me, his green eyes cloudy with lust. I brushed my thumb over his mouth.

"We have to stop."

A sexy grin curled his lips as he pushed down my jeans. "Not into hallway sex?"

"No. I mean, yes but…oh! What the…"

He lightly stroked the sensitive skin along my tailbone. The tingling sensation was euphoric, shooting up my spine, into my throat and back down to my toes.

"We won't limit this to the hallway. I plan to have you in every room."

Each caress heightened my arousal. No one had ever touched me there before and it was phenomenal. He pinned my arms against the wall again, holding on tighter. The overwhelming strength, both physical and sexual, was too much. I tried to wriggle out of his grasp.

"Ah, Lia," he said, his breath warm on my cheek. "Stay still. As much as I like it when you want to take charge, it's my house. My rules."

That dominant stare was not of this world. I'd seen variations of it before but never so raw and focused. The veil he usually kept locked in place vanished, unleashing a torrent of want. I loved it. My heart raced as though I'd just finished running a marathon.

Flexing his hips into mine once more, he grinned lasciviously.

"This look" - he kissed me - "will never leave your face this weekend."

Being caught in his seductive bubble was proving to be too much for me to handle. I considered going full force with him, monthly lady visitor and all. Thankfully, that thought only lasted a split second.

"I have my period."

A blurted phrase like that certainly alters the mood pretty damn quick. The world snapped into focus. Alastair paused, stared at me for a few seconds and stepped back. Confused, he cocked his head to the side.

"Now? I thought you said it wasn't due until Monday."

"I think being on a plane expedited the process."

"No hallway sex then."

The coy grin on his face stoked the inferno deep inside me. My mouth watered.

"Not so fast, Holden."

I shoved his body against the wall. Shocked, he exhaled harshly. I kissed his neck.

"You were saying about how you like it when I take charge? Don't move."

As I lowered to my knees, he grabbed my arms and pulled me back up. "Wait."

I looked at him, dumbfounded. "For real? You were just plastered all over me."

The thick cloud of want returned with a vengeance. His fingers dug into my skin as his grasp tightened. I could see him battling with himself internally. *But why?* Thinking as quickly as my love-fuzzed brain would allow, I placed my hands on his hips and leaned into his chest.

"Tell me what you want," I insisted, using the words he'd spoken to me time and again.

His expression faltered in a manner so subtle I almost missed the change. Releasing his hold on me, he aimed a laser stare in my direction. "I want you, love."

I unbuttoned his jeans, peeling them off as I sank to the floor. He made the male body look like a piece of art. I traced along his hipbone, savoring the v-shape. His labored breathing filled the hallway. I teased him a bit, running my nails along his inner thighs before taking his erection into my mouth. I loved hearing him sigh and moan as I took my time enjoying his body. Every little quiver, no matter how subtle, spurred me on. I had him exactly how I wanted him; vulnerable. He shoved his hands through my hair, pulling it. I responded by hollowing my cheeks, forming an airtight suction.

He groaned, his left leg shaking violently. I kept one hand on his hip and the other around his length. He was close. I could feel it. His body was rigid. Fisting his hands in my hair tighter, he held me in place. *Always the control freak.* I teased him again, releasing him from my mouth and letting my warm breath glide over him.

"Don't stop," he ordered in a hoarse whisper.

Looking up at him, my heart skipped a beat. Eyes closed, his head was pressed against the wall. Ecstasy was etched upon his face. *Mine.* Carnal instinct took over. Focusing on just the tip, I wrapped my lips around him. With a yell, he came hot and thick in my mouth. I didn't move until he finished.

Folding to the floor like a paper doll, he sat in front of me. I sat back on my heels, admiring his sated expression. Tilting his head to the side, he ran a hand through the tousled mass of dark red hair framing his gorgeous face.

"No hallway sex, huh?" I smiled.

"Bit of a minx, aren't you?"

I laughed. "You have no idea."

"So it seems."

"Are you blushing?"

"No." He smirked. "Come closer, please."

Scooting forward, I leaned over him, placing my hands on either side of his legs. The warm glow radiating from his emerald eyes made me so happy. He cupped my cheeks, smiling softly.

"Welcome back to Glasgow. I hope this is a weekend you'll never forget."

"So far, so good."

Still smiling, he pulled our foreheads together. "You probably want to freshen up after your long flight. Everything you need is my bedroom. I'll fix us some breakfast."

He stood up, redressing with ease. I grabbed his hand and walked with him toward the kitchen. Everything sat in its place in his immaculate house. It would look perfect gracing the pages of Architectural Digest with its luxurious furniture and ornate decorations. Neutral tones suggested a warm welcome, subtly accented with deep, rich colors. But there were no personal touches, nothing that gave anything away about the guarded man who lived here. My heart pinged with sadness. Buried beneath his hard outer shell was a broken soul trying to heal after years of self-reproach. Nobody saw that part of him except for me.

Slapping me playfully on the behind, he told me to take as much time as I needed. I scurried off to the bedroom. The door to his walk-in closet was wide open. I peeked in, stunned by the array of clothes bursting from each corner. One side held all of his suits, ties and dress shirts. Shelves stacked with more casual clothes lined the wall.

I swallowed, looking to my left. The rest of his closet was filled with clothes for me. Not just jeans and capris and other everyday items I wore but formal dresses and gorgeous high heels, too. Neatly folded on shelves were various satin and silk nightgowns and robes. *Jesus. There are enough outfits in here to last at least six months.*

"Too much?"

Startled, I spun around. Alastair leaned against the doorframe, concern flashing in his eyes.

"It's, um, there's a lot of stuff."

"I don't want you to think…Lia, are you alright?"

I held onto the doorknob. Everything that happened this past week flooded back into my consciousness. The room spun. I felt Alastair's arms tighten around my waist.

"Look at me."

I did as I was told, focusing on his firm hold. "I'm fine, sorry. Must be the jet lag."

His searing eyes scrutinized my face. I forced a smile, hoping to convince him nothing was wrong.

"Seriously. You know me and jet lag. Next thing you know I'll be tripping over carpets."

That seemed to work. He lifted my hand, pressing a small kiss to the palm.

"Did you buy all this yourself?"

"Of course I did. Who else would?"

"I don't know. I thought maybe you'd sent Paxton to do this."

"Paxton?" His eyes widened in amusement. "He's a great bloke and all but I don't think he'd appreciate being sent out with a list of women's clothes and beauty products to purchase."

"Well, I mean, he drives you around. I just thought he—"

"He drives me around for work purposes, that's all. He's my security detail, not my errand boy," he scowled, retreating a step behind his shield.

Dammit.

"Sorry. I didn't mean to imply you can't do things for yourself."

Too late. The relaxed, sated aura dissipated. He stared at me blankly for a few seconds. The silence was deafening. I'd much rather he shouted or complained about whatever it was that bothered him. The quiet added layers of tension but this was his way. I'd be able to see through his cracks if I was patient enough. Of course, he could see through me with zero effort. The give and take was a delicate balancing act we were still figuring out.

"I'll leave you to do whatever freshening you need. Come find me in the kitchen when you're done."

Without so much as a backward glance he walked out. I felt

sick to my stomach. Deciding not to dwell upon his abrupt mood swing, I went into the bathroom. Lined up on the counter were a variety of my favorite beauty products. *He remembered.* I grabbed the bottle of almond scented bubble bath. Stripping out of my clothes, I filled the white stone bathtub until it almost overflowed. Settling into the warm soapy water, I leaned my head back. Another unpleasant replay of the week's events consumed me. I had to stop thinking about it. All I wanted was to enjoy my time with Alastair. Nathan and those damn photos could wait. There was no way in hell I'd bring up the crazy accusation that his uncle hired a tabloid reporter to follow me. Not until I knew for certain.

"Room for one more?"

I jumped, opening my eyes. Alastair stood in the middle of the bathroom in all his naked glory. I took my time admiring every toned inch of him.

"I'll take that as a yes." He climbed in and sat down facing me. "Come here."

The egg-shaped tub was more than big enough for the two of us so I straddled his lap with my legs wrapped around his waist. He scooped a small handful of bubbles from my shoulder.

"I could smell this in the kitchen. I'm glad you like it."

I cupped his jaw, kissing him. "Of course I like it. It's from you."

A little smile curved his mouth. "You don't mind if I postpone breakfast a bit, do you? The thought of you sitting in here naked without me was distracting."

"I don't mind. You'll have to feed me eventually though."

Pulling him closer, I pressed our bodies together. This intimate skin-on-skin contact made us both shudder. Apparently the tense exchange by the closet was forgotten. I hugged him a little tighter, kissing his shoulder.

"You feel so good," he murmured, sliding his hands down my back. I leaned back to look at him. "Don't move. I want you close. I always want you to be close."

"I want that, too."

He squeezed my ass. "You'd better."

"Hey." I pulled back, greeted by a smug grin. "Watch your hands, chief."

"Oh, I am."

Another squeeze. I narrowed my eyes. "Enjoying yourself?"

"Quite. You have a nice, pert bum."

"So, you basically interrupted my bath to cop a feel?"

"I'll take what I can get. Although, I'd be lying if I said I didn't want to shag you senseless right now."

I laughed. "Shag? Honestly, you Brits are too polite."

His dark, challenging stare quickened my pulse. "I can be impolite if you prefer."

My skin tightened and warmed under the firm grasp of his fingers. He cupped my left breast, sealing his mouth around the nipple. It beaded under the warmth of his tongue. His other hand disappeared under the water. I jumped when his fingers slid between my legs.

"You can't—"

"I'm not going near anything you don't want touched. Trust me." His hot, commanding stare burned through me. I twitched in his lap, eliciting a small moan from him. This connection, this intensity we shared scared me as much as it turned me on.

Circling both arms around my waist, he brushed his fingers over my tailbone. I shivered, amazed at how sensitive that area was for me.

"What this look does to me." He traced one finger up my spine. "You own me with those beautiful amber eyes."

On cue, my body woke with ravenous desire. I wanted him and his come-hither stare. Figures my hormones would rage when I was, for all intents and purposes, incapacitated in the sex department. A devilish grin curved his lips as he cupped my jaw.

"Close your eyes."

I did, basking in the warmth of his skin on mine.

"Keep them closed," he whispered.

The heat from his hands left my face. I swallowed, wondering where I'd feel them next.

I waited.

Nothing.

I'm an idiot for sitting here with my eyes closed.

"Want to know what I'm doing?" His low, raspy question tickled my neck. It startled me.

"No."

He chuckled, pressing gentle kisses along my jaw, stopping at the corner of my mouth.

"You're so soft and silky," he whispered, gliding his lips down my neck. "And beautiful. And—"

"Alastair."

"I like the way you say my name."

Teasing along the edge of my lips with his tongue, he coaxed them open without any resistance. I was a rag doll in his arms, sighing into his luscious kiss. He invaded my mouth, claiming and savoring me. I kissed him harder, pressing into him. The desperation and intensity of his movements increased. So did the way he stroked the skin over my tailbone. Sparks of pleasure shot through me, filling every inch until I thought I might burst. Unable to control myself I rolled my hips, sending ripples through the water.

"Stay still, kitten," he ordered, his rich voice and velvety accent invading my senses. Pulling one hand away, he pressed his palm to my lower abdomen. I felt his thumb slide down, stopping just shy of where I wanted his touch the most.

"You're teasing me, Holden."

"Am I?"

Opening my eyes, I was greeted with a white-hot stare. The vulnerability behind it took my breath away. "Yes."

"I'm at a disadvantage, love. Unless," he paused, sliding his thumb lower, brushing it against my hypersensitive button of nerves. I nearly shot into orbit. Gauging my reaction, he pressed and held his thumb against me. "Is this impolite enough for you?"

Steam from the warm water mixed with our mutual desire, altering the climate in the bathroom. No longer were we just sitting in a tub. We were nestled deeply in our never-ending craving for each other. It was hard to imagine there had been a time when I shrugged off his advances.

Another firm press sent a shockwave of pleasure cascading through me.

"Look at me," he growled. "I'd better be the only thing dominating your thoughts, Amelia."

Crushing his lips to mine, he finished me off with expertise and finesse. The disorganized mess that doubled for my mind shorted out, succumbing to an orgasm so intense it took awhile for me to regain composure. If I owned him with just a look, he possessed me with one touch. Sagging into the water, I wrapped my arms around him, resting my head on his shoulder.

"Feel a bit more relaxed now?"

"Yes."

"Good." He kissed the top of my head. "I have something fun planned and need you stress-free."

I looked at him. "Am I stressed?"

"You've seemed a little off since we spoke yesterday."

His ability to see through me could be annoying. I rolled my eyes. "I'm fine."

Arching a brow, he squeezed my waist. "We both know something is bothering you. However, I'm going to give you a free pass this time."

"Gee, thanks."

"That smart mouth of yours will get you in trouble one of these days."

"Oh really?"

"Yes." He nipped at my earlobe. "Especially if I have anything to say about it."

"All bark and no bite, Holden."

He had my arms pinned behind my back so quickly there was

barely a ripple in the water. "Is that a challenge?"

"Only if you're up for it."

The look of surprise that crossed his face amused me. I wondered how many of his ex-lovers acted this way around him or if they just gave him what he wanted, no questions asked.

"Feisty."

"I try," I said, grinning facetiously.

"I like it."

"I like you."

The unguarded smile that blossomed on his lips was so beautiful it warmed my soul.

"I like you, too," he said, releasing my arms.

"You'd better, otherwise I'm sitting naked in a bathtub with the wrong guy."

He squeezed my waist so hard I yelped.

"I told you that smart mouth would get you in trouble," he smirked.

"Be gentle when you tickle me. I'm delicate." I could barely the get the words out and not laugh.

"You are delicate. And you're mine. No naked anything with other men."

"I wouldn't dream of it," I whispered, kissing him hard and wrapping my arms around his neck.

"Alright then. I'm hungry, so you must be famished." Carefully lifting me off him, he stood and climbed out of the tub. I pouted.

"None of that." He leaned over and kissed my nose. "Finish up in here. I'll have breakfast waiting for you."

I stared at his naked backside as he walked out. Grinning, I slid under the water. *Love, lust and infatuation. Girl, you've got it bad for him.*

CHAPTER FOUR

The lush Scottish countryside flew by in a green blur. I hung my arm out the car window, skimming my hand along the warm breeze. The sun shone bright in the sky, fending off the wisps of clouds that tried to spoil its celestial show. For me, this sky was far more beautiful than any sunny day in Orlando.

"Now are you going to tell me what we're doing?"

"Nope."

I looked over at Alastair. He flashed a brilliant smile and gave the car a little more gas. The Mercedes' engine growled, kicking into higher gear. I did enjoy watching him drive. Especially out here in the middle of nowhere. His fluid control and relaxed stance behind the wheel added another layer of hotness to his already scorching exterior.

The car rolled to a stop on a dusty patch at the side of the road. A large meadow spread out to our left. Aside from various clusters of trees, there was nothing to see for miles.

"We've arrived."

Leaving the engine idling, Alastair got out of the car. I followed him, spurred on by a healthy dose of curiosity.

"Where are we?"

"Carbeth."

"And what's so special about this place?"

He turned, a goofy grin plastered on his face. "Nothing. It's a bit out of the way and I thought it would be a good place for your lesson."

Now I was completely confused. Alastair kept that ridiculous smile aimed in my direction.

"You're going to learn how to drive my sexy little car."

"What?"

A loud laugh echoed through the breeze. "Don't look so excited. It's really simple."

I folded my arms. "Why do you want me to drive your car?"

"No reason. Just curious to see you behind the wheel."

"I told you I can't drive a stick."

"Yes, I know. Hence the lesson. Get in."

"So bossy."

I settled in behind the wheel and adjusted the seat so I could reach the pedals. Alastair folded his lean frame onto the passenger seat and grinned.

"Looking good, doll face."

"Oh my God. What did I say about faking the American accent?"

He chuckled. "Are you ready to learn?"

"I suppose."

"Alright. Press down on the brake and clutch. Put the gear in first and release the emergency brake."

"You might want to buckle up," I muttered, doing as he instructed.

"Now, gently give it some gas and lift your foot off the clutch slowly."

The car rumbled beneath me as I pressed on the accelerator. Tightening my grip on the steering wheel, I carefully lifted my foot off the clutch. The car stuttered a bit before rolling forward.

"That's it. Give it a little more."

Taking a quick glance to my right, I eased the car onto the road. *Stay on the left, stay on the left.* Driving on the wrong side of the road while sitting in the wrong side of the car was a tad disorienting. I kept repeating my little mantra as I accelerated, shifting into second. I'd only driven a stick shift a few times. My dad tried to teach me when I was sixteen. He thought it would be beneficial to know 'just in case.'

Okay, this might be easier than I thought. The road didn't have any major curves as far as I could see. I eased the car into third, feeling more confident I wouldn't end up upside down in a ditch. Adrenaline gave me an added boost of courage.

"Ready, Holden?"

I gunned it, charged by the power raging in the SLK55's engine. I heard a thump and looked to my left. Alastair clasped the door handle.

"Too fast?"

"No, love," he answered in a low, gravelly tone.

By the time I hit sixth gear I really had a feel for it. The car purred and hugged the road at my command. Alastair remained suspiciously quiet, observing every move I made. I couldn't wipe the smile off my face if I tried. This was almost as liberating as jogging along the coastline.

I glanced at him. His expression may have been blank but his eyes glowed a molten forest green. After several miles, I saw an area to pull over. Gliding the car to a stop, I put it in neutral, popped the brake and cut the engine.

"How d—"

I was silenced by a kiss.

"Impressive, Meyers."

He looked a little peaked but otherwise seemed fine. A twinge of guilt shot through me. Maybe my driving so fast had reminded him of the accident that killed his family. My stomach sank. *Not what I was going for.*

"Come with me."

Those words always sent a charge through me. Grinning, he got out of the car. I waited while he grabbed a blanket from the trunk and followed him to a large elm tree. After he spread the blanket he motioned for me to sit. Once I was settled he laid down, resting his head in my lap. I played with his hair, enjoying the quiet. Only the occasional chirping bird interrupted the relative peace of our little roadside pit stop.

"Everything okay at work?" I asked. There was a long pause before he answered.

"I suppose."

Here we go. The parade of vagueness begins.

"How's your grandfather been feeling?"

"Fine."

"And your aunt and uncle? How are they?"

"Same as always. Katherine keeps asking when I'm bringing you by the house again."

The house. I had to stifle a laugh. My whole apartment building could fit neatly inside the Holden Estate with room to spare.

"We should go back there and visit. I'm sure they'd love to see you outside of official family gatherings."

Alastair folded his arms across his chest and stared up at the sky. I could tell he hated the idea. He'd mentioned he avoided going to the estate unless it was necessary. His aunt was a sweet woman, though. I couldn't imagine why he wouldn't want to spend time with her. The uncle was another story. I'd noticed Alastair's relationship with him seemed strained.

"You look lovely today."

I came screeching back to the present and glanced down at him as he fingered the hem on the green chevron striped tank top I'd picked from the closet. I'd paired it with denim shorts.

"Thank you."

"Everything fits alright?"

"Um, yeah."

"But…?" He raised an eyebrow.

"Well, the bra is a little snug. But I think that has more to do with, you know, hormones and stuff."

"Snug?" He reached up, skimming his fingers over the swell of my breasts and cupped one of them. "Feels good to me."

"Smart ass."

"What? I think you look smashing. Sexy as always."

"Whatever."

A slight frown marred his otherwise serene expression. Anxiety rushed through my body. The late afternoon sunlight shone off his eyes as he looked up at me, turning them an even more vibrant green.

"What's on your mind?"

"Nothing."

He smiled bitterly. "Is this what I do to you? Give annoying one word answers when there is clearly something going on?"

"Sometimes."

He was quiet for a few seconds. "Okay then. This morning, when you asked about Paxton running errands for me? The reason I got upset is because when I was younger my uncle always drilled into my head that nothing should ever be handed to me. I should work hard for every advantage, just as he and my father did. It didn't matter that we were wealthy. The minute we let someone else do the most simple task for us, we lost our sense of independence."

The transformation in his manner of speaking was jarring. He sounded monotone, almost as though he were reciting an unpleasant oath. Regardless of my suspicions about his uncle, this seemed to be a decent piece of advice. But what did I know?

Some of the tension melted from his face. "Sorry I was so abrupt with you. It's a bit of a sore spot with me."

"You have a lot of sore spots." I poked him in the stomach. "I'm going to need a roadmap pretty soon to navigate through them."

"No you won't," he said softly, staring up at me with reverence. "You're gorgeous in this light."

Sitting up slowly, he twisted a piece of my hair around his finger. Sunlight reflected off the chestnut strands in shades of copper and auburn. More stunning for me was the way it set his hair ablaze with color.

"So are you."

He scrunched his nose. "If you say so. Come. I want to take you somewhere."

For the first time ever I didn't ask where we were going. I simply followed him back to the car and remained silent. I liked how this weekend was progressing. We felt more comfortable around one another, physically and emotionally. At least I did. I could tell he did to a certain extent. There were still an abundance of layers to peel away before I'd be secure enough knowing he fully trusted me with his emotions. Patience was the key. The last thing I wanted to do was rush him. *Or complicate matters with accusations of stalking.*

I winced, pushing the thought out of my mind.

"We've arrived."

I glanced out the window and saw a familiar looking thatched cottage.

"I remember this place," I grinned, following him to the front door. The same 'at home' feeling washed over me when I entered the cozy living room. Everything about this cottage was the exact opposite of his house. It was modest and lived in. The hard wood floors were a warm honey color partly covered by a soft cream throw rug. Small lamps and sconces cast a pleasant glow throughout. Even the low ceilings had charm with their exposed beams.

"What do you remember about it?"

Leaning against the crimson couch, I smiled. "I remember you being a gentleman after my unattractive display from too many martinis."

"Is that all?"

The longing in his eyes radiated through the room. In a heartbeat, he stood in front of me. A flurry of nerves rushed through my stomach. He brushed his cheek against mine, the stubble lightly tickling me. I lost myself in his delicious scent. The mix of shampoo, body wash and him was so enticing.

"This is where I first kissed you," he whispered, brushing his thumb over my lips. "This is where you made me feel for the first time in years."

Something about the cottage had a calming effect on him. He stood before me, devoid of any protective shield or mask. Seeing him so open melted my heart. He moved closer, gently running his knuckles down my cheek.

"Please tell me what's bothering you."

Panic streaked through me. *I can't.* Not moving, I struggled to maintain eye contact with him. He stayed silent, watching me carefully. Feigning aloofness was out of the question. He saw through me too easily.

"Rough week at the office, chief. That's all." I grinned, hoping it touched my eyes so he'd be convinced. There was truth to that. It had been a rough week.

Cradling my face gently as though he were holding porcelain, he studied me. It made me uncomfortable. I knew it was my own fault for not being forthcoming but I had to keep this from him. He hovered his lips over mine.

"We are so much more alike than I realized," he said, kissing me softly. "You'll tell me when you're ready, yes?"

"There's noth—"

His mouth covered mine, the pressure making my lips burn. I wrapped my fingers around the back of his neck, holding him tight against me. His impassioned kisses were just as magnificent as the tender ones. They lit my bloodstream on fire. Hazy and throbbing with want, I met his ardent stare.

"Are you going to keep kissing me like that until I tell you?"

"Yes."

"Then you'll have to wait."

Leaning his forehead to mine, he laughed. "You drive a hard bargain, Meyers."

I ran my hands up and down his back, gliding them slowly over the cotton t-shirt. A low moan vibrated in his throat. I loved the sounds he made when he was turned on. Lifting the hem of his shirt I snuck my hands under, caressing the warm, soft skin along his lower back. I felt his muscles contract.

"Don't control it," I said against the corner of his mouth. "Let go."

He jerked backwards, burning me with a blistering stare. The heat from his body still pulsed against me. His raw emotion was palpable. Teetering on the edge, he fought to retain control. I made him look this way. I broke his every defense.

"You're mine, Holden. You don't have to hide behind the mask with me."

I wanted so much for him to see me as his safe place, someone he could trust with his emotions. I think on some level he did. Our relationship was new and unchartered territory for both of us. Alastair standing there and looking at me with that bewitching stare made it difficult to concentrate. Even when he fought to corral his feelings, the strength of his desire hit me at full force.

"You are so goddam sexy." I didn't even recognize the sound of my own voice, mostly because that was supposed to be an inside thought.

A salacious grin tugged at the corner of his mouth. "Ditto, love."

He scooped me up off the floor and tossed me over his shoulder. I shrieked in surprise as he carried me to the bedroom, laughing when he placed me on the bed. He strode over to a small desk and opened a laptop. Slow, jazzy piano music filled the room.

"Who is that?"

"Jamie Cullum." He climbed onto the mattress. Poised over me, he lowered his head so our noses touched. "We're going to lie here and forget the world for a while, alright?"

Enclosed within his magnetic sphere I reached up, touching his cheek. "If that's what you want."

His jaw tensed, eyes flashing. "You are what I want. Only you. Always."

He kissed me with the feverish passion of a man who'd finally found the one thing that gave his life meaning. We made out like sex-starved teenagers, rolling around on the bed, yanking each other's shirts off. Hands and fingers moved greedily over skin, grabbing and caressing. His body was solid, lean muscle next to my soft curves. I had no definitive thought process, only where I should touch him next.

When we finally stopped, I had ended up on top of him, slowly kissing his neck.

"What are you doing with that smart mouth of yours, Amelia?"

"Staking my claim." I nibbled at his skin. He tensed briefly, then moaned and relaxed. I kissed down his chest, smiling as the reddish-brown hairs tickled my face. A quick squeeze at my waist stopped me.

"Hey." I sat up.

"I have to get something. Don't move."

He kissed my nose before standing up and leaving the room. I grabbed one of the oversized pillows and flopped onto my stomach, listening to INXS sing soulfully about afterglow. Resting my chin on my hand I smiled, looking out into the bedroom. Like the rest of the cottage, this room was warm and cozily draped in rich neutral colors. It reminded me a bit of the color scheme in his living room, only without the cold, sterile aura.

He seemed much happier and at peace here than he did anywhere else. But maybe that was just my wishful thinking. Anytime he let his guard down was a moment to behold. Oh, how I loved when he did. I could only hope he realized how much it meant to me.

I noticed something move out the corner of my eye. Looking to my left I saw Alastair standing by the door, pointing a camera in my direction.

"What are you doing?" I jumped.

Confused, he lowered the camera. I clutched the comforter, trying to tame my furiously beating heart. *Dammit. Control yourself.*

"You just," I stammered, "I wasn't expecting you to be taking pictures of me."

"I was going to say something but you looked so pretty lying there. Sorry." His shy little smile made me melt. So did the fact that he was shirtless wearing only his jeans. "Want to see?"

"Sure," I sighed, sitting up. Settling next to me, he turned the camera so I could look at the preview screen. There I was, stretched out on my stomach clad in only my bra and shorts, hair all mussed up. My pinky finger rested on my lips, which were curled into a lovesick smile. To top it all off, my legs were bent at the knees, feet pointing up to the ceiling. *Oh my God.*

"I look so…" I wrinkled my nose.

"Perfect."

"I'm far from perfect."

He frowned. "I want you to see yourself through my eyes. This is my favorite smile of yours. You have so many different ones but this one…it's…" He swallowed hard. "I like to think you smile like this when you're thinking about me."

I blinked at him, stunned.

"Too cheesy again?"

"No. It's, um…you have a favorite smile?"

"I have a lot of favorite things about you. At the risk of sounding too soppy, I'll end it there."

Regaining some of his trademark cool-as-ice demeanor, he leaned against the headboard. The guy who once declared he didn't do relationships certainly knew how to charm a girl. Always a master at disguising his feelings, the mask slid back into place, locking in any trace of emotion that tried to escape. Not what I wanted.

"Can I ask you something?"

He eyed me suspiciously. "Alright."

"How did you end up with this place?"

The switch from stoic to tranquil was subtle. He stared out in an almost dreamlike state. I was fascinated.

"It belonged to my mum's parents. They were from Scotland

and bought this cottage shortly after they married. I never met them. They died before I was born and left it to her. Years went by before anyone thought to do anything with it. I remember my parents talking about having it renovated so we could spend summers here. Obviously that never happened." His shoulders slumped. "When I turned eighteen and finally got the keys to the place I drove out here to see it. I'd never been before. It was rundown and needed loads of work to be livable. I hired some contractors, told them what I wanted and here we are."

Every layer I managed to peel away held an intriguing nugget of information.

"You never considered selling it?"

"No." His voice tightened. "Not an option."

"So, you're part Scottish then?"

A huge smile brightened his face. "Aye. My being a ginger didn't give it away, lass?"

"At least your attempt at a Scottish accent is better than your American one. What other tricks can you do? Got any kilts in your closet?"

Raising an eyebrow, he grinned wickedly. "You'd like that wouldn't you?"

"I like you just as you are now; half naked in your jeans, relaxed and playful. This cottage has an amazing effect on your whole being. It makes me happy to see you this way." The words tumbled out of my mouth faster than I could employ some sort of filter.

"I feel safe here," he said quietly, not breaking eye contact with me. "For someone like me, that's rare."

The strength of his admission hit me hard. This was his sanctuary, a place to lock out the world and be himself. I studied his body language, looking for any signs of withdrawal. He sat calmly, hands resting in his lap. I half expected him to start meditating.

"Is that why you brought me here?"

Staring darkly, he repositioned himself to kneel in front of me. Every muscle moved with controlled precision. I sat up on my knees so we were eye to eye. He still seemed relaxed but there was a hint of danger in his eyes.

"We all want to be understood, to find that one person who needs no explanation when they look at you. I've wandered through most of my life shutting out that possibility. And then I met you." He paused, tracing his finger along my jaw. "Nobody has seen me so completely. We're two sides of the same coin, Amelia. I am yours and you are mine. Always."

A pleasurable shiver ran down my spine.

"I told you once that you made me feel so much, it hurt. Even now, in the safety of this cottage, it hurts. I don't understand it but I know I can't live without it." He used both hands to cup my jaw, fixing a stare on me so hot the intensity burned straight to the pit of my stomach. I grabbed his waist, pulling him closer.

"I hate to break it to you, Holden, but you have it bad for me."

"Is that so?"

"Yup."

"Your way with words is stunning as always, Meyers."

"I love you, too." I leaned in, brushing my lips on his. "The thing I mentioned before about you being so goddam sexy?"

"Yes?"

"Thought I'd, you know, bring it up again."

He kissed my forehead. "Tell me what you want. I'll give you the world if you asked."

"I have everything I want right in front of me."

He slowly traced his fingers along the contours of my body, savoring each curve with gentle strokes. "I'll be right back. Don't move."

"Why?"

The atmosphere shifted as an unrelenting tempest of want and need gathered around us.

"Because I said so, love," he said in a low, commanding tone. Only the feral gleam in his eyes betrayed the outer shell of control. When he spoke to me like this my whole body came alive.

I watched him saunter out of the room and trembled with anticipation. Not even the stress of the past week could derail the frenzy of lust that continued to build. I became more attuned to my deepest, most intimate desires with him. He brought out a side of me I'd never allowed myself to set free with anyone else.

I barely noticed the lights turning off as they were replaced by the flickering glow of candles. A haunting piano melody filled the room rounded out by a slow, seductive electronic beat. Alastair had me caged against the mattress and locked in a deep kiss as wisps of the lyrics floated through what was left of any conscious thoughts in my mind.

"This song," he whispered on my lips, "is called *Bloodstream*. It describes exactly what you do to me."

Too overwhelmed by him and how he covered every inch of me in magnificent kisses, I neglected to pay attention to the song.

CHAPTER FIVE

The mattress moved as Alastair stirred next to me, draping an arm over my stomach. His face held none of the dispassionate, guarded façade it did while he was awake. Sleep almost gave him a seraphic glow. *My tragic angel.*

Carefully removing his arm, I almost managed to get up without waking him.

"Lia," he mumbled, his voice thick with sleep. "Stay with me."

"I'm just getting some water," I whispered, kissing his forehead.

"Hurry back, love."

He was sound asleep before I left the bedside. I tiptoed to the living room. The cottage floors were old and creaky so I made sure to move as quietly as possible. I noticed the green light on my cell phone blinking from the coffee table. I grabbed it and took a small blanket from the couch. Taking a deep breath, I unlatched the door and went outside. A chilly breeze swept over my bare skin. Even in July Scotland had a way of reminding me not to get overly comfortable with the warmer temperatures.

Hugging the blanket around me, I unlocked the phone. Several text messages from Nathan waited for me. I was about to respond when the phone vibrated in my hand.

"What?" I hissed.

"I thought you'd be sleeping," Nathan drawled. "Did I wake

you?"

"No. Why the hell are you calling me in the middle of the night?"

I heard him sigh in a way that suggested he was rubbing his hand over his face. I'd seen him do that a million times, usually when he was frustrated. "When do you get back to Orlando? I need to see you."

I scrunched my toes into the cool grass. "No, you don't."

"Listen," he snapped, "do you want my help or not? If you do, we're doing this my way."

"I don't take orders from you. We don't ever need to be in the same space."

"Dammit Lia, stop being so difficult."

My anger at him and with myself for reopening this door flooded my body. "I'm not say—"

The phone was ripped from my hand. I spun around, coming face to face with one pissed off Englishman. Alastair put the phone to his ear and said in a deadly calm tone, "Leave. Her. Alone."

Moonlight cast a silver glow on his stony expression, accentuating the unfiltered animosity in his eyes. He remained still as a statue, holding my phone in a death grip. Seconds passed by with slow torture.

"Call or talk to her again and it will be one of the last things you do." Ending the call, he lowered his hand and stared at me. "Is this what's been bothering you?"

I couldn't answer. I just pulled the blanket tighter. Reaching out as though he was going to touch my cheek, Alastair stopped and scowled. Vulnerability hovered behind his eyes like smoke before disappearing, wrenching my heart.

"I—"

"Tell me why you were on the phone with *him*, in my front garden, at two in the morning."

This wasn't a request. Gone was the relaxed, playful man I'd spent the day with. I was now presented with his public persona, the one so guarded and locked it gave weight to the reputation that he was standoffish and didn't want to be bothered. I hated knowing I caused this side of him to materialize.

"He's been after me all week about some exclusive interview." The words flowed out of my mouth with little effort. I had no idea my brain could even work let alone react with such logic. "He won't tell me what it's about and already," I raked a hand through my tangled hair, "finagled a dinner meeting out of me this week."

A raised eyebrow was his only response.

"I hated every second of it," I blurted. "He kept apologizing for everything and wanted to make amends. I didn't—"

"Do you want to be with him?" he interrupted with strained agony in his voice.

Air rushed out of my lungs forcing me to bend forward and clutch my thighs. "No. Jesus, Alastair, why would you even think that?"

"You know his demons. You don't know all of mine. Familiarity can be comforting even in the most undesirable circumstances."

"That's crazy talk and you know it." I moved closer to him. "This is all on me. I fucked up and should have told you but I wanted this weekend to be about us. No drama. No stress. Just you. And me."

Dropping the blanket, I put my hands on his bare chest. I felt the ferocious vibrations of his heart beating and waited for him to push me away or shrink further into his shell. How could I expect him to see me as his safe place if I treated him this way? A hot, gritty lump forced its way up my throat.

"Look at me." He wrapped both hands around my neck, pushing his thumbs into my jaw and compelling me to look up. Passion and determination blazed from his eyes. "I've never worked harder at anything in my life. Every instinct I have tells me not to get attached to you, not to let you in. But you are my clarity. I've never felt as strongly for someone as I do for you and it scares the shit out of me. I will move heaven and earth for you but if I am not what you want—"

"You are the only thing I want," I yelled, my voice echoing through the darkness.

"—I will step aside."

The weight of his words hung in the air, dulling the stars and muting the moon's glow. I couldn't breathe. I could only stand and shiver. Letting go of my neck, he bent down and picked up the blanket, draping it over my shoulders. I wilted under the heaviness, feeling it more as a burden than comfort.

"I'm sorry." Thick tears rolled down my cheeks. Wiping them away with his thumb, he considered saying something. Instead, he kissed the corner of my mouth. I grabbed the back of his head, pulling his lips to mine, desperate to show him how much I loved him. He held me tightly, kissing down my neck, whispering words of affection. *You are my world…my everything…always… always…always.*

Scooping me in his arms, he carried me back into the cottage.

* * *

Buchanan Street was apparently *the* place to be on Sunday afternoon. Scores of high-end retail stores lined both sides of the pedestrian friendly street. For someone as well-versed in shopping as me, this was heaven. Warm sunlight shone down as Alastair and I walked hand in hand on the strikingly beautiful granite stonework. I drank in the intricate mix of Victorian architecture and urban design. Glasgow had quickly become one of my favorite places on earth.

"This way." Alastair tugged gently at my hand, guiding me down another street lined with shops. We stopped in front of a jewelry store. My pulse skyrocketed when he reached for the door.

"Are we going in there?"

"Yes, love."

Either I swayed or a rare earthquake shook the sidewalk.

"Relax, Lia. It's not what you think. Not yet."

52

He led me to a display case filled with glittering diamonds, emeralds, sapphires and every other precious stone imaginable. Bypassing those, he stopped at the far end of the display. Inside sat the most unique, beautiful ring I'd ever seen. A gorgeously polished cognac amber nugget was nestled beneath a swirling setting of white gold encrusted with small diamonds. The nugget was huge and oval within its imperfect shape. The setting was wrapped around the amber, almost mimicking a hug.

"Mr. Holden. Welcome back," a well-dressed man from behind the counter greeted him. I glanced at the lapel of his dark suit and noticed a nametag. *Alright, Robert. What do the two of you have in store for me?*

Alastair squeezed my hand and grinned. "Been getting many inquires about this?" he gestured toward the ring.

"Several. It's not often we keep a custom designed ring on display when it's already spoken for."

I swallowed. Hard. Robert opened the display case, removed the ring and laid it on a piece of velvet in front of me. My free hand flew to my neck, grasping the necklace Alastair had given me only a few weeks ago at the beach. I ran my thumb over the platinum 'A.'

"Try it on," he encouraged, letting go of my hand.

I picked it up and slid it onto the middle finger of my left hand, immediately feeling its weight. Holding up my hand, I admired the way the amber glowed and the diamonds sparkled under the soft light.

"The stone's color reminded me of your eyes," Alastair said, brushing his thumb over the ring. "I hope you—" I silenced him with a kiss. Feeling the firm pressure of his lips moving with mine negated any reservations I had about public displays of affection.

"I love you. So much," I declared, tightening my grip on his shirt. "Always."

Little by little, fragments of the impenetrable outer shell were breaking away, revealing the man I adored. It wasn't a complete shedding of the barrier. He kept enough in place to let me know there were still some issues we had to work through. "I want everyone to know you're mine. Off the market, so to speak."

By *everyone*, I knew he meant only one specific person. His penetrating stare was sultry but it made me nervous.

"I only have eyes for you, Alastair Holden."

The slightly arched eyebrow did nothing to quell the undeniable disdain he held for my ex. "Good."

Grinning, I pulled him close for a soft kiss.

Two women took it upon themselves to pick this moment to stand next to us and peruse the jewelry in the case. It was clear they knew exactly who he was. They shot sideways glances at me while pretending to coo over the rings. He probably didn't appreciate these people being so intrusive. Much to my surprise, he fisted his hand in my hair and kissed me with such force I almost fell backwards. Sliding his tongue around mine in long slow strokes, he kept us locked in this heated embrace far longer than I would have expected. Not that I minded.

"My Lia," he breathed. "Let's get out of here."

I swear I saw the two women fanning themselves as we left.

* * *

The level of concentration on his face was staggering as he flipped through a large cookbook. I stood on the opposite side of the breakfast bar, not hiding the amused smile growing on my lips.

"You're staring."

"So are you. I'm hungry. Get started, chief."

He flicked those bright emerald irises at me, making my heart race. "I'd rather not have this go pear shaped if you don't mind."

"C'mon. It's only dinner. Don't be so…" I paused, looking for the right word, "British."

He smirked. "You don't know what pear shaped means, do you?"

Tapping my nails on the counter, I shrugged. I knew what it

meant but was more interested in the stare being leveled at me than his use of slang. Those eyes could stop time. Oh, and that mouth. Even twisted in a wry grin it made my insides quiver. *Mine.* Every inch of him was mine.

"What are you thinking about?" The rich, velvet tenor of his voice curled my toes.

"You. Duh."

"Very articulate."

"What can I say? You're, like, totally hot and I wanna see you naked." I twirled my hair in an exaggerated manner and winked.

He smiled slightly. Since we returned to his house in Bearsden after the jewelry store I'd been trying to draw out his playful side. The emotional roller coaster from last night had a strong hold on both of us. I'd hoped it would have weakened by now. Strumming his fingers on the counter, Alastair sighed.

"How about we order food instead and do…couple-y things?"

"Couple-y things?" I scrunched my nose. "Who's being articulate now?"

He shrugged. "I have this big living room that I never use. I thought maybe we could watch a movie or listen to music or… have a snog or two."

"Oh, *those* couple-y things. You mean, what normal people do?" I teased.

"Cheeky." His pretty eyes dropped their shield sending a rush of happiness through me. "What do you prefer? Chinese, Indian or Italian?"

"Keep it simple. You can't go wrong with pizza."

Shooting me an exaggerated eye roll, he rifled through one of the drawers and pulled out a menu. Judging by the name of the restaurant, it was something Italian and most certainly not pizza. He disappeared to his office without asking me what I wanted. I made myself comfortable in the museum-like living room. The couch cushions were so puffy I had a feeling I was the only one to ever sit on them. I was afraid to touch anything. Even the remote control for the flat screen television looked unused. The only thing in here that had any personal feel to it was the photo he'd taken of Big Ben with a red bus driving past it.

I smiled to myself, wondering what he was going to do with the pictures he'd taken of me last night. It wasn't too big of a stretch to think he'd display them somewhere in the house. Preferably the bedroom. Although from my understanding nobody ever came here so he could blow the pictures up poster sized and hang them all over the house if he wanted. *Silly, silly thoughts.*

"You look like the cat that got the cream," he remarked, striding through the room. "I'm going to pick up the food. It's just down the street so I won't be long. Make yourself comfortable."

I grabbed the remote and stretched out on the couch, saluting him. "Yes, sir."

His gaze darkened as he hovered over me. "Be careful, kitten. I could get used to you saying that."

Spurred on by the heated stare leveled at me, I ran a finger down his shirt. "Is that so, Mr. Holden?"

"Vixen," he muttered, nipping at my earlobe. "I'll deal with you when I come back."

"I'm counting on it."

"Wow." The throaty laugh I loved so much filled the room. "Someone is extra feisty tonight."

I heard him chuckling all the way to the door. Once he was gone, I decided to take another self-guided tour of his house. Strolling past the master bedroom and home office, I noticed a closed door at the far end of the hallway. I twisted the doorknob and was surprised to find it locked. My curiosity shot off the charts. I figured it was a second bedroom but why keep it under lock and key? *What is he hiding now?* Scolding myself for always assuming the worst, I went to his bedroom. The camera sat on his bureau. I grabbed it, turned on the preview screen and almost dropped it.

A picture of me sleeping popped up. Thank goodness I wasn't slack jawed or drooling in the photo. I actually looked quite peaceful with one hand curled under my chin. Taking a deep breath, I scrolled through more photos. They were all of me. He must have taken a dozen while I was sleeping. The rest were from when he'd been lurking by the door.

His aunt once told me he had a soft spot for fragile beauty. She'd mentioned he was drawn to how delicate and unexpected it was. I guess that was how he saw me. I thought back to last night when we were standing outside.

I've never worked harder at anything in my life.

Underneath all the expensive clothes and rigid exterior, there was a broken man who yearned to love. I knew he didn't trust his emotions. I knew he retreated to a dark place when he felt overwhelmed. Inadequateness surged from the pit of my stomach to the tips of my fingers and toes. My own insecurities could be just as crippling.

Stretching out on the bed, I held the camera on my stomach and closed my eyes. A frisson of electricity jolted me. My hairs stood on end. I knew he was in the room. I could feel him.

"Do you always take pictures of sleeping, unsuspecting women?" I asked with a grin.

The mattress jostled when he sat down.

"Only ones who find themselves in my bed."

The tone of his response suggested there was a cocky grin crossing his lips. I confirmed my suspicions as soon as I looked at him.

"You must have quite the collection."

He hesitated, uncertain if he wanted to continue. The uneasiness was brief. "I do now. And I think I want to add more."

The sultry timbre in his voice, coupled with those hooded bedroom eyes, roused all the right parts of my body. I sat up, nuzzling my nose to his. "After you feed me."

"Why am I not surprised?" he smiled. "Come on."

Two plates of pasta were arranged on the coffee table along with some garlic bread and a small salad. We ate in silence mostly because I was petrified I'd spill something on his pristine rug. He cleared the dishes, instructing me to stay on the couch and wait for him.

Andrea Bocelli's clear, tenor voice floated through the room joined by the powerful vocals of Sarah Brightman for their popular duet *Con te partirò*. I turned, noticing Alastair standing in front of the media cabinet. He held a remote and scrolled through a list of songs.

"Do you have a preference?" he asked.

"Whatever you like to listen to is fine with me."

"Alright." He set down the remote and flopped onto the couch next to me. Sighing into the cushions, he draped his arm over my shoulders. "This is rather comfortable."

"Don't tell me you've never sat in here before."

He shot me a sideways glance and grinned. "I have, once or twice." Tucking me into his side, he continued, "There's not usually a gorgeous girl next to me though. This relationship thing may have its advantages."

I laughed. "I've been upgraded to arm candy for your living room? Sweet."

Resting my head on his chest, I lost myself in the rhythmic beating of his heart. It sped up when I placed a hand on his thigh.

"Do you have to fly home tomorrow?" The soft warmth of his lips brushed against my forehead. I squeezed his leg.

"Yeah."

Enveloping me in his arms, he repositioned himself so we were both lying on the couch, fitting together like pieces of a puzzle. Leaning his forehead to mine he whispered, "Stay. Live with me."

A full brigade of butterflies and fireworks exploded in my stomach. I froze in the midst of his stare.

Unaffected, he continued, "I want the sound of your laughter to fill this house. I want to fall asleep next to you every night and wake up with you every morning."

"I—"

"If you're worried about your job, don't be. I have it on good authority a highly rated news magazine program is looking for a new executive producer. I can get you an interview tomorrow."

"Christ," I muttered. "Does your company own this show?"

"No."

This had to be a joke. It wasn't possible for me to drop everything and move to Glasgow at a moment's notice, let alone switch jobs on a whim.

"Your brain is overheating, kitten."

I rolled my eyes at his smug grin. "Well, you try being me for a second with some hot English guy saying all these super romantic things. It's not easy for me to say no to you, Alastair."

"I know," he kept grinning. "Think about it. And then say yes."

"Oh my God," I snorted. "You're impossible."

Keeping that ridiculous grin plastered to his face, he leaned in and kissed me softly. It turned my brain into a useless pile of gray matter.

"Will it always be like this? Will it always feel this way?"

The innocence and wonder reflecting in his eyes brought tears to my own. I didn't know the answer to that. Nobody did. I told him the only thing I felt in my soul.

"It will as long as we love each other."

Swallowing hard, he nodded and held me tighter. "I hope you're right," he whispered.

CHAPTER SIX

"Amelia Grace, why do you never answer the phone?" my mother's chipper voice blared through the receiver. "Your father and I have booked a flight to Orlando. We arrive on Friday. It would be nice if we got to see our daughter."

I erased the voice message and rested my head on the steering wheel. I loved my parents dearly and missed them but I sort of wanted this weekend to be all about vegging out on the couch. They usually took an impromptu vacation every summer to the west coast or Bermuda or somewhere that wasn't Central Florida. I could only imagine why they were gracing me with their presence.

I glanced up at the threatening black clouds. The second I stepped out of my car, the sky opened up and poured its wet bucket of sadness all over me. Grimacing, I ran toward the restaurant wishing a magical dome would appear and save me from the downpour. Nope. I ran right through a puddle instead. My feet squished in the now soaked sandals I thought would be so cute to wear today.

"Stupid summer rain," I grumbled.

I saw Stephanie as soon as I walked through the restaurant doors. She sat at the bar, flirting mercilessly with a guy who exuded the casual air of a California surfer. When I first moved to Orlando we had flirting down to a choreographed science when we'd go out. She was a master. No man was safe when she turned on the charm.

"Lia," she called, waving me over. "Come sit."

Smoothing down my damp hair, I perched on the stool next to her.

"This is Bradley." She introduced us.

Unassumingly handsome with shaggy blond hair and chocolate brown eyes, he was the poster-child for the type of man Stephanie drooled over. I leaned forward, shaking his hand.

"Bradley just moved here from Maine," Stephanie informed me, poking my side with her elbow.

"Yeah. A really, really small town called Castine," he said. "I was offered a job down here, so I packed up my car, threw the dog in the backseat and headed south."

"Maine, huh? I'm originally from Connecticut." I smiled.

He laughed. "A couple of displaced New Englanders in all this Florida heat and humidity. How long have you lived here?"

"Almost six years."

"How about you?" he turned to my best friend, "Are you from New England, too?"

"Oh God, no. I was born and raised here. I grew up in Oviedo."

"My first native Floridian? I didn't think any of you actually existed."

"We do." She laughed coquettishly and morphed back into full on flirt mode. The protocol was for me to remain nearby and only intervene if she flashed the signal. Catching the bartender's attention I ordered a glass of sparkling wine and fiddled with my phone. Alastair's invitation to live with him flitted through my mind. I would love nothing more than to be with him permanently.

"Come on, Lia. Our table's ready."

Looking up I saw Stephanie hug her new conquest goodbye before following the hostess. We were seated at a table by the window.

"You two seemed to hit it off," I remarked, raising an eyebrow.

"What? Yeah. He was nice."

Stephanie was flustered. Unbelievable.

"*Nice*? Who are you?"

"Huh?" She blinked. "Oh. He was okay. We're going out on Friday."

"Are you inviting him to your big new job celebration?"

Her face brightened immediately. "I still can't believe they hired me. And I'm moving to Glasgow in two weeks. This is crazy. You have to come with me."

"I just got back yesterday," I laughed.

"So?" she exclaimed. "You have to help me move and get all settled. It's only fair. Tell Bruce this is more important than the show and writing thirty second stories and editing stupid video."

The panicked look on her face would have been priceless had she not been serious. Getting hired at Finley Marketing and Advertising as a graphic designer may be a dream job for Stephanie but leaving the city she loves and all her friends behind weighed heavily on her.

"I'll see what I can do. At this rate Bruce might tell me to stay over there."

"That would be the best news ever. Live with me, find a fabulous job and we will own that city."

"You make it sound so simple."

"It is." She looked me up and down. "Besides, you're still glowing from the weekend so I know at least one other person would be thrilled if you moved there."

"Let's not get a—"

"It's the next logical step." She waved her hand to brush off my protest. "I mean, my God, look at that ring. I'm surprised you got on the plane to come back. Don't give me that look. You know I'm right. Besides, long distance relationships are tough. Especially when it's across an ocean."

"So now you're pro-Alastair?" I sat back, folding my arms.

"I was never really anti. He's a little moody and stiff sometimes but he treats you like a queen. Darren likes him and he would tell me if there was something off about him. The other stuff is... I shouldn't have given what Cassie said so much stock. I worry about you and hearing all that negative gossip about him pissed me off."

I watched her squirm in the chair. She hated apologizing. I sipped my wine to hide the amused smile growing on my lips. Nothing fooled her though. She narrowed her ice blue eyes.

"You're enjoying this too much," she grumbled.

"Maybe."

"Listen, I will support this relationship one hundred percent. But," she leaned forward, "I swear, if he pulls another stunt like he did in England I will go after his ginger ass like a princess on fire."

"Your enthusiasm for that is scary."

"You're my unofficial-little-sister-official-best-friend. He hurts you, he hurts me by default." A chagrined look crossed her face. "Besides, he did fly four thousand miles to patch things up with you. The romantic in me is jealous and swooning at the same time."

"I can probably ruin this relationship without his help," I mumbled.

"That sounded ominous. Is something going on?"

"Oh, you know," I sighed. "Just my awesome self-doubt."

"Stop it. He loves you. You love him. Enough said."

"Anyway," I chuckled, "my parents are coming to visit this weekend. Know anybody who can get them tickets to a show or the ballet or something so I don't have to be a one-woman entertainment stop?"

"Ah, I love your parents," she exclaimed. "Your mother kills me. And your dad is a riot. Nobody at the station has tickets to anything?"

"Yeah but I was away so I missed out."

"There's a Predators game on Saturday if they're into arena football."

"My dad will love it."

"I'll ask Justin to give me his suite tickets. That way we can go with them." She flashed a mischievous smile. Justin owned the salon where she worked and was currently dating the Predators' public relations manager.

The server arrived to take our orders before I had a chance to give Stephanie a snarky reply. We spent the next couple hours brainstorming ideas for her party and being silly. We probably drank more wine than was necessary. It dawned on us that she'd be living in Glasgow for the next milestone in her life: the illustrious thirtieth birthday. Always one to find an excuse to celebrate, Stephanie declared she'd have a massive party at one of the nightclubs downtown. Of course, I'd have to fly out there to join the celebration. Seeing her so excited made me so happy.

"Ugh. My bladder is getting old," she complained. "I'll be right back."

I laughed watching her dart off to the ladies' room. She hadn't been gone five seconds when I felt a presence behind me.

"Lia."

The voice saying my name sent a small shiver down my spine. Steeling myself, I turned. Standing in his tan dress pants and crisp white button down shirt, Nathan looked like the poster child for a L.L. Bean catalogue. He moved closer and held my arm. I stiffened, ready to make a scene.

"May I sit?"

"No."

Ignoring me, he sat in Stephanie's seat. "Have a nice weekend?" His tone dripped with acid.

"Spectacular."

Nathan leaned back in the chair with an air of over-confidence. "Nice ring. You didn't tell him about the photos, did you?"

Anger squeezed my chest in an unrelenting grip. "No."

"I figured you wouldn't. Knowing you the way I do, all the facts have to be tied up in a neat little package before you attack. You should have been a prosecutor."

I wanted to burn the smile off his face with a blowtorch. "What do you want?"

"Look, I know this situation hasn't been pleasant for you. I'm afraid it'll only get worse."

"How do you know that?"

"There's something that family doesn't want the general public to know. His uncle went to great lengths to keep it hidden. From what I've learned it has something to do with your boyfriend and an incident from his early twenties. I don't like where this is going, Lia. He's not good for you."

The room spun violently. More secrets? An incident? I clasped my hands together and stared at Nathan. I needed to play this smart.

"Stop being so dramatic. It's not like you didn't do stupid shit in your early twenties."

"Right. But my stupid shit isn't sealed in a file. Something big happened. I want to know what and I want you to see the light about him."

Rage simmered deep within me, giving me a strange quiet calm. My focus sharpened along with my instincts. This was a game for Nathan, a battle of wills. I wouldn't - *couldn't* - let him win.

"So much for you wanting to gain my trust, then."

He bristled at my tone, displaying an expression I'd seen a million times before - disgust. "Wake up, Lia. Whatever my faults were in our relationship at least I never hid anything from you."

"Yeah. You were a real keeper."

"What is it about him that's so goddam special? He's a womanizer sitting on a mountain of cash. You're not a gold digger so his bank account means nothing to you. It certainly can't be his sparkling personality."

I smiled slyly, holding his piercing stare. Frustrated, Nathan rested his forearms on the table. I folded my hands in front of me. There was a time when his look would frighten me or make me back down. The realization that I'd been so blinded by what I thought was love for him burned brightly. I'd never loved him. I was only trying to win his approval. In the process, I'd lost part of who I was deep down.

"Jealousy has always been an ugly color on you," I said with a smug smile.

Nathan grabbed my hand, squeezing tightly. Determination flashed through his eyes like a building storm. "I don't want things to be like this between us. I'm not your enemy."

We stared at one another, which made me slightly uncomfortable. Regardless of his envious outburst, nothing but sincerity bled from him.

"I don't know what you want me to say," I said cautiously. "We don't have the best history."

"That's not true. Remember the first time we went away together?"

The memory flooded me with unexpected warmth. A genuine, glowing smile bloomed across Nathan's lips. He gently squeezed my hand.

"You do remember. We went to Sanibel Island for Memorial Day weekend. I took you sailing and paragliding and snorkeling. I think it was the second day we were out on the Gulf, when you saw a dolphin. I'll never forget the look on your face as long as I live. You were so excited and awed by it. I knew at that moment, you were the one."

The unsullied joy of that weekend away filled every fiber of my being. The recollection was so vivid I could almost smell the salty air. As much as I hated to admit it to myself, he was right. Not all of our history together sucked. Moments like that weekend in Sanibel were living proof.

"Try to focus on those moments, Lia. I only have your best interest at heart."

My whole body vibrated, not knowing how to react to anything. *I shouldn't have had all that damn wine.* I broke out into a cold sweat.

"Let me handle this thing with Rachel," he continued. "I'll get her off your back and convince her to focus her interests on that baseball player who knocked up some college freshman. That's more her speed anyway."

"But if she's getting paid to—"

"I can ruin her reputation in a heartbeat. Nobody respects or trusts a so-called journalist who takes money under the table to print gossip. She's looking for the big score to get a flashy by-line. You don't have any dirty little secrets. I'm pretty sure she's figured that out by now."

"Are you positive the money is coming from his uncle?" My voice shook.

Nathan almost looked sympathetic. "It's coming from a trust account that he deposits money into every month."

"How did you find out about this?"

"That's not important."

I clenched my jaw. What a dumb question. This guy was a master at stalking. Although, and my God how I hated to admit it, his skills would be beneficial in getting to the bottom of why Alastair's family wanted to dig up information on me.

"Okay," I said quietly.

"Okay what?"

Every piece of my soul fought against what I was about to say. Nathan gave my hand a reassuring squeeze. *I hope I'm doing the right thing.*

"Do what you have to do," I nearly choked on the words. "But promise me you'll stay away from Alastair and you won't confront him."

He scowled. "If I find out something that—"

"Nathan. Promise me or I walk away forever."

"Fine," he relented, looking at me softly. "Thank you for trusting me."

"Don't make me regret this." I snapped my hand away.

"Get the hell away from her."

Stephanie's outburst caused several people to turn in our direction.

"Thanks for the talk, Sparkle," he said, standing up. Fixing a cold stare on Stephanie, he smirked. "Nice to see you, Steph."

She flipped him off as he walked to the exit. "What an asshole. Why did you let him sit down?"

"I didn't *let* him do anything. He just sat." I rubbed my temples, wishing I had stayed in Glasgow.

* * *

Torn Between a Senator's Son and a Billionaire Media Mogul
By: Rachel Jameson

Do we smell reconciliation? WMZB's Lia Meyers has been spotted out on the town not once, but twice with former flame Nathan Greyson. The attractive pair dined together last week at a cozy table for two in one of Orlando's hottest restaurants. Last night, they were canoodling downtown in a more casual setting. And yes, she is sporting an expensive ring close to that finger. The news producer has turned heads recently with her highly publicized relationship with British media mogul Alastair Holden. The sexy English redhead spent two weeks in the city wooing his American lady, alongside working as CEO at Holden World Media, but has since returned to the United Kingdom. Were his efforts enough to keep her from rekindling a romance with Orlando's most eligible bachelor? The senator's son has been nursing a broken heart since his ladylove broke things off earlier this year. Only time will tell. Stay tuned.

The accompanying photos weren't much better. One picture showed Alastair and I walking hand in hand through Cranes Roost Park. The others made me physically ill. A seemingly intimate moment between Nathan and me from last night showed our hands clasped together as we stared at one another. A similar one from last week's dinner turned my stomach. At first blush, it looked like a tender moment. What the average gossip-loving person didn't know wasn't important. Pictures spoke a thousand words and that one proclaimed *reconciliation*.

Glaring at Rachel Jameson's name in the byline, I resisted the urge to call her. The whole article made it sound like I was playing both guys, as if I couldn't decide who I wanted more. It was laughable but again, the average person who lived for gossip didn't care about the validity.

"Another appearance in the gossip column? You're becoming notorious."

I shot Tyler Garrett a nasty look. The assignment editor perched himself on the edge of my desk, grinning with glee.

"How have you managed to hold back on the comments for so long?"

"C'mon, Lia. Lighten up. I'm only teasing."

"I know, I know. Sorry. It's just so annoying."

"Let's face it. Orlando is boring and this is the most exciting thing going on aside from the theme parks and shuttle launches. You should feel honored."

In spite of my annoyance at the article, I laughed at his nonchalant attitude. "I don't know about that but thanks."

"Ignore it. This will do more to bolster Greyson's ego than anything. Your guy probably won't even see it."

My stomach dropped. *Oh shit. He's going to go ballistic.* I fought off nausea while attempting to keep a normal expression in front of my co-worker.

"Are you coming to the event at Lane's tonight?" Tyler asked, standing up. "I know Wes and Katie are going. Sounds like it'll be a good one."

One of the players from the city's basketball team was holding his annual charity bowling event. A good majority of people from the other television stations would be there along with fans who purchased tickets, local sports celebrities and corporate guests from various companies sponsoring the event. I wanted to go. *I should go.* I was just so emotionally drained from last night. Sleep was elusive and my brain didn't stop creating horrible scenarios about what I'd agreed to.

"Probably not," I answered. "I want as many nights to myself as I can have before my parents get here Friday."

"Bring them by the station. We'll dazzle them with our hurry-up-and-wait television schtick."

I laughed. My mother would love nothing more than to be paraded through the newsroom. She thought my job was so glamorous.

"Can you handle three Meyers at once?"

"I put up with that one all day." He gestured toward Gus at the assignment desk. "Your family will be a breeze."

"Hey, Lia." Cynthia Steele, one half of our evening anchor team, walked towards my desk with purpose. Tyler ducked out just before she arrived. Already dressed in her royal blue pantsuit for the broadcast, she looked network TV ready.

"I have a question about this health story on vitamins. The script doesn't make any sense."

She pointed to the rundown. I read it, paying close attention to the wording.

"What's confusing you?"

"It says women who take vitamins every day have a higher risk of dying early. But then it says there's no conclusive result. Which is it? Am I going to die young because I take vitamin B or not?"

"I'll polish up the wording. It should say the study only showed an association, not cause and effect. It's also missing the part about researchers not asking the women about underlying health issues."

"Who wrote it?" She narrowed her eyes and fingered a piece of immoveable auburn hair.

"Um, one of the new writers. I'll talk to him and make sure he knows to add as much info as possible." I grinned, amused by Cynthia's theatrics over the smallest details.

"You're the best, Lia. Thank you." Her strong, melodic voice echoed through the newsroom as she strutted back to her desk. I became so lost in my work that I didn't even notice the hours flying by. An unsettled feeling paraded through my stomach when I also realized I hadn't heard from Alastair yet today. *He must have seen the article by now.*

Sheer panic seized me as I opened my inbox and saw nothing from him. I called his cell phone. It went directly to voice mail. Shaking, I typed an email.

To: Alastair Holden <aholden@holdenworldmedia.co.uk>
From: Amelia Meyers <ameyers@wmzb.net>
Subject: Missing you…
I can't reach you, chief. Please call me when you can.
Lia xoxo

I carried on with the rest of my evening and all of Thursday fully expecting a response. One never came.

CHAPTER SEVEN

Peace, quiet and a lovely bowl of spaghetti and broccoli in a light cream sauce with sun-dried tomatoes greeted me when I arrived home Friday night. I flopped on the couch and let the activity of the week slide off me bit by bit. My parents were settled into their hotel, relaxing before their visit kicked into high gear this weekend. Stephanie was at some swanky restaurant grand opening with the guy from Maine. She'd asked me to join them but I turned down her invitation politely, preferring to curl up on the couch.

I was still in my work clothes. The lure of food was too strong for me to waste time changing first. That was certainly next on my agenda for this lazy evening.

The doorbell scared the ever-living shit out of me. I dropped my fork, splattering spaghetti and cream sauce all over my skirt. Cursing under my breath I got up to open the door. I blinked, not believing what I saw. Standing in front of me looking casual and hot in his jeans and green t-shirt was Alastair holding a small paper bag. Judging by the amount of stubble on his face, I'd guess he hadn't shaved all week. And boy did he look pissed. *Shit. He'd seen the article.*

"Did I come at a bad time?" He flicked his eyes to my soiled clothes.

"Considering you've shown up unannounced and you live

across the Atlantic, I'd say yes."

"May I come in?"

"You know you don't have to ask. Why are you here?"

"I can't pop in to see my girlfriend?" he smiled, but the amusement didn't touch his eyes.

My heart started pounding. His arm brushed against me as he walked through the door, simultaneously giving me a rush and making me nervous. This was going to be interesting.

"Are you home alone?" He casually glanced around the living room before placing the bag on the kitchen counter. Turning to look at me, he folded his arms and stood as still as a statue.

"Of course. I was just having something to eat."

"I can see that," he said dryly, casting a frigid glance at my pasta stained skirt. I generally kept the temperature in my apartment comfortably cool because it was always so hot out. At this moment, it was downright arctic in here.

"Is the bearded look a new thing you're trying?"

Expressionless and stoic, he leaned against the counter. No emotion, not even anger, reflected in his eyes. He was a blank canvas and it scared the hell out of me.

"Don't be coy."

"What are—"

"What the fuck, Lia," he interrupted, clamping his arms around his torso.

I stared at him, unable to form a sentence.

Scowling in frustration, he raked both hands through his hair. A few cracks appeared in his impenetrable shield. "Stop doing this," he growled. "Or do you enjoy sneaking around behind my back with that fucking tosser?"

Each bitter word stabbed my skin with its sharp edges. Moving with calculated strides, he stood in front of me, dominating my line of sight. I was enveloped in his suffocating aura, caught between my desire to protect him from what I knew and collapse in his arms, asking for forgiveness.

"Why are you seeing him?"

"I'm not."

Clasping my chin in his hand, he tilted my head up. Hurt and confusion stained his beautiful green eyes. He kissed me forcefully, gasping for breath when he pulled away. "Why are you seeing him?"

"Alastair, I'm not seeing him."

He kissed me again. The strength of it caused me to lose my balance and fall onto the couch. I'd never felt this level of desperation emit from him. Caging me against the cushions, he squeezed his eyes shut. "You're mine," he said in a husky whisper. "Don't leave."

"I'm not leaving." I freed my arms from his grip, running my hands through his hair. "Look at me."

His laser stare nearly burned a hole through my skull straight to the floor. Completely shrouded in his protective shell, he waited for me to say something. I traced along his hairline, running my thumbs over his eyebrows, cheeks and lips. He remained so still it unnerved me. There was zero emotion on his face. His body hovered above me, rigid and unyielding. It was almost as though he was caught in a nightmare with his eyes wide open. I couldn't bear to see him like this.

"Do you want him back?" His flat, lifeless tone echoed through the room.

"Someone is following me," I blurted hoarsely. "I needed his help."

All the color drained from Alastair's face. Without saying a word, he climbed off the couch and made a phone call.

"I want you and Scott on round the clock duty for her. Tonight. I'm at her flat now. I'll make sure you both have clearance to come and go as you please."

Hearing him spout off orders over the phone to who I could only assume was Paxton jolted me out of the murky haze I'd been stuck in. I stood up, waiting for him to finish.

"I don't need bodyguards."

"But you need that knob?"

We exchanged heated stares.

"It's not as black and white as that," I glowered.

"Explain it to me."

Exasperated, I paced the room. In a moment of pure frustration, I grabbed the envelope of photos and tossed it at him. "Here. This is what I found waiting for me when I got home from work last week. I thought Nathan was behind them but he's not. It's some tabloid reporter. He's helping me get her off my back."

Alastair sifted through the photos slowly. His eyebrows shot up when he presumably saw the one of us at the beach.

"Why didn't you tell me about this?" he asked quietly. "You spent all last weekend keeping it to yourself. Why?"

"I didn't want to stress you out over something that's really not a big deal."

"Lia," he said, dropping the photos and appearing in front of me in two steps. "Your safety is a big deal. I couldn't live with myself if something ever happened to you that I could prevent. Promise me you won't do this again."

He held my chin firmly, locking a determined gaze on me. I didn't like being scolded but at least some emotion crept back into his eyes.

"I don't need bodyguards. And stop being so dramatic."

"It's not up for discussion. Be thankful I'm not having them drive you everywhere."

"Jesus Christ, Holden," I exclaimed. "What is it with you and this bossy, overprotective shit?"

Tension thinned his mouth into a firm line. "Tread carefully, Amelia."

"What? Now you don't trust me? Are they going to make sure I don't have any more secret meetings with him?"

"I never said I didn't trust you. This is for your protection."

"From what?"

Clenching his jaw, he looked away. "I don't want to fight with you."

I closed my eyes and inhaled deeply. *What are you hiding?* "I don't want to fight with you either."

"Good." He straightened his spine, appearing satisfied with the outcome. "Paxton will monitor you to and from work—"

"You can't dictate my day to day routine," I nearly shouted. The echo from my outburst bounced off the walls. Alastair stared at me impassively, waiting for my tantrum to end.

"I know," he muttered. "I'm not dictating anything. This is an extra precaution. A buffer, if you will. Now please, I don't want to fight, Amelia."

I folded my arms, sighing. "No offense, but sometimes it's exhausting being in a relationship with you."

The corners of his mouth perked up. "Ditto, love."

I rolled my eyes, focusing on the bag he'd sat on the counter eons ago. "What's in that?"

"A peace offering."

"Are we at war?"

The deep, throaty laugh that curled my toes filled the room. He pulled a bottle of vintage port out of the bag. "Not anymore. Would you like some?"

"Yeah, sure."

He gave me a once-over. "You might want to change first." *Right. The spaghetti.*

"Thank you, Mr. Blackwell."

His puzzled look made me laugh as I walked toward my bedroom. My jeans were haphazardly tossed on a chair by the window. I threw those on with a fitted, red scoop-neck cotton shirt. I caught a glimpse of myself in the mirror and ran my fingers through my hair quickly before going back to the living room.

Alastair was sitting quietly on the couch, elbows propped on his knees, chin resting on folded hands. Two wine glasses sat on the coffee table in front of him. He motioned for me to have a seat. I was momentarily struck by how that gesture made me feel like a guest in my own home. I sat gingerly next to him and grabbed a glass. The port was smoky and savory with a hint of chocolate. A slight smile curved his lips when he saw me enjoy it.

"Is this an official truce then, Holden?"

"Do you want it to be?"

"I suppose."

"Your lack of enthusiasm is worrisome," he said, taking my glass and putting it on the table. "I want your undivided attention." I could almost hear his heart pounding as he leaned in close. "My Lia. My stubborn, feisty, frustratingly enchanting Lia."

"Poetic as always." I ran my fingers over the reddish-brown beard covering his youthful face. "Not sure if I'm into this mountain man look."

"No? I thought American women liked a rugged man."

Maybe it was the way he looked at me with that little grin or the way his eyes flickered with flirtatious mischief but I couldn't help myself and climbed onto his lap, straddling him.

"I'll take you any way I can get you, chief. Now stop talking and kiss me."

Amused by my order, he obliged and treated me to a passionate lip-lock. It was skillful, sensual and confident. I enjoyed this one much more than the frantic, desperate ones from earlier. Part of me still vibrated with guilt for not being completely honest with him about the pictures and why I'd enlisted Nathan's help. For now, I focused on him and savoring this moment.

"Do you have plans this weekend?" he asked.

"No."

"You sure about that?" he chuckled.

"The only thing I'm sure about right now is I like kissing you."

"Even with all the scruffy facial hair?"

"Yes." I slung my arms around his neck. "You're insufferably hot. Hairy or otherwise."

"Ah, the truth finally comes out. I knew you only wanted me for my body."

"I prefer your cooking skills to be honest."

He smiled, leaning his forehead to mine. Placing his hands on my thighs, he caressed me with devotion and adoration. I cherished our relaxed intimacy even though I knew he remained partially shielded.

"So you're free this weekend, then?"

"My parents are in town. We're going to an arena football game tomorrow."

He regarded me with great interest. "Your parents? Can I meet them?"

Struck by the wide-eyed nature of his request, I nodded. "Yeah, of course. Do you want to come to the game with us? I can see if Steph can get another ticket."

"If it's not too much trouble. And if you don't mind being seen with a hairy ginger Englishman."

"Seriously? This is a thing, this look?"

He laughed good and loud. "No, love. Stop panicking. I worked from home all this week and got a little lazy with the shaving." Something in his eyes gave me pause. He sounded cheerful but I sensed he wasn't telling me everything.

"Lia." He tilted my chin up. "Look at me." He scanned my face, searching for God knows what. "Want to shave me?"

The request caught me off guard. Sliding a razor across his face wasn't something I'd fantasized about specifically. My goal, at some point, was to shampoo all that gorgeous hair on his head.

"The longer you think about it, the longer this beard will grow." He squeezed my waist.

"Hey." I flinched.

"Do I have to enforce the no overthinking rule again?"

"Okay, fine. I'll do it. But don't blame me if I mark up your precious face."

"Positive thoughts, please," he teased, sliding me off his lap. I followed him to my bathroom and watched him rummage through my toiletries for the shaving cream and razor. Once he had everything set up, he peeled off his t-shirt and sat on the counter.

"You're sure you trust me to do this?" I asked, squirting some shaving cream into my hand.

Inexplicably, the mask locked into place, hardening his expression. Neither one of us moved. We stared at one another silently. I desperately wanted to know what thoughts or feelings plagued him but he was unreadable. Frustrated, I rinsed the shaving cream off my hand and walked out. Nothing about tonight sat well with me anyway. I wasn't fully convinced he'd shown up at my door just because he saw the online gossip piece. A nine-hour flight for that seemed excessive.

And why the hysterics with having Paxton and that other guy keep an eye on me? I stood by the windows, staring out into the darkness. Alastair continued to be a multi-layered puzzle. Sadly, I was nowhere near figuring him out.

"Amelia."

The hairs on the back of my neck stood up. Every cell in my body gravitated to the dark, carnal voice that spoke my name. It pulled me, an unrelenting force I was powerless to stop. Aware that my breathing had become deep and labored, I turned. Alastair's half naked body filled the doorway; a tall, powerful figure exuding raw sexuality.

"Come to me."

The dangerously seductive command was intensified by his primal stare. I froze, momentarily caught in his lusty haze. Shaking it off, I went to him. The room almost hummed with the energy radiating from our bodies. Running his hand through my hair, he pulled it, forcing my head back.

"This look," he murmured, pressing his lips to my neck. The pressure from his kisses gave me a thrill. It intensified as he sucked on a soft patch of skin at the crook of my neck. I arched my back, pushing into his chest. He had me locked in a heated embrace with one hand knotted in my hair and the other tightly clasped on my backside. The world went fuzzy as I let the stress and tension of tonight melt away.

When he stopped, I was surprised to learn he'd sat me on the kitchen table. Without saying a word, he removed my shirt and bra. I watched him, fascinated. He was focused and methodical in his movements, taking off the rest of my clothes along with his own. Wrapping my legs around his hips, he leaned into me, catching my bottom lip in his teeth.

"You provoked me in a way I've never experienced," he said, low and domineering. "I am not sharing you with him. For any reason."

Fiery embers of possession flickered through his eyes. I'd never seen this side to him. It didn't trigger me the way I expected because I knew deep down he wasn't a possessive bastard. This envious, controlling outburst came from a fearful place that I don't think he realized existed. Gripping the edge of the table, I was surprised my fingers didn't sink into the wood.

"I don't want to be shared, Alastair."

Liquefied emerald irises drifted over every inch of me before connecting with my own fervid stare. I cried out from the fullness and pressure as he staked his claim on my body swiftly and with renewed determination. Leaning back, I closed my eyes.

"Look at me," he ordered, torturing me with the leisurely way he moved in and out.

I did, tangling my fingers through his hair. Hovering my mouth over his I whispered, "You feel so good."

The table shook as the velocity of his thrusts increased. I clawed at his back, pulling him closer. The animalistic way he stared into my soul unraveled me, exposing my irrefutable need for him. Before he snapped his eyes shut, I saw the same nakedness in them.

With a harsh groan, he grabbed my hips and stopped thrusting. I pressed my fingers into his lower back, urging him to continue.

"Tell me what you want," he growled.

"You," I answered, breathless. "I want you."

"Only me?"

"Yes." I grabbed his hair. "You're mine."

He flexed his hips slowly, teasing me. The gradual movements drove me insane. I was hypersensitive and throbbing, wanting him to finish what he started. He leaned his athletic body against mine, our sweat and scents mingling.

"My Lia," he whispered, stroking his tongue along my bottom lip. "The things you make me feel."

His lustful desire for me filled the room, suffocating my sense of reality. Barely aware of his feverish movements, I succumbed to the delightful chaos of sensations taking over my body. He'd stripped me to the core, elevating the most intimate act two people can share to something not of this world. And he did it in the most ungentlemanly way by ravaging me on the kitchen table.

We climaxed within seconds of one another, breathing hard and collapsing onto the wooden surface. Like he'd done many times before, he stayed inside me for a few minutes, keeping our bodies fused together.

"Bloody hell," he marveled, pulling out.

I could only grunt a response. I was spent. I couldn't sit up even if I wanted to.

"Come with me, love," he whispered, lifting me off the table and carrying me to the bedroom. I melted into his arms, resting my head on his shoulder. He placed me on the bed, stretching out next to me. Unable to open my eyes, I snuggled against him, inhaling his delicious scent and savoring his warm embrace.

"You smell good," I mumbled into his chest.

"So do you."

Slivers of contentment and joy spread to every part of my body. As we lay together, arms and legs tangled in post-coital bliss, I wondered how much more in love I could be with him. It scared me on so many levels. At any moment he could decide it was too much effort to be in a relationship. He could also choose to reactivate his *I-don't-date-I-just-get-laid* thing. Or he could just get bored with me. Any of those scenarios would shatter my heart beyond repair. I shivered.

"Are you okay, love?"

I finally managed to open my eyes and drank in his satisfied, calm expression. There was even a small smile playing on his lips.

"Yep."

"Are you cold? There's a jumper in my car if you want it."

"A jumper?" I asked, mimicking his accent. "Why are you driving around Florida in July with a sweater?"

"Because people like you keep the air conditioning at temperatures rivaling Antarctica."

"Would you rather I opened the windows and let all that disgusting humidity in here?"

He squeezed me tight. "Fair point."

Snaking my hand behind his head, I pulled him in for a kiss. He nuzzled into my neck, brushing that damn beard against my skin.

"You need to shave, buddy. That tickles way too much."

He smiled against my neck, pressing a quick kiss to it before looking at me. "As you wish, m'lady."

An overwhelming surge of guilt flowed through me. I swallowed it down, choosing to stay in this moment rather than let my thoughts run rampant.

"Your brain is on overload again," he said, tucking a strand of hair behind my ear. "None of that."

I traced my thumb along his sculpted mouth. "Are we okay?"

Shadows of uncertainty glided through his otherwise serene expression. He furrowed his brows, wrinkling the patch of skin between them. "I've never lost control like that before," he murmured. "I'm sorry."

"Are you apologizing for shagging me senseless on the kitchen table?"

The left corner of his mouth ticked up. "Not quite."

"Good."

Retreating behind his shield, he looked me squarely in the eye. "I trust you implicitly, Amelia. This is all new to me, this relationship stuff. You know that. If you were to leave me or—"

"I'm not leaving you. Stop saying that."

"You have to understand," he paused, brushing his knuckles on my cheek, "my desire to protect you and keep you safe is important to me. I don't want you turning to that prick for help." His jaw tightened. "He doesn't respect you. In his eyes, you're nothing more than a prize to be won."

I sank into the mattress, the weight of my guilt pressing heavily against me.

"You have a good heart. You want to see the light in everyone. If not for that, I probably wouldn't be here with you. I've been shrouded in darkness for so long I didn't know there was any light left. You saw it. You made me see it. But there isn't any light in Nathan. He's a con artist. He knows which strings to pull and if you're not careful, he'll play you right back into his arms."

I bristled at his insinuation. "I'm not that easily manipulated, Alastair. I know his game, trust me. I can hold my own with him."

"Retract those claws, kitten." A cocky grin spread from ear to ear. "I come in peace."

"And you say I have a smart mouth."

He brushed the pad of his thumb along my lips, fixing a molten stare on me. "Your mouth is meant to be covered in my kisses."

Love and lust pooled together in the pit of my stomach. Only one man could play me perfectly into his hands and I was already tangled in bed with him.

CHAPTER EIGHT

The plaza in front of the Amway Center teemed with people. Various radio station vans and television trucks were parked in the drop-off circle. Almost lost among them was a gunmetal gray Mercedes SUV. I stared at it, noticing the silhouettes of two grown men sitting in front. *Overprotective, party of one.* Shrugging off my annoyance at the adult babysitters, I turned my attention to Alastair and Stephanie. They were engaged in friendly conversation, thankfully.

"Looking forward to starting your new job?" Alastair asked her.

"Yeah. I'm nervous though. I've only done some freelance work on the side. This is, you know, the big time."

"You'll do fine. Sarah runs a great company and you're part of one of the best graphic design teams in the UK."

"Do you know what projects you're going to work on yet, Steph?" I asked.

"Nope. They mentioned magazine advertisements to start but that could all change once I get there." She shrugged. "They'll probably put me on something low key to see if I know what I'm doing."

"Maybe not," Alastair said. "Sarah mentioned they just closed a deal with Summit Enterprises for their new ultra lounge called Pulse. It's owned by Brent Garrison." He looked in my direction.

"I'm sure you remember meeting him."

I did. Brent was around the same age as Alastair and successful in his own right in real estate. There was obvious tension between them thanks to Alastair's previous relationship with his sister. Brent took it upon himself to enlighten me with some of the details while at the garden party last month. I still didn't know exactly what happened and really had no interest in delving deeper into my boyfriend's history of getting laid and discarding women when he 'got what he wanted.' But I knew now that side of him was triggered by his decision to avoid any and all emotional attachments. We'd obviously managed to make a breakthrough in that department, but his reputation still preceded him.

"You'll most likely be working on that campaign," Alastair concluded.

Stephanie's eye widened. "Really? How do you know?"

"I know everything, Stephanie," he smirked.

She rolled her eyes and elbowed me. "Seriously, with this one?"

"Welcome to my world," I laughed.

"Do you have a place already lined up?" he asked, ignoring both of our comments.

"I'm staying with Darren for a bit until I get settled into the job and I'm confident they won't fire me. Then I'll probably look for my own place."

"If you need help, I know a few realtors in the area who can find you something spacious without it costing an outrageous amount of money."

Her eyes widened again. "Thanks, Alastair. I'll keep that in mind."

A tiny smile pulled at his mouth as he scanned the growing crowd. I had no idea what he was looking for. He'd been a little on edge all morning, which made me anxious. Even now, standing on the sidewalk in his designer jeans and pale gray Henley shirt, he looked uncomfortable.

A loud cheer erupted to our left. One of the radio stations

started whipping everyone up into a frenzy by tossing out t-shirts and recruiting people for a game. It was rather basic. Contestants were blindfolded and had to throw a football into a garbage can. Out of the six people chosen, only one was lucky enough to have the ball land inside the can.

"Is that my girl, AG?"

Before I could turn to see who it was, a pair of strong arms lifted me off the pavement and spun me around once.

"Oh my gosh, Grant," I exclaimed, giving him a big hug. "I haven't seen you in ages. How are you?"

"Ah, you know, same old, same old. What about you?" He draped an arm across my shoulders. His dark chocolate skin was warm against mine.

"Nothing too exciting. My parents are visiting so we're taking them to the game." I motioned toward my best friend. "You remember Stephanie?"

"Absolutely. How are you, beautiful?"

Stephanie grinned and shook his hand.

"And this is—"

"Alastair Holden. Good to meet you, Grant." His introduction was more professional than friendly. A look of surprise flashed on Grant's face.

"Uh, wow. Wasn't expecting to run into the big boss today," he laughed, extending his hand.

Alastair shook it, studying him with a cool, dispassionate gaze.

I gave him a look. "Grant is the sports producer at WTDO."

"If this is your first time at an arena football game, you picked a good one. These two teams don't like each other so it'll be an exciting one to watch. They don't call it the War on I-4 for nothing."

Thawing out a little, Alastair grinned. "I'll take your word for it."

"Alright, I should get inside." Grant gave me a quick squeeze good-bye. "Great seeing you, AG. Nice to meet you, Mr. Holden."

Stephanie waited until he was out of earshot before snickering. "Mr. Holden. I'm sorry, that's hilarious."

"You find my employee's respect amusing?" he lifted a brow.

"No. It's just funny to hear people refer to you so properly. I mean, you're Alastair, the guy my best friend tripped and fell into. You're not," she made air quotes, "Mr. Holden."

"I'm not?"

"Ugh, you're so stuffy and British. Loosen up," she chided.

Running an index finger across his lips, he smiled. "Stuffy and British. Where have I heard that before?" Tilting his head, he eyed me with delight.

"See?" I poked him in the side. "I'm not the only one."

"The two of you share the same brain," he said dryly. "I thought one smart mouth was bad enough."

Stephanie and I exchanged glances and laughed. I liked teasing him, especially when I had a partner in crime to add to the fun. Maintaining his cool-as-ice demeanor, Alastair shook his head and continued scanning the crowd.

"I'm gonna go check out what that radio station is doing. Be right back." Stephanie bounded off in the direction of the large crowd.

I sidled up close to Alastair, placing my hands on his waist. It was like touching marble.

"You okay, chief?"

"Yes."

I stood on my tiptoes and kissed him. "Can I ask a favor?"

He stared at me blankly, not moving or answering.

"I would really appreciate it if you told Paxton and that other guy to take the afternoon off. They could go to Disney World or something."

The muscle in his jaw twitched. I knew he hated this.

"They're here for your protection."

"I know," I said quietly. "But you're here with me. And my parents are on their way. I just…it would mean a lot to me if their first time meeting you didn't include a private security team tailing us."

He scanned my face with eyes as hard as granite. Getting him to back down was going to take a huge effort on my part.

"No."

Swallowing back a bitter response, I looked away. His whole demeanor was off-putting and this just added to my annoyance. Lacing my fingers through his, I gave his hands a quick squeeze.

"Please. Just for today."

"Lia, don't argue with me. You're being followed. They stay."

My temper flared. "By a tabloid reporter, not a psychopath."

Tension from our combined stubbornness blossomed and spread around us. He was immoveable but so was I.

"They. Stay," he said through clenched teeth. "This discussion is over."

The finality of his words shackled me. I didn't like feeling as though I'd been backed into a corner. That was usually when my claws came out.

"Jackass," I snapped.

"Feel better now that you've gotten that off your chest?"

"Do not stand there and make a joke out of this. You're being ridiculous. I don't need baby-sitters. I'm about two seconds away from telling all three of you to get back on your goddam plane and leave."

Softening his expression marginally, he bowed his head. "You have to trust me," he said. "I'm not doing this to be difficult. I'm doing this to keep you safe."

A cold chill swept through my body. Much like last night, I had a feeling he wasn't telling me everything. The way he looked at me pretty much confirmed my suspicions.

"Hey you two, look who I found." Stephanie's sing-song voice sliced through the murky gloom hovering over us. My parents stood next to her, beaming at me. Flashing my biggest, brightest smile I hugged them.

"Ready for some football, kiddo?" my dad asked, ruffling my hair. I laughed. That gesture drove my sister crazy but I didn't mind it.

"Not really."

"I'm ready for the air conditioning," my mom stated, fanning herself. "How do you put up with all this heat?"

"I only go outside early in the morning or late at night," I joked.

Their attention turned toward Alastair, the lone stranger in the group. He waited patiently to be introduced, studying them in the same guarded, curious way he'd done when we met. I took a deep breath.

"Uh, Mom, Dad, this is Alastair."

His abrupt switch from stony to charming was lightning fast. As many times as I'd seen it, I was still amazed at how smoothly the mask morphed from 'don't talk to me' to 'tell me your life story,' especially around people he met for the first time. His expertise at showing only what others needed to see was second to none.

"Alastair Holden," he smiled, extending his hand. "Pleasure to meet you both."

The accent alone did it for my mother. I thought glitter and stars were going to burst from her eyes.

"Joseph." My dad shook his hand. "This is my wife Lillian. My daughter tells us you're from Scotland?"

"England, actually. I moved to Scotland several years ago to work for my grandfather's company."

"Family business, huh? What do you specialize in?"

And just like that my dad and Alastair spent the next half hour talking about market analysis, financial projections and other sleep-inducing topics. Thankfully, the suite was stocked with food and beverages. Stephanie, my mom and I snacked on raw vegetables and cookies.

"Those two hit it off," Stephanie remarked.

"Yeah. My dad can talk the ears off a deaf person. I'm not surprised."

"He seems like a nice young man, Lia. A little shy but nice."

"Shy?" I laughed at my mother. "Alastair is many things. Shy is not one of them."

"I have to agree with her on that, Mrs. M. I prefer to say he's—"

"Stuffy and British," we said in unison.

"You girls," she shook her head. We settled into our seats and watched some of the game. A loud cheer erupted as the Orlando Predators scored a touchdown against the Tampa Bay Storm. I looked over to my right to see if my dad and Alastair were still chatting. They were. I was floored by how at ease he seemed to be with my family. His whole demeanor, though guarded, was friendly and approachable. Our eyes met briefly. As frustrating as he could be at times, he still took my breath away.

Images of our rendezvous on the kitchen table filled my mind. His sounds, movements and the way he kissed me all flashed through my memory. An ache steadily grew at my core. I parted my lips slightly in order to get more oxygen. Alastair's eyes darkened as he watched me.

"Lia."

I jumped, whipping my head around to see what my mother wanted.

"Do you know where the ladies' room is?"

"Uh, yeah. Down the hall to the left."

"Thanks."

"You have that deer in headlights look again," Stephanie whispered after my mom walked away. "You okay?"

"Yeah, I'm good."

She looked at me skeptically. "If you say so. Oh! So, Friday night. We have the VIP section reserved, right? I think the entire staff from ShortCuts is coming." Her whole face lit up talking about the upcoming going away party. Out of the corner of my eye I noticed Alastair stand up and pull his cell phone out of his pocket. He scowled at the screen. My heart sank.

"If you'll excuse me, I have to take care of something," he told my father. Stopping next to my chair, he tilted my chin up and brushed his thumb over my lips. The small, intimate gesture was just enough to let me know our heated discussion was a distant memory. I smiled, comforted by the warm glow in his eyes.

His phone rang, putting an end to our little moment. Answering with a gruff, "Holden," he walked out.

My dad came over and sat with us.

"All done talking his ear off?" I teased.

"He's very personable. Smart, too. To be that young and run a successful worldwide company is impressive. I don't know how you kids do it these days. I'm tired just thinking about it."

"Oh, stop," I laughed. "You wouldn't know what to do with yourself if you ever retired."

"I did retire."

"Yeah but then you started doing consulting work. Mom is right. You have busy bee syndrome."

My mother rejoined us a couple minutes later. "You finally let that poor boy out of your clutches, Joe? I saw him in the hallway on the phone. I hope he's not working on a Saturday."

Another loud cheer filled the arena as the Predators scored their fifth touchdown. While they watched the game, I waited for Alastair to return. After twenty minutes passed I started to feel uneasy. The phone calls never lasted this long unless there was a major problem. Tempted to go out in the hallway, I crossed my legs in an effort to remain centered and relaxed. Didn't work as well as I wanted it to. My leg bobbed up and down in a nervous rhythm. I willed the anxious energy to subside but all it did was relocate to my foot, which tapped against the glass window.

Muffled conversation between my parents and Stephanie floated around me. I caught bits and pieces of it. *Where should we go to eat…They sure do score a lot of points in arena football…Why didn't the quarterback just run with the ball…When do you start your new job…We should go to games this way back home.*

The beeping of my phone cleared the fog from my head.

4:48pm Have to go take care of a few things. Paxton will take

you home.

That was it? That was all he had to say? I shoved the phone back in my pocket, created an excuse to tell my parents and made no effort to pay attention to the rest of the game.

* * *

I stared into the darkness, trying to make sense of the shadows on my walls. Insomnia had a pretty good stranglehold on me. I hadn't heard from Alastair since his terse text at the game. Paxton was no help either. He just said there were some issues at the office and Alastair had to be on an emergency conference call. I didn't believe a word of it.

Glowing digital numbers taunted me from the nightstand with their giddy declaration that it was only three-thirty in the morning. I groaned, burying my face into the pillow. It still smelled like Alastair, immediately causing me to miss him like crazy. I rolled over and reached for the cell phone. As my eyes adjusted to the bright home screen I saw I had no messages.

Tossing the phone back on the nightstand I sighed. Heat lightning lit up the sky outside, illuminating my bedroom. I closed my eyes and willed myself to fall asleep. When it became clear that wasn't going to happen, I got up and did laundry. I thought maybe the mundane task would lull me to sleep. Nope. I paced the apartment, watched some TV and took a shower.

I couldn't stand being trapped between these walls any longer so I drove out to Lake Eola. Early morning joggers loped along the path, focused on their pacing. I wasn't dressed for a serious run but did manage to get in a lap around the lake. I noticed one guy casually walking near the water's edge carrying a camera. Eying him suspiciously, I slowed down. He raised the camera and snapped a few pictures of the swans floating gracefully on the lake.

Shaking my head at my own paranoia, I went back to my car.

I stopped dead in my tracks. An envelope sat on the windshield, stuck under the wiper. Looking around, I saw no one. Paxton wasn't even following me. He'd gone back to the hotel after dropping me off at home last night. Whoever did this knew I didn't have any eyes on me.

Angry, I grabbed the envelope and tore it open. There were only two photos inside this time; one of me and Nathan from the other night and one of me with Alastair, Stephanie and my parents in front of the Amway Center. *So much for the adult babysitters being on top of things.*

A slip of paper floated to the ground. I picked it up and unfolded it.

Tell your ex-boyfriend to back off or photographs like this will be the least of your worries.

CHAPTER NINE

I stormed out of the elevator before it opened all the way and banged on the penthouse suite door. No answer. I fumed, pacing the small hallway. Reaching for my phone, I checked to see if I had any messages. Nothing. I knocked on the door again. From inside, I heard footsteps on the marble floor.

"I can hear you in there," I called out.

The door opened. Paxton stood solemnly in front of me.

"Good morning, Miss Meyers."

"Hi, Paxton. Is he awake?"

"No."

"I'll wait in the—"

"I'm sorry. I can't let you do that." He blocked the doorway with his sizable, bodyguard frame. "Mr. Holden would prefer if you stayed at your flat until he can come to you. You shouldn't even be here right now. It's not safe."

I nearly exploded. "Not safe? If it's not safe why aren't you or that other guy acting like my shadows?"

"Scott had to take care of something for him. I'm meant to stay here."

More vague answers. More hard to read, blank expressions. *Did they all go to the same School of Stoicism?* Royally pissed off, I dropped the envelope at Paxton's feet.

94

"Well, this was on my car when I finished my run at Lake Eola."

He narrowed his eyes. "What were you doing out there? I told you not to leave the flat when I dropped you off last night."

"I am not a caged animal," I yelled. "I can come and go as I please. Why can none of you get that through your thick skulls?"

"It's not up to me, Miss Meyers. I'm only following what Mr. Holden wants."

"Of course," I grumbled. "He always gets what he wants."

Bending down to pick up the envelope, he frowned. I had the distinct impression he was keeping something from me. My head spun. I'd had enough of all this secrecy bullshit.

"Look, I'm all set with whatever covert thing you guys have going on. Alastair shows up at my door unannounced, you two follow me everywhere to protect me from some mysterious danger and now I can't wait in my boyfriend's hotel room because it's not safe. I'm done. When you see Alastair tell him I said to have a good flight back to Glasgow."

Tears pooled in my eyes more out of anger than anything. I practically threw myself into the car and pounded on the steering wheel. As exasperated as I was, I knew deep down this was all happening because I didn't tell him his uncle hired Rachel to follow me. My own stubbornness had come back and bitten me in the ass.

* * *

Brunch with my parents was torture. They gushed and gushed about how lovely Alastair was, how much of a gentleman he was, blah, blah, blah.

"He's a good egg, Lia," my dad proclaimed. "Smart, personable, straightforward. He does play his cards close to his chest, though. Then again, every good businessman should."

I forced a smile, shoving a piece of Belgian waffle into my mouth. *You have no idea how close. No idea at all.* I helped the waffle slide down my throat with a big sip of mimosa. The restaurant hummed with conversation as I soaked in the scenery. Or tried to at least. I couldn't focus on anything. The food was excellent but I didn't enjoy it as much as I should have.

"Your father and I are driving up to Saint Augustine after we finish here."

"I hear it's nice. I've never been there."

"You've lived here almost six years and have never gone to Saint Augustine? Why not?"

I shrugged. "Never really thought about it."

"Amelia," my mother sighed, "there is more to life than being in a newsroom. Go out and experience things."

"Seriously, mom? You honestly think I spend all my free time at work? I like my job but not that much. That place drives me nuts most days. I mean, my God, I was in Glasgow last weekend. Where else do you want me to go?" My nerves were so fried the smallest things irritated me.

"Alright, alright." She put her hands up in retreat. "Both my daughters have demanding jobs. I worry. You're only young once."

"I think she's doing just fine." My dad patted my hand.

The rest of my time at brunch passed by painlessly. Well, in a manner of speaking. Spending time with my family was always a treat and to some extent it did help get my mind off Alastair's abrupt departure. When I returned to my apartment I paced the living room. Paxton was on my tail again. I'd noticed the SUV while we were at the restaurant. This surge of overprotectiveness grew tiresome.

Deciding not to dwell on this, I called Stephanie and asked if she'd like to do some clothes shopping for her going away party. Never one to turn down a retail excursion she agreed enthusiastically. I found a sassy, shimmery slate gray cocktail dress that I absolutely loved.

"So, are you going to tell me why Alastair's driver has been following us all day?" Stephanie asked while I tried on the dress.

"You noticed."

"It's hard not to. He sticks out like a sore thumb in that Secret Service outfit. Jesus, it's Florida in mid-July. Nobody wears that many clothes."

"I think they call it MI5 in the United Kingdom," I giggled, walking out of the dressing room. "What do you think?"

"Ooh, so pretty. It makes you look all hour-glassy and hot. I wish I had your figure."

I stared at myself in the mirror, smoothing down the dress. The sleeveless, fitted bodice was covered in a delicate design of tiled crystals. It did hug my curves in all the right places. Plus, it showed off just enough leg to be sexy without looking like I was trying too hard. "Give me some of your height and you can have some of my hips and boobs."

"Touché. So, why is the suit and tie following you?"

I sighed. "I'm assuming it's because of Jameson. I can't think of any other reason."

Stephanie looked uncomfortable. "Maybe he's doing this because he's jealous and doesn't want you seeing Nathan behind his back." She glued her eyes to the floor, fidgeting with her purse.

"You and I both know that story was a fabricated piece of shit. They made it look like I was on a date with him."

"Did you tell Alastair that was what happened?"

I sighed. "He knows I'm not seeing him. He knows that whole thing is crap. He's more concerned about Nathan manipulating me." I turned toward Stephanie. She had a worried look on her face. "What?"

"Well," she stammered, "no offense but you did ignore his shitty side for so long that maybe you can't tell when he's playing you."

"I know. I was an idiot back then. It's different now. I can see through his act way easier."

"Can you?"

I clenched my fists. "Yes. He's damn good at being a smooth talker but I can handle myself."

"Why turn to him though? Why didn't you come to me?"

"It's complicated."

"In what way?"

I sat on the plush, velvet-covered bench next to her. The flood-gates threatened to open and spill out everything to my best friend. I wanted to tell her. *She'll overreact.* "There's something…off about why Rachel is following me. I don't have all the facts yet. It could be nothing. Once I know, I'll tell you. I promise."

Discouraged, she folded her arms. "I don't like when you clam up about stuff."

"I know."

"Then tell me. Maybe I can do something to help so you don't have to rely on that ass wipe."

"I wish there were something you could do," I said quietly. Silence suffocated the dressing room, reaching into every corner.

"Have you heard from him?"

"Which one?"

She rolled her eyes. "Nathan."

"Nope. Not since the night we were at dinner. He's been radio silent all week."

"That's a good thing then, right?"

"Of course it's a good thing," I hissed, exasperated. "Do you think I like having to lean on him for help? It makes me sick but I have no choice."

Silence again. I caught a glimpse of our reflections in the mirror. We both looked agitated.

"You know what we haven't done in awhile?" Stephanie asked, brightening the room.

"What?"

"Gone to a theme park to ride the roller coasters. What do you say? I have nothing to do the rest of the day."

"You are a genius. Let's go."

I changed and bought the dress, then drove off to spend the afternoon acting like a kid. Something about roller coasters helped relieve stress in the best way. All the yelling and screaming and high speeds were a great catharsis. We must have gone on the rides a dozen times before deciding to have dinner and drinks at one of the many countries in EPCOT. After spending a substantial amount of time in France drinking slushy, candy-flavored concoctions at the Pavilion, we made our way to the Rose and Crown pub in Great Britain. Drinking around the world seemed to be the perfect way to spend the night.

There were a good number of guests milling about the traditionally decorated British pub. The park was open late thanks to "extra magic hours" and people kept coming in. I sipped on some strong apple cider and people-watched. Sitting alone at a table in the corner keeping a watchful eye on us was Paxton. I grinned, raising my glass to him. He nodded slightly and came very close to smiling.

"We should send him a drink," Stephanie suggested.

"I'm willing to bet my paycheck for a year he's not allowed to drink while," I pulled a serious face, "on assignment."

Clinking our glasses together we both giggled.

"I wonder if Alastair has a code name for you. You know, like how they call the president Blitzen or Hawk Eye or whatever."

I snorted. "I wouldn't put it past him."

"I've heard him call you kitten before. Maybe they use Duchess, like the white fluffy cat in Aristocats."

"Nah. It's probably something boring like Rosebud."

"He knows you like to run. Maybe, Roadrunner? Or something totally British, like scone or haggis."

I nearly fell off the barstool from laughing. "Scone or haggis? So he sees me as a quickbread or sheep organs? Oh my God. I can't."

We hadn't laughed this hard together in a long, long time. It felt good. A twinge of sadness crept through me as the realization dawned that I didn't have many more of these silly girls' nights left with her. She'd be in Glasgow soon, ready to start her new life. *Next weekend at this time I'll be helping her pack.*

"Oh no. Why the sad face?"

I swallowed my drink. "No sad face, my friend. Cheers." We clinked glasses again and ordered another round along with a small pizza. Once we finished our food, we strolled through the park back to my car. Paxton stayed a good ten paces behind us. I felt bad for the guy, having to follow me wherever I went. My normal daily routines were so boring. I stopped short and turned around.

"Hey, Paxton," I called out when he was closer. "Have you ever been here before?"

"To this park? No." He stood in front of us, scanning the crowd.

"Walk with us," Stephanie offered. "We promise not to do anything too embarrassing."

Oh my goodness. He smiled. *I don't think I've seen him smile since the night we all went to the benefit in Glasgow.*

"Very well." He fell into step with us, listening to our conversation while keeping a watchful eye on our surroundings.

"How long have you worked for Alastair's family?" I asked.

"Fifteen years."

"Do you like working for them?"

"I have no complaints."

"Does he ever give you a day off?" Stephanie chimed in. I elbowed her in the side and gave her a look. "Ow. Hey, it's a valid question."

Paxton seemed amused. "I get to enjoy a holiday now and then when I'm not scheduled to be in the States."

I lifted an eyebrow. "Was that sarcasm, Paxton?"

"Yes it was, Miss Meyers. Any more questions from the press corps?"

"Ooh," Stephanie's eyes glittered with enthusiasm. "Someone's snarky. I like it."

We stopped next to my car as he chuckled to himself.

"I do have one more question," I said.

"Fire away."

"Will you please stop calling me Miss Meyers? I think we've reached a point in our relationship where you can call me Lia."

Standing with his hands clasped behind his back, he thought about my request for a few seconds. "I suppose that will be alright. Drive safely, Lia. I'll be watching." He gave me a stern look before walking to the SUV. I came very close to mock saluting him. Stephanie got in the car and laughed most of the way back to her condominium.

"That man is a hoot. You just know there's a big personality hidden beneath that damn suit." She paused and laughed again. "I'm a poet and didn't even know it!"

I groaned. "Stop it. See what happens when you have too much wine? You think you're Tina Fey."

"Then you must be my Amy Poehler. Although I always thought we were more Rachel and Monica. You know, from Friends?" She launched into the show's theme song. By the time I pulled up to the curb in front of her condo she'd sung the song half a dozen times.

"Alright TV Tunes, get out," I teased.

"You'll miss me when I'm gone," she chirped, climbing out of the car. "Good night, my fair Lia. May your news days be filled with riveting stories." She did a little dance up the walkway while singing another song. I shook my head, filled with adoration and love for the greatest friend a person could ever want.

CHAPTER TEN

"And this is where we do the weather." Vance Winters spread his arms in a grand gesture. The evening anchor was giving my parents a tour of the newsroom during some down time on Tuesday afternoon. My dad walked over to the back wall where a long desk held several computer monitors. Weather graphics, maps, projections and all types of forecasting information flashed on the screens.

"It looks so involved," my mom marveled. "All this just to say it's going to be sunny and hot?"

"Don't let Charlie hear you say that," Vance laughed. "It's an exact science with not so exact results at times. Mother Nature is a fickle beast."

They strolled through the set, mindful not trip over the camera cables.

"This is pretty much it," I said. "You've seen the newsroom, green room, control room and weather center. Hours of excitement, isn't it?"

"Sure is," my dad said, putting an arm around my shoulders. "And you're in charge of all this?"

I laughed. "Not quite. I just try to keep these yahoos on time when we're on the air." I looked pointedly at Vance. "Easier said than done."

"You don't like my banter with Cynthia?"

"I love it. I just need you two to wrap it up and toss to the break the first time you hear me in your ears."

"And that's why this little spitfire is my favorite producer." Cynthia chimed in, walking towards us. "You must be Lia's parents. It's so nice to meet you."

Cynthia had the ability to talk without ever coming up for air. She shared about six stories in the two minutes it took all of us to walk back to my desk. Sydney popped up off her chair to say a quick hello before dashing to the edit suites. Tyler waved from the assignment desk, cradling a phone at his ear. And Wesley? Well, he stared at his monitor a bit too intently for anyone to risk interrupting him.

"Everyone seems so busy. We're not keeping you from anything important, are we Lia?"

"No, mom. We just like to make it look like we have more work than we actually do," I smiled. "Especially when there are visitors."

"Thanks for showing us around, kiddo. Get back to work." My dad hugged me and thanked Vance and Cynthia for taking time out of their day to give them a tour. I escorted them to the main lobby and said my goodbyes. They were off to Miami for a couple days before flying back to Connecticut.

I wasn't settled at my desk for more than five minutes when the phone rang.

"Lia Meyers."

"Lia, it's Bruce. Can you come to my office real quick?"

"Sure."

Tyler fell into step with me as I walked across the set. "Where are you off to?"

"Popping into Bruce's office for a second."

"Good times. Hey, what time is your friend's party on Friday?"

"It starts at eight but you can show up whenever. We have the VIP lounge reserved for the entire night so we'll just be hanging out there."

"Cool."

We went our separate ways at the end of the hallway. When I walked into Bruce's office the atmosphere felt amiss, almost as though a dark cloud hovered just below the harsh fluorescent lights. He tapped a pen on the desk, staring into the computer monitor.

"Sorry to drag you in here like this, Lia." He gestured for me to have a seat. "There's a problem with one of the stories we aired last week. The one about the murder investigation in Lakeland?"

"What's wrong with it?"

"The way it was worded. The script referred to the suspect as the murderer, not the alleged murderer. His attorney called and was not pleased that we apparently tried and convicted his client already. He's threatening to sue for slander. I've already said we'll do an on-air apology but he's not having any of it." The tapping of the pen increased. "What makes it worse is the story aired that way during your show and then again on the morning show."

I broke into a cold sweat. "I don't usually miss something that important."

"I know you don't. Neither does Jeanie. Unfortunately, this isn't going away. Do you remember who wrote it?"

"It was either Rene or Gwen."

"Okay." He wrote something down in a notebook. "I'll talk to them. Our legal team is being briefed on the situation. You may be called in again to give your side to the story. Don't worry. You didn't do anything malicious or intend for this to happen. Neither did the writers. In the meantime, I need you to have clean, tight shows with no errors in the writing. I'll give final approval on all packages and scripts of this nature until further notice. Thanks, Lia."

For the rest of my shift I was hyperaware of everything I read. It got to the point where I second-guessed every word that was written. I had a feeling I'd missed that mistake in the story because I'd been so distracted with my own personal crap. It made me angry. I wasn't willing to risk my career or the integrity of the station because I was wrapped up in ridiculous drama.

Cynthia and Vance were in rare form as well. They harped on anything in the scripts that felt abnormal. For a fleeting moment I pitied Jeanie. She looked frazzled and stressed trying to make sure all the stories were factually correct and worded properly. *Then again, if she didn't spend so much time online shopping, this wouldn't have happened in the first place.*

"Lia," she huffed, making a beeline to my desk. "You really need to make sure this doesn't happen again. It's bad enough we were late with a breaking story because of you last month. This pattern of irresponsibility won't go unnoticed."

Indignation boiled through my veins. *How dare she throw something back in my face that wasn't even my fault?*

"If you'd like to have this conversation, there's an empty conference room," I seethed.

"No, we don't need to have this conversation. Get your act together."

"Or what? You'll throw me under the bus for something else?"

Her face turned red as a tomato. "Your blasé attitude needs adjusting. I'm not going to look bad because you can't do your job."

The shrill tone of her voice echoed through the newsroom. Everyone carried on with their work but sat up a little straighter and perked their ears so as not miss anything. These theatrics didn't intimidate me at all. If anything, they made her look petty and small in front of the staff. We all had at least one knife in our backs thanks to Jeanie's own incompetence and penchant for blaming anyone but herself.

I bit the inside of my lip to keep from retaliating. Sinking to her level of immaturity wasn't something I planned to do.

"Jeanie," Gus yelled from the assignment desk. "Vanessa is on the phone. She wants to read her package script you."

My executive producer grimaced, glared at me one last time and went back to her desk. The day's unscheduled middleweight fight may have concluded for now but I was heated. I ground my teeth so hard I feared I might break them.

"Don't let her get to you." Sydney's soft voice floated through my consciousness. "We all know final approval rests with her and she missed it."

"I don't care about that," I grumbled. "I'm just all set with everything right now."

"I'm sorry, sweetie. If you need to vent or talk, let me know."

Half smiling, I thanked her. Mercifully, the afternoon passed quickly and I escaped the newsroom without any additional unpleasantness. What I wanted most was to run but the humidity was so suffocating I could barely breathe. I kept a spare gym bag in the trunk of my car so I decided to head straight for the gym.

I managed to hop onto the last free elliptical. Churning my legs at what felt like warp speed, I pushed myself to the limit. Sweat poured off me in rivers even though I didn't set any resistance on the machine. It whirred beneath my feet, carrying me nowhere but taking me away from all the frustration of the past few days. I made it a point not to dwell on Alastair's departure and subsequent silence. I wasn't the type of girl who was clingy or needed to know what he did every second of the day. I usually mocked people like that. But here I was, desperate to know why he'd left and if he was ever coming back.

I longed for a time when we could just be and not have obstacles thrown in our direction at every turn. Maybe this wasn't meant to last. Maybe our relationship started too fast and we were clinging to one another because we didn't know what else to do. I wasn't even looking for this. My heart and soul had been sideswiped when he walked into my life.

A cold blast of air conditioning swept over my glistening skin forcing me to abandon my current thought process and come back to the present. Men and women of various shapes and sizes quietly worked out around me, each lost in their own private world. The clanging thud of weights and steady thumping of feet pounding on treadmills saturated the room. My quad muscles screamed for mercy, burning under my skin. Intent on going until I dropped, I ignored their impassioned pleas and pushed harder.

Turning to my jackass ex was the worst thing I could have done. I knew it from the start. I should have hung up on him when he called about the alleged exclusive interview. What a load of crap that turned out to be. All he did was trick me into believing that he wanted to change. I forced my legs to move faster. *Idiot. I'm smarter than this. What the hell was I thinking?*

Thick drops of perspiration landed in splotches on the digital monitor. A weird wheezing sound caught my attention. I looked around to see who was having trouble breathing. *Oh Jesus. It's me.*

I slowed my pace, suddenly aware of how fatigued I'd become. I had zero strength left in my arms or legs. Fitting, seeing as how I had zero strength left when it came to my personal life. I grasped the metal handles to check my heart rate. It was well over one-hundred-seventy. *Great. I'll probably give myself a heart attack if I continue.* I spent about five minutes cooling down so I wouldn't collapse walking back to my car. I didn't even bother showering at the gym. I just wanted to get home and put this day to bed.

Weaving through traffic proved relaxing in the oddest way. I turned up the radio and sang along with every song, even ones I didn't like. By the time I pulled into my complex and parked, I felt a little better. Gross and sweaty, my only goal was to take a long, hot bubble bath. I walked into my apartment, dropping the gym bag in the living room. It was dark. I'd forgotten to leave the light on over the stove in the kitchen. The hairs on my arms stood up as I passed through the room. Glancing around quickly, I saw nothing but lumpy shadows. A funny rustling sensation tickled through my stomach. Apparently my anxiety was still hanging around. I turned on the stove light and went back to the living room, flipping on another light.

Stopping short, I clamped a hand over my mouth to keep from yelling. Sprawled out on my oversized couch was Alastair. He was fast asleep, his head bent at an uncomfortable angle into the cushion with an arm flung behind it. The other rested on his stomach. The gray hoodie he wore was unzipped and open, revealing a plain white t-shirt. One of his long denim-clad legs dangled over the edge of the couch. I stared at him for what felt like ages, watching his chest rise and fall in deep, measured breaths.

I didn't know if I should be relieved or annoyed. He had disappeared for two days without saying a word. Stirring gently, a low moan vibrated in his throat. The sound quickened my pulse. The closer he came to waking up, the faster my body reacted to his close proximity. We were even breathing in unison. Scrubbing his hands over his face, he sat up slowly. Pieces of his hair stuck out in every direction. Bleary, exhausted emerald eyes met mine. He looked so worn out I forgot that I was supposed to be mad at him.

"Hello, love." His voice was barely above a whisper. Fighting an urge to wrap myself around him, I forced a tiny smile. Noticing that I stood before him in running shorts and a spandex sports bra, he grinned. "You're quite sporty."

All the frustration I thought I'd run out of my body returned with a vengeance. "Where the hell have you been?"

He held my ice cold stare, steeling his expression. "London."

"What? Why?"

Massaging the back of his neck, he shrugged. "I had to take care of something."

"Oh no you don't," I yelled. "You will not answer me with this vague bullshit. You left without so much as saying one word. All I got was a text. A fucking text."

"Amelia, calm down."

"I will not calm down." I paced the room, fully aware that I was coming apart at the seams.

He stood up, reaching for my hands. His touch was like a soothing balm, relaxing me almost instantly. Pulling me against his chest, he hugged me tightly. I wanted to stay angry. I wanted to give him a hard time for disappearing but I was so glad to see him. Secure within the warmth of his arms, I held onto him with all my might. He stroked my hair, whispering apologies as he buried his face against my neck.

Breaking our embrace, he placed his hands on either side of my face. Fatigue and stress ravaged his features. "I don't deserve you," he said, shaking his head. "I don't."

The same desolation that stained his voice wrapped its fingers around my heart. *He's pushing me away again.* He kept repeating how he didn't deserve me in a low whisper.

"Stop," I pleaded, pressing a kiss to the corner of his mouth. "You do deserve me. I love you. Please don't shut me out."

Imprisoned by something only he could see, Alastair withdrew so far into himself I was left completely alone even though I held him in my arms. This had to be way beyond survivor's guilt. I knew he blamed himself for his family's death all those years ago but this had to be something bigger. The internal scars he kept covered were jagged and long. My love for him only eased the pain so much. I was so helpless, so useless. All I could do was touch him, let him know I'd be there even if he didn't want me to.

"Come back to me," I implored. "Whatever it is, we'll fight through it together."

CHAPTER ELEVEN

A pitiful whine echoed through the room. I was wide-awake, unable to sleep. I'd finally convinced Alastair to come to bed with me but he found no refuge in slumber. Tension still had a strong hold on his face. Stretched out next to me, he rolled onto his stomach. Another soft moan filled the space between us.

"Don't go, please," he whimpered.

My heart broke, wondering if these nightmares would ever stop plaguing him. Lightly running my fingers down his back, I leaned close and kissed his cheek. It was damp with tears.

"Stop. Fucking. Pitying. Me."

I froze, stunned more by the harsh tone than his words. His lips curled into a snarl, his hand clenching the sheet tighter. Moving away slowly, I repositioned myself so as not to wake him.

I shuddered against the mattress. *He doesn't mean it. He's dreaming.* I watched his eyes dart from side to side beneath his lids, looking, searching for whatever haunted his dreams.

"You're nothing. Get out. *GET OUT.*" He thrashed under the blankets, turning violently onto his back. I let go of the sheet, watching it twist and bunch in his hands. Shallow, harsh breaths parted his lips. Staring in disbelief, I climbed out of bed. This wasn't the same dream I'd seen him have before. This was angry. *Vengeful.* Padding slowly out of my bedroom I sat on the couch.

Darkness and an acute sense of loss suffocated me. Hugging my knees to my chest, I strained to hear if he was still lashing out. Silence, thick and heavy, permeated through the apartment.

Alastair.

"Can't sleep?"

His silky accent floated through the room. I drank in the beautiful silhouette standing gracefully in my living room. There was no malice. No harsh words. If anything, he surveyed me with caution.

"No. I guess not."

Moving closer, he clutched his stomach. Outdoor lights seeped through the blinds, deepening the shadows of worry and confusion carved in his face.

"I woke you with another nightmare, didn't I?"

Our eyes locked, a fission of electricity spurring my heart. He knew. He knew this one was different.

"Sit with me," I said.

Not taking his eyes off me, he sat to my right. I ran my knuckles down his cheek, a gesture he'd so adoringly showered on me time after time. He nuzzled into my hand, kissing the palm, moaning softly.

"I didn't mean it," he whispered. "Whatever I said, it wasn't aimed at you."

Tracing my thumb along his mouth, I leaned in and kissed him. His lips were still salty from the tears. "I know." My insides trembled. "You can tell me about it, if you want."

The intensity behind his verdant eyes nearly illuminated the room. Any traces of vulnerability slid away, replaced by a fierce, controlled stare. Locking his fingers through mine, he pulled me off the couch and led me to the bedroom. Collapsing on the bed together, he wrapped his body around me like a vine.

"I need you," he murmured, pressing his fingers into the small of my back.

"You have me," I said, running my hand through his hair. "Get some sleep."

Sighing heavily, he relaxed into my arms.

* * *

I put up no fight when Alastair announced Paxton would be driving me to and from work for the rest of the week mostly because I was exhausted and he had morphed into über bossy mode. He'd defrosted from last night's events but that impenetrable shield was padlocked. I sipped on my coffee while he finished getting dressed. Emerging from the bedroom in a ridiculously expensive chocolate brown suit, he grinned. If quiet control and power could be bottled up, wrapped in lavish clothes and given a face, this was it. From that gorgeous head of dark red hair down to his designer shoes, he was perfection. The obnoxious beating of my heart vibrated to my toes.

"Jesus," I muttered.

"Like what you see, love?"

"Smart ass." A small smile played on my lips as I drank more coffee. Moving with the speed of a cheetah, he caged me against the counter. I nearly dropped the mug.

"You can't smile at me like that and expect it not to drive me crazy."

"You're awfully frisky this morning, chief."

He nuzzled his nose into my hair. "You're awfully sexy this morning, kitten."

"Too bad we're all dressed up with places to go."

Veiled eyes darted over my body, settling on the hem of my sundress. "I could take you on this counter." He lazily dragged his finger up my inner thigh. Normally, I enjoyed when he came on strong but this was different. He was detached, going through the motions of seducing me without any feelings behind them. I was basically being eye-fucked by a hot guy in a three-piece suit.

"Maybe later." I wiggled out of his arms. "Do you have a permanent office in the WTDO building yet? They must love having to

112

be on their best behavior all the time."

"They're letting me use the supply closet. It's small but quiet."

"British humor again?" I smirked.

He lifted an eyebrow, ushering me to the door. We walked out to the waiting SUV together. I covered his hand with my own after we settled into the backseat. The muscle in his jaw twitched.

"I want us to go away for a couple days. I have to be in New York on Monday so I thought we'd spend the weekend in Manhattan."

Stunned, I looked at him. "Really?"

"Yes. I think getting out of Orlando will do us both good."

I liked the idea but wasn't a fan of his chilly demeanor. Red flags popped up in my head. There was obviously something he wanted to keep me away from. Glancing in my direction, he frowned.

"You don't approve?"

"It's fine. Just a little out of the blue, no?"

"Do you have plans otherwise?"

"I was supposed to help Stephanie pack but she hired movers to do all that for her. I guess I'm free."

Straightening his spine against the seat, he smoothed down his tie. "Brilliant. We'll fly out Saturday morning."

"Is there a specific reason why you have to be in New York next week?" Sometimes words fell out of my mouth before I could tell my brain to corral them.

Keeping his eyes locked on the back of Paxton's head, Alastair shrugged slightly. I was beginning to dislike that little shrug. "Work. I need to be in the main offices for some meetings."

"Sounds magical," I grumbled.

The SUV rolled to a stop in front of my building. Paxton got out, presumably to give us some privacy. Alastair sat in stony silence for a few seconds. I had no desire to go to work but I also dreaded staying in this car one minute longer.

"See you later," I said, reaching for the handle.

"Wait."

The gravelly command halted me. His eyes flashed behind the

veil.

"We need this weekend, Amelia. No interruptions. Just you and me." He brushed his knuckles on my cheek, sending a shiver through me. "I need to make this right."

Confused, I climbed onto his lap. Straddling him, I titled his chin up so he had no choice but to look me in the eye. Not saying a word, we communicated the only way we knew resonated with us both - by touching one another. Holding me with restrained passion, his cloaked eyes brightened as I stroked his tie. Little by little, pieces of the shield fell away revealing the unguarded man who melted my heart. The world bustled outside the tinted windows but as far as I was concerned we were in our own universe, alone and entwined.

"I could stay like this all day."

Leaning my forehead to his, I smiled. "Ditto, love."

"Dinner tonight?"

"Are you offering to make it?"

He cupped my backside, squeezing gently. "I'm offering to feed you. I seem to remember you liking when I did that."

I flushed at the memory of him feeding me chocolate bread pudding. We'd barely known each other at the time but the act had been so intimate it stuck with me. I still haven't been able to enjoy dessert properly since. A satisfied grin spread across his stunning mouth.

"Go to work, kitten, before I decide to keep you here."

Giving my behind one last squeeze, he released me. I climbed out of the SUV and waved goodbye to Paxton. I felt a zillion times better than I did last night. I was almost to the studio door when I heard my name called.

"You are so difficult to pin down." Rachel Jameson's perky voice cut right through my good mood. "Figured I'd catch you before you disappeared in there."

Her bright smile lit up the lobby. I mentally prepared myself for the battle of wits I was about to join.

"Do you want to come into the newsroom? There's a conference room we could use."

"I don't have that much time. I'm due at a press conference in twenty minutes for the performance enhancing drug scandal at the university." She looked at me curiously. "I was wondering if we could meet for coffee later, after you're done with the evening show. There's a little shop right down the street."

I nearly rolled my eyes at her using the phrase 'press conference' when I knew quite well she'd be camped outside the locker room, chasing down anybody willing to give a sound bite.

"I have plans tonight. Sorry."

She grabbed my arm as I turned on my heel. "Listen," she said under her breath, "I need to talk to you. There's some weird shit happening and I'm stuck in the middle of it all."

A sense of urgency streaked through her vivid eyes.

"What do you mean?"

"I don't want to get into it here."

Fed up with any vague or cryptic answers, I laughed bitterly. "Look. I'm sorry. I can't." I swiped my badge in front of the detector and walked into the newsroom.

The morning passed by swiftly enough. When lunch rolled around Sydney and I decided to make a quick run to the smoothie shop at the corner.

"Peanut Butter Banana or MangoMadness?" she asked.

"I think I'll go with the high protein chocolate one today."

She placed the orders and we sat at a table in the back corner to wait. This shop was one of our favorite lunchtime haunts. Most days we sat at our desks but on the rare occasion when it was slower than normal we allowed ourselves to have at least thirty minutes away from the newsroom. I liked watching the different types of people come and go. Tourists were the easiest to spot. They moved slower and most had that glazed *it's-so-hot-outside* look. There were several art museums in the downtown area as the city did have more to offer than theme parks and International Drive.

"This is so good," Sydney gushed, sipping on her smoothie. She handed me mine and sat down. "Did your parents have a nice visit?"

"Yeah. They're easy to please for the most part. I think my mom was overwhelmed with the studio tour. She didn't know where to look." I laughed.

"We do have a snazzy newsroom. Too bad they couldn't stay for the actual broadcast."

"Just gives them an excuse to come back."

"Have things settled down between you and Jeanie? I noticed y'all haven't said more than six words to each other."

"Whatever." I waved my hand. "She's convinced everything is my fault. There's not much I can do to change that."

Sydney pursed her lips, eyes narrowing. "Well, she needs to stop blaming everyone else for stuff. That breaking story last month wasn't your fault. She wanted to go live with no information just so we could be first."

"I know. The art of confirming information is apparently lost on her. Oh well. I'd do it again in a heartbeat. I'd rather be late and correct than early and wrong."

"Cheers to that." She tilted her cup in my direction before sipping through the straw. "Violet wants to know if you're coming to the lake house next weekend. She made something for you."

"Really?" I grinned. Sydney's precocious seven-year-old daughter was the cutest thing. "What is it?"

"A surprise. She won't even tell me."

"I love it. She's too precious. Of course I'll be there. It's your big cookout. I wouldn't miss that for anything."

By the time we finished our smoothies, we were relaxed and ready to tackle the rest of the day. We chatted non-stop on the walk back to work. I stopped short after entering the newsroom. A colossal bouquet of roses sat on my desk. Sydney jogged over and buried her face in them, inhaling their scent.

"These are beautiful," she sighed. "You're so lucky."

Amused by her dreamy expression, I touched one of the velvety petals. The perfumed scent of love swirled in the air, leaving behind a giddy trail of smiles. I was well aware of the stupid grin taking over my face. As much as I fought against becoming a swooning, mushy mess I could not deny this was totally romantic. Feeling lighter than air, I sat down and opened my email inbox.

To: Amelia Meyers <ameyers@wmzb.net>
From: Alastair Holden <aholden@holdenworldmedia.co.uk>
Subject: You…
…either think I'm a complete ninny or haven't been by your desk in the past forty-five minutes. Put me out of my misery and let me know which one it is.
Yours, Alastair x

To: Alastair Holden <aholden@holdenworldmedia.co.uk>
From: Amelia Meyers <ameyers@wmzb.net>
Subject: You…
…might be the cheesiest self-professed no-relationships-non-dater I've ever met.
They're beautiful. Thank you.
Lia xoxo

To: Amelia Meyers <ameyers@wmzb.net>
From: Alastair Holden <aholden@holdenworldmedia.co.uk>
Subject: Back to cheesy?
I make no apologies. The non-dater in me has no idea what he's doing. I bet you're smiling though.
So does this give me any chance to get lucky this evening?
Hopeful, ARH xx

To: Alastair Holden <aholden@holdenworldmedia.co.uk>
From: Amelia Meyers <ameyers@wmzb.net>
Subject: Chivalry Is Dead
Wow. You skipped right over "gentleman" and settled on

"horny guy." I would say the odds are good seeing as you've managed to charm most of the women in here with all these long stemmed beauties. In fact, one of the editors is staring at them right now with starry eyes.

To: Amelia Meyers <ameyers@wmzb.net>
From: Alastair Holden <aholden@holdenworldmedia.co.uk>
Subject: Decisions, Decisions
As flattering as that sounds, I'm only interested in the brunette American wearing a pinkish coloured dress. Is she available?
Yours,
Stuffy and British

To: Alastair Holden <aholden@holdenworldmedia.co.uk>
From: Amelia Meyers <ameyers@wmzb.net>
Subject: Out of luck
She's taken. Her boyfriend probably wouldn't appreciate her being propositioned in an email. Too bad for you. Rumor has it she puts out when roses appear on her desk at work.

To: Amelia Meyers <ameyers@wmzb.net>
From: Alastair Holden <aholden@holdenworldmedia.co.uk>
Subject: Smart Mouth
You, Amelia Grace, are filling my head with inappropriate thoughts. Thank goodness I'm protected by the walls of the supply closet.
I'm glad you liked the roses. See you in a few hours.
Yours,
Alastair xx

CHAPTER TWELVE

Traffic snarled through downtown, paralyzing cars at every opportunity. I looked out the window, glad I wasn't the one driving through it. Orlando has its own special type of rush hour. Not only were the locals trying to get home after a long day, tourists were trying to go out and experience the city's nightlife. Delays like this didn't bother me too much. My adopted home had a certain charm I couldn't deny. There was a reason its nickname was The City Beautiful.

The sun still burned in all its golden glory overhead, glinting off the glass windows of high-rise buildings. Living in perpetual summertime gave Orlando a uniquely debonair vibe. Everything was sun-kissed.

I relaxed into the SUV's leather seat. Nagging questions regarding Alastair's sudden trip to London still dominated my thoughts. Not wanting to work myself up over the unknown, I focused on the simplest reason; it was work related. He'd been spending a lot of time over here and probably needed to devote more time and attention to his company. The last thing I wanted was for him to neglect his duties. I could only imagine the pressure he was under from his grandfather. Samuel Holden might be retired but I had the impression he kept a close watch on the vast media empire he'd built. Alastair was more than capable of holding his own though.

The congestion cleared and it was smooth sailing back to my complex. Paxton didn't say much even though I tried to engage him in conversation. He seemed preoccupied. Then again, he was driving. I waved goodnight after climbing out of the car. Not really knowing what to expect from Mr. Cool-As-Ice, I unlocked the door and walked into my apartment.

All the blinds were drawn. Only the soft glow from about a dozen or so candles lit the room. They were on the windowsills, end tables and coffee table circling everything like a warm and fuzzy ring of fire. I was not expecting him to go down this route at all. Studying my surroundings even closer, I noticed he'd rearranged the furniture.

A cozy pile of oversized pillows and blankets beckoned from the spot he'd cleared in the center of the floor. Shocked that he'd put so much thought into this, I remained immobile. I thought this was just supposed to be dinner. I should have known. *Nothing is simple with him.*

"Are you hungry?"

He leaned against the kitchen table, hands in pockets, gauging my reaction. He was still in his suit but had removed the jacket and vest and untucked his shirt. The tie hung loosely around his neck. Yeah, I was hungry. I wanted to peel the rest of his clothes off with my teeth.

"Keep looking at me like that and all this food will go to waste." *Jesus, that accent.*

"You've been busy," I finally managed to say. "First the roses, now the candlelight dinner. Don't use up all your romantic moves at once."

He maintained a guarded expression. "I'm not romantic. I just wanted to make you smile."

There was something off about him. My insecurities ran rampant. *The roses. The candles. The cozy dinner. He's going to break up with me.*

"Why such a serious face?" I hoped my voice didn't sound as shaky as it felt. Raising an eyebrow, he flicked those bright irises at me.

"Amelia." Calm severity wrapped around each syllable. "This is important."

Unsure if he was teasing me, I laughed nervously. "It's only food. Don't be such a curmudgeon."

"How long have you been waiting to toss out that one?"

"Long enough."

"Cheeky." Uncoiling from his stoic stance, he grinned in a wickedly sexy way that made me want to spread him out on the counter. "Come."

"Are you going to feed me?" I asked, slowly walking toward him. I swayed my hips just enough to bring attention to the way the soft cotton dress moved against my legs. He shook his head, running a finger over his mouth. Without saying a word, he pressed a kiss to my forehead.

"That's all I'm getting?"

"For now, love."

Disappointed, I turned my attention to the food. Two plates were sitting on the table. One was filled with various cheeses, the other with fruit. A bottle of champagne sat between them. My stomach snarled. He'd also ordered a pizza.

"There's dessert, too," he said, twisting a strand of my hair. "If you'd rather start with that."

Unable to shake off this uneasy feeling, I tugged on his tie. "What's going on in that head of yours, chief?"

His mouth curved. "Have a seat."

Nudging me with his elbow, he tilted his head toward the pillows on the floor. I fluffed up a couple of them and sat. He joined me, stretching out to my left. My anxiety subsided the second he ran his hand along my thigh.

"Excited for Manhattan this weekend?"

"Yeah. I haven't been in ages. Do you have anything planned

for us?"

Hooking his arm around my waist, he pulled me down so I was lying face to face with him. The heated, intensely sexual stare he leveled at me answered the question. "Do you really want to know?"

"I think I can figure it out."

"Contrary to popular belief I do plan to enjoy my time in the city with you in public doing tourist-type things."

"Oh really?"

"Yes."

I sat up. A brief glimmer of vulnerability illuminated his eyes, signaling a yearning I hadn't seen in him before. I couldn't stop my mind from racing, trying to figure out why it was so important that we went to New York this weekend.

"Such deep thoughts have been known to expedite the appearance of worry lines around the eyes."

Jolted out of my own head by his silky voice, I looked up. He was at the table, holding the plates of fruit and cheese. Rejoining me on the pillowed floor, he set the plates between us and picked up an apple slice.

"How do you know my thoughts were deep?"

"Your face is an open book." Grinning, he touched the apple to my lips. "Do you want this?"

I bit into it without breaking eye contact. He popped the rest in his mouth and reached for some cheese. We ate in silence for a few minutes, sizing one another up.

"Why did you go to London?"

Not breaking stride, he picked another apple slice off the plate and ate it. "There was an issue with a former client that needed to be fixed."

He's lying. I felt it in the pit of my stomach. His calm, measured response sounded rehearsed.

"What kind of issue?"

"The kind that demanded I handle it immediately." His posture and tone indicated this discussion was over. For once in my life

I chose to let it go and not press the issue. Besides, he'd gone through all the trouble of setting up my apartment for our dinner date. The least I could do was appreciate the here and now and not dwell on something I had no control over. I kicked myself mentally. Hard. Sometimes I was my own worst enemy.

"Again with the overthinking, love."

His fiercely affectionate gaze took my breath away. Moving the plates out of the way, he urged me closer, circling his arms around my waist. We sat facing one another, legs entwined. I fidgeted with his tie, loosening it even more.

"Tell me something about yourself that no one else knows," I said, unknotting the tie and sliding it off his neck.

"You've cornered the market on that already, kitten. There isn't much else to tell."

"Oh please. I've known you what, five minutes? There's a ton of things about you I don't know."

"Like what?"

"When's your birthday?"

Paling slightly, he tightened his hold on me. "It passed already."

"Shut up. When was it?"

"April."

"Really? Before or after we met?"

"It doesn't matter. It passed already."

"Come on." I batted my lashes. "I might want to bake you a cake next year."

He was *not* amused. "I don't like talking about my birthday."

"Why? Because you're over thirty?" I teased.

The temperature in the room plummeted. His distant, cold stare shattered me. "No," he said in a strained whisper.

"Okay," I replied quietly. "You don't have to talk about it."

Baring his teeth, he exhaled sharply. "Shit. If I can't talk about it with you then—" His fingers dug into the small of my back. "The twenty-ninth of April." Staring at me with wide eyes he continued, "The accident that killed my parents and Grace happened because of my birthday. The picnic we were driving home from was for me."

Heavy sadness washed through me. Not only did he blame himself for causing the accident, he also viewed a simple birthday picnic as the culprit. I did the only thing I could and hugged him tight. He sighed into me, unintelligible whispers tickling my skin.

"What kind of cake would you bake for me?" he asked after several minutes.

I broke our embrace. "What's your favorite flavor?"

A shy, unguarded smile curled his mouth. "Amaretto."

"Aren't you fancy." I snickered, wrapping the tie around my hands.

"That's a Robert Talbott you're twisting through those pretty little fingers." He lifted an eyebrow in mock disbelief.

"Well excuse me," I scoffed, slinging it around my neck and making a loose Windsor knot. "Is this more acceptable?"

He fingered the chocolate brown silk, wetting his lips. "You make everything better, love. Even this boring necktie." He lowered his tone. "Even me. I can't wait to take you away this weekend and pamper you properly. I've held back on showering you with lavish gifts and all the best this world has to offer for fear of scaring you off. That ends now."

"Oooh. Are you going to send me to the spa?"

"If that's what you want."

"Is there a pool at the hotel? We can go swimming."

"We're not staying at a hotel. My family owns a penthouse on the Upper West Side. It overlooks Central Park," he said matter-of-factly.

I stared at him, shocked. The piece of cheese I'd planned to eat sat suspended in midair between my fingers. A brilliant smile lit up his face.

"I told you. All the best the world has to offer."

Even though I'd known him for a handful of months the staggering reality of his wealth never really registered with me. Yes, his family's media empire was, well, an empire. He never flaunted his money. Most times he seemed uncomfortable with it. I was slowly being introduced to yet another side to him; Alastair Holden, the filthy rich orphan who had the world on a silk string.

"To answer your question, there is a pool. It's on the roof and it's heated. You can swim to your heart's content. I'll be more than happy to watch."

"You're not going to join me?"

He fidgeted with one of the pillows. "I can't swim."

"What?"

He narrowed his eyes. "You heard me."

I laughed in disbelief. "I'm sorry, I don't mean to laugh but really? This sort of makes you," I paused, "mortal."

"What was I before?" he asked dryly. "A demigod?"

I playfully shoved him. "Shut up. I just figured you knew how to do everything. At least that's the way you present yourself."

"Sorry to disappoint you," he chided.

"You could never disappoint me."

The room imploded with desolation and despair. He retreated back to that horrible place he did last night. My God, he looked so broken and defeated. Not one shred of his control or self-restraint was visible. I'd never seen him more exposed than in this moment. It scared me. His inability to mask the darkness inside him shattered me.

"Alastair," I whispered.

"After this weekend, you'll know everything." His words held none of the melodic beauty from his accent. They fell flat. I didn't know what he meant by this but figured it had something to do with why he went back to London so abruptly.

Lifting his hand, I kissed the palm and placed it over my heart. "There is nothing you could ever tell me that would change the way I feel about you."

Wincing, he scowled and shook his head. "You're so eager to give your love away to me."

"And you're so scared to give me yours. It's a precious gift,

Holden. One I don't give freely and one I would be honored to receive from you. I know you love me. Your actions, the way you touch me, the way you look at me." I paused, caught in his gaze. "The way you make love to me. You have me, body and soul."

His eyes widened in fear and revelation. "I can't…I haven't said those words in so long," he admitted in a hoarse whisper. Fixing a glossy-eyed stare on me he wet his lips. I pressed my forehead to his, hoping to soothe him.

"*I love you.*"

The whispered words tickled my ear and floated through my hair like a feather. If it hadn't been so quiet in the apartment, I probably wouldn't have heard him. The ferocity of his beating heart vibrated against me as he pulled me closer. I wanted to see him. I had to. Breaking our embrace, I looked at him. Overwhelming fear etched itself across his face. Oh, but those eyes. They burned with love. A quiet, intense calm consumed me.

"I love you, too."

Relief flooded through him so powerfully he sank into the pillows. "Right then, I survived that." He sighed.

"Did you really think I'd say anything different back?"

Shrugging, he grinned sheepishly. "Anything is possible."

"Ugh, you are so infuriating sometimes," I exclaimed, shoving him onto his back so I could straddle him. "I. Love. You. Get it through that stubborn ginger skull of yours."

"Put your claws away, kitten. I'm wading into new territory with you. However, and let me make myself crystal clear, you have been eternally etched upon my mind and on my heart since the night we met. That is where life as I now know it began. As far as I'm concerned, it has no end. I loved you before you fell into my arms. I will love you until I take my last breath."

Captivated by his words and unwavering resolve, I trembled. The skin warmed on my arm as he caressed it slowly.

"Seems I've found a way to make you speechless, Meyers."

"It won't—"

With great quickness and agility, Alastair flipped me onto my back, straddled me and pinned my arms against the floor. "You were saying?"

"Always have to be on top, don't you?" I grinned salaciously.

"Figuratively? Yes. With you? Frequently."

"Control freak."

A lopsided grin spread easily, brightening his face. "I haven't heard any complaints so far."

"I'd like to log my first, then."

"Would you?" He lifted an eyebrow. "By all means. Far be it for me to have a dissatisfied customer."

I wriggled out of his grasp and sat up. He knelt in front of me, leveling an amused stare in my direction. The change in his demeanor from just a few minutes ago was lightning fast. Determined to keep things light and playful, I grinned.

"My boyfriend—"

"You have a boyfriend?"

"I do."

"That's a shame. I rather fancy you. Break up with him."

I laughed. "Can't do that."

"No? Maybe you need some convincing." He leaned forward and planted a lush, wet kiss on my mouth. "Change your mind yet?"

"Sorry, mate."

"Wow." His hearty laugh filled the room. "You're stuck on him, then? Who is this wanker?"

I scooted closer to him, wrapping my arms around his waist. "He is my best friend, the other half of my heart, the love of my life and the best shag this side of the Atlantic."

"He sounds like a lucky man," he said, nuzzling his nose against mine.

"He is."

"Your modesty is earth shattering."

"Shut up and kiss me."

"Ah, you're a bossy one. He can have you then."

Smiling, I shoved my fingers through his hair and pulled his mouth to mine. Our lips moved together effortlessly.

"We should eat the pizza before it gets cold," he said, nibbling on my neck.

"I'm not hungry."

"Stop the presses." Cocking his head to the side, he grinned. "Best shag this side of the Atlantic?"

All talk of food ceased. Skipping dinner had never been so much fun.

* * *

The coffee shop bustled with people popping in for an after work caffeine jolt. I sat at one of the small tables waiting for Rachel to arrive. She'd left me half a dozen messages throughout the day so I figured it would be best to get this annoyance out of the way. I crossed my legs carefully, mindful of the delicious soreness lingering between them. Last night's dinner date still had me floating on cloud nine.

Humid air swirled through the cafe as Rachel walked through the doors. She saw me and made her way over to the table.

"Thanks for meeting with me," she breathed, sitting down. Her usual confidence seemed shaken.

"Sure."

Tucking a strand of dark brown hair behind her ear, she leaned forward. "When was the last time you spoke to Nathan Greyson?"

"Shouldn't you know," I lashed out. "That's what you're getting paid for, right?"

Taken aback by my animosity, Rachel frowned. "I don't understand."

"Oh please. I've known about this little arrangement all along. Don't play dumb with me."

"I really have no idea what you're talking about. Those photos of you with him at dinner were emailed to me anonymously. You know, like a tip. I only ran the story because I'd seen you out with him the week before." A little smirk crossed her glossy lips. "If you date high profile men, expect to see yourself in the gossip columns."

I sipped my iced coffee, processing what she'd said.

"Listen," she continued, "your love life isn't a high priority on my list of things. I wanted to talk to you about something else. So when was the last time you talked to Senator Greyson's son?"

"Why does it matter?"

"Nobody has seen or heard from him since last week. As far as I know, you're the last person he was with."

My mind raced as I worked hard to keep a neutral expression on my face. Nathan's whereabouts weren't a major concern of mine but if he'd fallen off the radar…

"I don't know what to tell you," I shrugged. "He sat with me at the restaurant for a few minutes then left. I was having dinner with a friend. He took it upon himself to sit down when she went to the bathroom."

"Oh. I was under the impression it was something more."

I snorted. "Of course you were. That anonymous tip you got was chock full of facts, wasn't it?"

Sitting up a little straighter, Rachel regained some of her confidence. "I don't appreciate being in the middle of whatever feud you have with your ex. He tells me one thing, you tell me another. I get anonymous emails daily from God knows who enticing me with some huge scandal that involves you."

She stopped short, aware that she'd let something slip. I froze, unable to tame the erratic beating of my heart.

"What are you talking about?"

The only response I received was a shake of her head. Panic closed my throat, cutting off the necessary flow of oxygen.

"Someone has it out for you, Lia. I don't know who it is or what they have but they seem to think it'll destroy you."

CHAPTER THIRTEEN

I sat in the cafe long after Rachel left trying to get my thoughts under control. The first thing I had to do was find Nathan. It certainly wasn't like him to drop off the face of the earth like this. As I gathered my belongings, I noticed Paxton keeping a watchful eye on me by the entrance. *This isn't going to be easy.*

I walked out into the wall of humidity and made my way back to the station. Paxton was no doubt following me on foot. He'd parked the SUV in a small public lot across from my building and probably sat there all day. My car was still at home, thanks to Alastair's proclamation that I had to be driven to and from work every day.

Air conditioning slammed against my heated skin in welcome relief when I walked into the main lobby. My reprieve was brief though.

"Lia."

Alastair's voice echoed through the expansive atrium. His presence dominated all the other sights and sounds that surrounded us. I gritted my teeth, mentally preparing for what I had to do.

"Hey."

"Is something wrong?" he asked, tilting my chin up.

"No. I need a favor."

He lifted a brow. "What kind of favor?"

"I need to go to Windermere." I stared at him, searching for a reaction. He narrowed his eyes but remained expressionless. "I need to go on my own."

"No," he responded flatly.

"Yes, Alastair," I said as calmly as I could. "I won't be long."

People were milling about the lobby, slowly walking toward the exit. The acoustics in this place would make for one hell of a show if I raised my voice. I had to work really hard to keep my emotions in check. It wasn't easy when a suspicious, stony glare was being leveled in my direction.

"Paxton will take you."

"He can't. I have to go by myself."

"Where exactly is it that you're going?" he asked in menacingly calm tone.

"The Greyson estate."

I said it so matter-of-factly I think it shocked both of us. For a split second I thought he might lose his cool. A tremor of anger streaked through his statuesque façade. We stood smack dab in the middle of the atrium, eyes locked in determination.

Placing my hands on his chest, I leaned closer. "It's a gated community. They know me and my car. Showing up with Paxton will only delay—"

"I'm coming with you," he snapped.

"No, you're not."

His chest rose in a deep, heavy sigh as he fought to remain in control. My only saving grace at the moment was the fact we were standing in a very public place. Locking his fingers around my wrists, he pushed them down in a firm, slow motion. "We're not doing this here. Come with me."

I let him lead me out to the small lot and climbed into the SUV. Silence flooded the interior as Paxton drove through the evening traffic. Apprehension and displeasure seeped from Alastair no matter how hard he fought to keep it locked behind his shield. I reached over and placed my hand on his thigh. The muscle twitched.

"I know you hate this. So do I. I promise, this will be the one and only time I have to go there."

Deftly unbuckling his seatbelt and sliding closer to me, Alastair forced me to look at him. His fingers pressed into the flesh of my cheeks. "Why are you running to him?"

"I'm not," I whimpered, unable to concentrate under the irate jade glow in his eyes. "I would never."

Seeing him swathed in a possessive, jealous rage triggered my disdain and repulsion for men who behaved this way. I wasn't helping matters by adding fuel to his inferno.

"Tell. Me. Why," he ordered.

Holding that stare was not easy. As angry as he was I could also see his fear. "Rachel, the tabloid reporter, was being paid to follow me. Or so he claimed. He says he knows who's paying her. I just want this whole thing to go away."

"Who is it?"

Panic streaked through me, paralyzing my heart. I couldn't say it.

"Amelia, tell me."

Tears sprang from the corners of my eyes. They burned my cheeks in their rapid descent. "Your uncle," I whispered, nearly choking on the hot lump stuck in my throat.

Alastair released my face, exhaling as though he'd been punched in the gut. The onslaught of emotion was short-lived. Steeling his feral gaze, he turned his attention toward Paxton. "Drop her off at her flat then take me to the hotel." He looked at me. "You are not to go anywhere, do you understand?"

"But I—"

"Do not argue with me," he shouted. "For fuck's sake Lia, do as I say for once."

Emotionally drained, I sank back into the leather seat and rode the rest of the way to my apartment silent. An unbearable weight had been lifted from my shoulders. I'd be lying if I said I wasn't relieved to have finally told him. Running my eyes over his immobile exterior, I studied the lines of his profile. He was unreachable. He kept his eyes fused to the back of the driver's seat. His only movement was a slight fidgeting with his cufflinks.

I reached out to touch him, wanting to feel him against me. His body stiffened before I made contact. Pulling my hand away, I rested my head against the window and closed my eyes.

I'd lost him to thoughts only he could see.

* * *

The quiet in my apartment was so heavy and suffocating I couldn't breathe. Not knowing when or if I'd see him again chipped away at my heart. If I hadn't been so stupid, this would never have happened.

Curling up on the couch, I hugged a pillow close and regretted it immediately. Alastair's scent engulfed me. I buried my face in the pillow and cried.

* * *

"This legal matter is turning into a nightmare." Bruce rubbed his eyes and sighed. I sat in his office along with Cynthia, Vance and Jeanie. "Not only is the guy not the alleged murderer, he's not even a suspect anymore," he continued.

The woes of the wrongly worded story weren't going away any time soon. Jeanie shifted in her chair, shooting me a dirty look.

"Maybe if people paid more attention to detail," she huffed.

I ground my teeth, willing myself not to lash out at her.

"We all missed it, Jeanie," Bruce said, giving her a look. "Now we all have to fix it. This attorney isn't backing down. He says his client's name was slandered and now he's unable to work or go out in public without people hounding him. Apparently, this guy hasn't left his house."

"What does he want?" Vance asked.

"I'll do another on-air apology," Cynthia said. "What else is there?"

"They want a million dollars for emotional distress and damages."

A chorus of disbelief rang out in Bruce's office. Cynthia stood up and paced the room.

"Are they high?" she exclaimed. "It was a missed word. We didn't do it on purpose."

Bruce nodded, rubbing his eyes again. "I know. Everyone knows that, even the damned lawyer. But that's what his client wants. Our legal team is working out some sort of settlement." He paused, looking around at each one of us. "He also wants whoever was responsible for writing it to be fired and the producers suspended without pay."

I sat up straight, shocked. Jeanie's mouth dropped open.

"Jesus Christ," Vance muttered. "You're not going to do that, are you?"

Leaning back in his creaky chair, Bruce shrugged. "I don't want to. We have to wait it out and see what legal comes up with. Until then, do your jobs and do them well."

We left his office in a quiet, single file line. Take us out of the newsroom and we'd pass rather nicely for a funeral procession. Only Cynthia simmered in anger. She stalked back to her desk and immediately made a phone call. I sat heavily in my chair dreading the rest of the day. Sydney didn't make a move to say anything. She continued writing and offered small smiles of solidarity.

I forced all the unpleasantness to the pit of my stomach and powered through the afternoon. I didn't even stop for lunch. If I worked hard enough and fast enough the time would fly, right? Sort of. Sitting in the control room was like being at an oasis. The crew left me alone for the most part and the only human interaction I had was with Cynthia and Vance. The closer the red digital numbers crept to six-thirty, the more I smiled internally. Tonight was Stephanie's party and I couldn't wait to let loose and have a great time.

Thankful to be done with this annoyance of a workday, I drove home singing at the top of my lungs. For reasons known only to the enigmatic British guy in my life, I was free to drive myself to and from work today. Whatever he'd rushed off to do last night required him to bring Paxton with him. I didn't even care. I wasn't going to let anything spoil my best friend's special night.

I wanted to look great for the party. It might enhance my efforts to feel great as well. The new dress I'd bought certainly helped. The slate gray looked amazing against my sun-kissed skin. Tousling my hair a bit, I let it fall naturally on my shoulders in big, soft waves. I grinned as I slipped into a pair of sparkling gray high heels. *Alastair will love these.*

Giving myself one final glance in the mirror, I nodded in approval and dashed off to meet Stephanie.

* * *

Scores of people dressed to impress were lined up outside the main entrance of the dark brick building. Stephanie was chatting with one of the bouncers at the door.

"Yay, you're here," she squealed, running over. "Come on. Marcus says everything's all set up for us upstairs."

She grabbed my wrist and pulled me in her overly excited *you're-going-to-miss-all-the-fun-if-you-don't-come-now* way. A dizzying mash up of rock and hip-hop bounced off the dark cherry wood walls. The space was intimate and dimly lit, giving off a lavish vibe that screamed 'exclusivity.' High-backed, plush leather couches lined the wall of the VIP section. The amber-lit curved bar was just a quick walk to our right.

I loved the feel of this place. The decor and lighting projected power and prestige but in a non-threatening way. For a split second I wondered if this was what Alastair's house would feel like if he injected the softer side of his personality into it.

A two-tiered cake decorated with pink, brown and white stripes, and flanked by a sugary pair of edible hot pink heels, sat between several bottles of top shelf alcohol on the table near the leather couch. Stephanie grabbed my arm when she noticed it.

"Did you make that?" she asked.

I laughed. "No. I wish."

"It's gorgeous. I almost don't want to eat it."

"The cake is pink champagne flavored."

"Shut up," she exclaimed. "Where did you order it from?"

"That little bakery we always walk by in Altamonte. I hope it tastes as good as it looks."

"It does, lass," a male voice wrapped in a Scottish accent answered. "I've already licked the frosting."

We both spun around, shocked to see Darren standing behind us.

"MacCourty," Stephanie yelled, throwing her arms around his neck. "What are you doing here?"

"I never miss a party, you know that," he laughed. "Besides, I wanted to hang out with my new flatmate to see if we were compatible."

"I had no idea you were coming." She turned to me. "Were you in on this?"

I just smiled and shook my head.

"This was a covert operation," Darren grinned. "The only ones who knew were yours truly and Alastair."

Stephanie and I both looked at him.

"I was going to tell you, Lia," he continued, "but Holden said you'd accidentally slip up and spill the beans."

"Oh he did, did he?" I folded my arms, smirking. "Such a smart ass."

"Where is he, anyway?" Stephanie asked.

I shrugged. "Probably still holed up in his little office."

"Call him and tell him to get his ginger ass over here. It's Friday night and he should be living it up with the rest of us, not pushing paper or whatever the hell it is that he does."

"Can I quote you on that? 'Get your ginger ass over here' by decree of Stephanie?"

"Yes," she said, ice blue eyes gleaming. "We're going to ply him with alcohol and party that stuffy Britishness right out of him."

Darren draped his arms around our shoulders and squeezed. "Ladies, ladies. Enough about him. You have me. I'm better looking anyway."

Stephanie laughed and attempted to ruffle his immobile spiky blond hair. Some of her co-workers showed up, along with my friends from the station. Tyler and Wesley looked sharp for once in their lives.

"You guys clean up nice," I teased. "If I didn't know any better I'd think you two were regulars here."

"This is my scene, Lia," Wesley grinned. "Good threads, lots of drinks and hot girls. I'm in my element. If you'll excuse me, I see my first love of the evening."

Tyler and I nearly doubled over from laughing. Wesley was a good kid but he was no Lothario. Cute in his own right with an impish grin and mischievous cobalt eyes, he carried himself with a forced impression that he owned the world. The girl he sidled up to knew it as well. She humored him and let him buy her a drink but that was as far as it went.

Stephanie positively glowed as the center of attention. Her co-workers showered her with cards, gifts and drinks. Before long we all gathered on the dance floor as the DJ continued to spin great song after great song. Feeling relaxed and stress free thanks to being in the company of my friends, I let go and danced like there was no tomorrow.

As nice as this club was, the dance floor was a little cramped. One couldn't help but become entwined with the ebb and flow of gyrating bodies. I must have bumped into and brushed against a dozen people before finding a somewhat safe space to dance. I lost myself in the mesmerizing bass, closing my eyes and swaying my hips to the beat. After the week I'd had, this was what I needed.

I was so caught up in the music I barely noticed when a pair of hands grasped my hips from behind. I spun around and grabbed them, ready to give the guy a piece of my mind. A weird sense of deja vu crept through my body as I locked onto the wide emerald eyes staring at me. Casually elegant in his fitted black button down shirt -with the top button undone- and black dress pants, Alastair owned the room. At least he did for me. Especially with that look in his eye.

Still holding onto my hips, he pulled me closer as a new song started to play. I'd only ever slowed danced with him so this had the potential to be mind-blowing. Oh, and he did not disappoint. Thank goodness the lights were so dim. The way he moved his body with mine - grinding his hips and grabbing my backside - almost felt like we were having sex in the middle of the club with our clothes on. Neither one of us had a predilection for public fornication but wow, this could easily sway my position on it.

I think he whispered something in my ear. I felt his breath but didn't hear anything. All I could hear was Britney Spears purring about giving her more and the never-ending pulse of the music. I gave his bottom a squeeze and surveyed the dance floor. Bathed in blues, greens and reds from the lights everyone else had the same glossy, trance-like expression as they danced with a potential one-night stand or significant other. Alastair and I were just another two random bodies mixed in with the sea of movement.

"I'm thirsty, love. Let's go get a drink," he spoke clearly into my ear, jolting me out of the seductive cocoon I'd been enjoying. I followed him to the bar and waited while he ordered the drinks. Freed from the unrelenting grip of the dance floor, I was finally able to see where Stephanie and everyone else had disappeared to. They were all laughing and drinking in the VIP section.

"Here you go," he said, handing me a glass of water. The cool liquid felt amazing sliding down my throat. The temperature must be near ninety in here. Sweat beaded on my forehead, threatening to run down the sides of my face.

Alastair grinned in his crazy-sexy way, driving me nuts. "One more round on the dance floor?"

Nodding, I grabbed his hand and pulled him back into the churning tide of people. Feeling his hands on me and his body pressed into mine negated all the tension from last night. That was another lifetime as far as I was concerned. All I cared about now was falling into a deep, messy oblivion with each sway of my hips.

Fisting his hand in my hair, he held me tightly and lowered his mouth to my ear. "You realize if we keep this up I'm going to have to find a secluded corner and have my way with you." The velvet tenor of his voice slid through my bloodstream, igniting everything in its path.

We stopped dancing. As tempting an idea as it was, I wasn't about to sneak off into a bathroom stall and bang him. *Who am I kidding? I'd do it right here.*

"I know that look, kitten," he grinned. "Come. Let's go back to your friends and cool down a little."

Disappointed, I followed him back to the VIP section. We found a spot on the couch and sat down. Stephanie and Darren noticed we'd arrived and joined us.

"Glad you could make it, mate," Alastair smiled and shook Darren's hand. "Were the girls surprised?"

"Yes. Couldn't have been more perfect."

"Brilliant."

"You seem pretty satisfied with yourself," I teased, nudging Alastair. "Is it because you kept this from me so I wouldn't 'spill the beans'?"

"I'm more surprised Darren didn't slip up and tell you," he said, tilting my chin up. "He can't keep a secret to save his bloody life."

"Just like the English to rag on the Scot." Darren feigned a hurt look.

Stephanie giggled and reached across him to tap my arm. "I think we have a bromance forming with these two."

"He wishes," Darren snorted. "Can't say I blame him though. I am a catch."

"Jesus," Stephanie muttered. "You're a nut. Come on. Let's go dance." She stood up and grabbed Darren's hands, yanking him off the couch. "Feel free to join us," she called over her shoulder.

I settled into the luxurious leather cushions and snuggled into Alastair's side. He draped an arm across my shoulders and kissed my forehead.

"You threw some pretty decent shapes out there," I said.

Laughing, he squeezed my shoulder. "Think so? Reckon I looked more like a brick on marionette strings."

"If that's how a brick dances, you're doing just fine."

"You're just saying that because you want to score with me later."

I looked at him, lifting an eyebrow. "If I wanted to score with you I would have said you're a well-dressed brick who smells amazing and has hot dance moves."

His already sultry gaze darkened even more as he grasped my waist and squeezed. I jumped, stifling a squeal. Sliding his hand under the hem of my dress, he leaned in close.

"You look so sexy in this dress. I can't wait to see what you have on underneath."

And just like that, I became a useless pile of perfume, sparkles and lace. His fingers crept up my inner thigh, giving me a rush. Snared by his very presence, I had to keep reminding myself that we were in public, surrounded by people I knew.

"I think we should fly to New York straight away and not wait until morning." His lips tickled my ear as he spoke in a low, seductive tone. "I want to start this weekend with you immediately."

"Okay," I breathed.

"If I had my way," he murmured, brushing his lips to mine, "I'd take you back to Glasgow with me now."

"We'll see about that, chief."

Giving my thigh a squeeze, he kissed me. "I hated not waking up next to you this morning. I don't want that to happen again."

I stopped myself from launching into a thousand questions about what happened last night, where he went and why. He seemed to sense my thoughts and ran his knuckles down my cheek. "Soon, love. You'll get your answers soon."

CHAPTER FOURTEEN

I rejoined Stephanie and Darren on the dance floor after I couldn't take anymore of their pleading. Alastair chose to stay in the VIP section and watch from the couch. I laughed to myself when Tyler and Wesley cornered him for what would no doubt become an interrogation, rather than conversation. *And he thinks I'm curious.*

"Oh my gosh, Lia. You look *a-maz-ing*."

I turned toward the perky voice and came face to face with my co-worker, Katie Vitale.

"I hope you don't mind that we're so late," she smiled, flipping her strawberry-blonde hair over her shoulder. "We figured these things don't get really exciting until later anyway."

The morning show reporter was joined by Vanessa Jaxson, who usually worked the evening shows. They were both dressed to the nines and scanning the room. I cringed internally. Everyone in the newsroom knew about this party but I'd hoped only the people I was actually friends with would show up. I had a sneaking suspicion these two weren't here to see Stephanie or me.

"Is your boyfriend here?" Katie asked.

Bingo.

"Yeah. He's up there talking to Wes and Tyler."

They both looked up and dragged their eager eyes all over his well-dressed figure. "Oh great. We're just going to introduce ourselves real quick. Thanks, Lia." They sashayed away in a cloud of perfume and hairspray.

"What did the Wonder Twins want?" Stephanie asked.

"To check out the main attraction," I said, motioning toward Alastair.

"Oh my God," she snorted. "They're unbelievable."

"They're fit," Darren observed. "Are they single? Dating? Dating each other?"

I rolled my eyes and laughed. "They're both single. Go get 'em, cowboy."

"I do have the better accent, you know. They'll be putty in my hands."

"Darren, when's the last time you had an actual girlfriend?" Stephanie folded her arms.

He paused and thought for a second, then shrugged. "I don't know. Last year maybe? Why?"

"Just curious."

Darren smiled broadly and wrapped her in a bear hug. "Are you sweet on me, Stephanie?" She scrunched up her face and tried to wrestle out of his grip. "Ah, come on, lass. Give us a kiss."

Stephanie's protests were almost as loud as the music. She laughed so hard I thought she might pass out from lack of breathing. It dawned on me that she'd be leaving for Glasgow in less than a week. A wave of sadness washed through me.

"And you," Darren exclaimed, pulling me in for a hug, "need to get your pretty little self to Scotland immediately. This one over here won't make it long without you. I have room at my place. The door is always open for you."

"Thanks." I smiled.

"She'll be over before we know it," Stephanie grinned. "I have a feeling you-know-who wants you in Glasgow just as much as we do."

Laughing, I turned toward the VIP section. Alastair was flanked by Vanessa and Katie, while engaging in an animated discussion

with Wesley. He caught me looking and lifted an eyebrow. I just
waved and blew a kiss in his direction.

"He always attracts a crowd no matter where he goes," Darren
mused. "Sort of feel bad for the guy. He has loosened up a bit
since you two started dating though."

"Really?" I asked.

"A little. Don't get me wrong, he'd still rather put in his allotted
time for public appearances and then bugger off somewhere
private. But he's a little less frosty these days. I suspect you've
had a lot to do with that."

I couldn't wipe the smile off my face if I tried. Seeing Alastair
reveal more of his true self was something I wanted for him so
much. I watched him interact with my co-workers. His natural
charm and charisma commanded attention. Make no mistake, he
was still as guarded as ever but his easy manner of speaking with
people he barely knew masked it perfectly. I meandered back to
the VIP section and stood off to the side, continuing to watch him.

He embraced their general curiosities. Katie and Vanessa fired
off question after question. Alastair smoothly deflected a few of
the more probing ones but managed to satisfy their hunger for
information. When they'd finally exhausted every avenue to pry,
inquire and interrogate, the foursome scurried off to the bar. Tyler
gave me a thumbs up as they brushed past.

Alastair sighed, running a hand through his hair.

"Did they wear you out, chief?"

"Not at all," he grinned, hooking his arms around my waist.

"You do realize I'll probably never have another peaceful day
at work. Ten bucks says you charmed the pants right off them."

"The novelty will wear off soon. I'm not that interesting.
Besides," he leaned his forehead to mine, "the only pants I plan
to charm off anyone are yours."

"Cheesy," I smirked.

"You love it."

"Maybe." I pulled him in for a kiss. A bright light flashed, ruining the moment. I opened my eyes just in time to see some random girl lower her smartphone and stare at the photo she'd presumably just taken of us.

"Hey," I shouted, bolting towards her.

"Let her go, love," Alastair said, holding my arm. "It's not worth it."

I watched her disappear into the sea of dancing people.

"It's not fair to you," I grumbled. "You shouldn't have to put up with it here."

His lips curved. "I've been dealing with it all my life. It happens everywhere I go. I block it out most of the time."

"Yeah but still—"

"Enough," he interrupted with a laugh. "Would you like to dance some more with your friends or are you ready to leave for New York?"

"Can we bring them on the plane with us and have a dance party at thirty thousand feet?"

"Not this time," he smirked, lacing his fingers through mine. "Come on. Let's dance a little more."

*   *   *

I hugged Stephanie for the longest time on the sidewalk after we left the club. I'd see her again this week before she flew to Glasgow but I still felt so, so sad that this was our last weekend together. Darren made me swear up and down that I'd fly out for her birthday. Obviously I would, without a doubt.

"Have fun in New York," she whispered, squeezing me. "If you get engaged call me immediately."

My eyes nearly popped out of their sockets as I looked at her incredulously.

"Don't give me that look. It's coming, whether you're ready for it or not."

Still speechless, I glanced from her to where Darren and Alastair were chatting. *Neither one of us is ready for marriage.*

"This right here," she continued, touching the amber ring on my finger, "is the opening act. I watched you two all night. He is so in love with you it's almost unreal. He tries to hide it, just like you do. Y'all are the same person. Just get married already." She smiled.

I couldn't convince her otherwise. Stephanie was the biggest romantic I knew and when she made a proclamation like that, nobody could sway her. Too bad she never applied that outlook to her own love life. Since I'd known her she'd had exactly one boyfriend. As amazing and fabulous as my best friend was, she had a habit of sabotaging her relationships with unrealistic expectations.

"How about we relax with all that?" I said, folding my arms.

"Still so jaded," she sighed.

"I'm not jaded. I prefer to say 'cautiously optimistic.'"

"Whatever you want to call it, it's happening."

"What's happening?" Alastair asked, draping an arm over my shoulder.

I felt my cheeks heat up as a ridiculous blush commandeered my body. Stephanie giggled.

"Your amazing weekend getaway in New York," she answered. "Now get out of here. If my calculations are right, Darren is starving and probably wants something unhealthy and greasy."

"You're a gem," Darren said. "Those food trucks look mighty tempting." He turned to me. "Have fun this weekend, Lia. I'll see you in Glasgow soon, yeah?"

"I hope so."

Stephanie linked her arm with his and the two strolled off to find some food. Alastair gave my hand a tiny squeeze.

"Ready, love?"

"As I'll ever be," I grinned up at him.

The ride to the airport was quick thanks to the late hour. Since we were leaving ahead of schedule I didn't have any of my belongings with me.

"Uh, I don't have my suitcase or anything, Holden."

"It's already on the plane."

"What?"

"I may have stopped by your flat before coming to the party and gathered your things."

Shaking my head, I climbed out of the car and walked toward the waiting aircraft.

"Is this new?" I asked, turning toward him.

"No."

"It's different though, right? I mean, it's bigger."

Alastair shrugged nonchalantly. "I have more than one plane, you know."

I stopped short and stared at him. "Like a fleet?"

"You could say that. Are you going to stare at it all night?"

I sized him up with my best *you're-a-show-off* look and boarded the plane. Comfort and class hit me right away when I walked on. The flight attendant smiled pleasantly and motioned for me to sit wherever I pleased. He was as well-dressed and elegant as the rest of my surroundings. Draped in warm neutral tones of cream, beige and gray, the interior boasted large leather seats, a section with a couch and two doors that led to what I assumed were a bedroom and a bathroom.

Alastair chatted briefly with the pilot before joining me.

"Buckle up, kitten. We're taking off now."

I settled onto one of the leather seats and fastened my seatbelt. Staring out the window, I watched the ground move faster and faster as we taxied down the runway. Once we were airborne Alastair nudged me with his elbow.

"You're pretty."

I laughed. "Working on some new opening lines?"

He rested his chin on his hand and grinned. "Just admiring the view."

"What do you want?"

"That's an easy question."

"Is it?"

His intense, heated stare was unavoidable. "Yes, love. I want you. I always want you."

Hearing that really never gets old. I smiled and looked down, fidgeting with my dress. Sometimes he made me feel like such a lovesick puppy.

"No interruptions this weekend, right?" I asked.

I looked up in time to see his expression harden a little. There was still that whole business of him taking off last night after I told him about his uncle paying Rachel to follow me. I didn't want the stress of that hanging over us but it needed to be resolved. My heart jackhammered in my chest the longer he went without saying anything.

"No interruptions," he finally responded. "Except for the fancy dinner we're going to later tonight."

"I didn't really bring anything for a…" My voice trailed watching his lips curve in a wide grin. "You have clothes waiting for me there, don't you?"

"Maybe. Is that alright?"

"This whole playing tag-a-long with the billionaire thing is going to take awhile to get used to."

"Don't be so dramatic," he teased. "Think of it as a gift."

"But I didn't get anything for you," I pouted.

"None of that. You're with me. That's the greatest gift I could ask for."

"You are quite the charmer."

"You still think so?"

"Yep."

"Care to join me someplace a little more comfortable?"

I lifted an eyebrow. "Where would that be?"

Flashing his hundred-watt smile, he guided me to the back of the plane.

"Door number one or door number two?" he asked.

"Does it matter?"

He stood between them, leveling a dark stare on me that quickened my pulse. "I'll choose then."

Opening the door to his right, I saw a decent sized bedroom. The skin on my shoulder warmed immediately from his touch.

"We have two hours. I'm going to get you out of this dress and make the most of them."

Completely ruled by my overwhelming desire to tear all his clothes off, I followed him into the room and became intimately acquainted with the mile high club.

CHAPTER FIFTEEN

Windows surrounded me, rather than walls. No matter which way I turned, I had a fantastic view. The window to my right boasted the emerald green foliage of Central Park. At this moment I preferred the one to my left. Rolling onto my side, I drank in the never-ending beauty of Alastair as he slept. We'd arrived at his family's penthouse at around three in the morning, exhausted from our in-flight entertainment. Smiling, I stretched my legs along the soft sheets. Bright and airy, the bedroom was drenched in gorgeous earth tones giving off a relaxing, almost resort-like vibe.

I rested my head on his bare chest, content with listening to his steady breathing and rhythmic heart beat. It sped up a little when I placed my hand on his stomach. Stirring gently, he covered my hand with his.

"Good morning, beautiful." His voice always sounded richer and way more sexy when he first woke up.

"Morning. Did you sleep alright?"

"Yes, love," he said, nuzzling into my neck.

"That tickles," I giggled.

"My hair again? I'll shave it off."

"You will do no such thing," I scolded him in mock horror.

Reaching for my waist, he gave it a few quick squeezes. I made a half-hearted attempt to stop him. I hadn't been the victim of one of his tickle assaults in a while and sort of missed it.

"Do you know what time it is?" he asked, curling his body into my side. Something warm and hard poked into my thigh.

"I can take a guess."

"Can you?" He hovered over me, his eyes clouded with sleep and lust. Leaning back, he sat up and pulled off his boxers then removed my cotton pajama bottoms and underwear with a wicked grin. Caging me against the mattress, he pressed his forehead to mine and used his left knee to part my legs. I shifted beneath him, my breathing becoming shallow and quick. Honestly, I could do this all day and night. Every nerve ending tingled.

"I love waking up with you. My Lia," he sighed, sliding into me slowly. Burying his nose in my hair, he whispered, "My love."

I hooked my legs around his hips, allowing him to push in deeper. He filled me completely, the slight discomfort from his size an added sensation of pleasure. Running my hands over the toned, knotted muscles in his back, I sunk my nails into his skin.

"Look at me," I requested. My pulse raced seeing his raw emotion. The love that burned in his eyes was so pure and so unfiltered it gave me chills. "I love you, Alastair."

"*Lia*." Breath hissing through his teeth, he pulled out to the tip then thrust in as deeply as he could, over and over.

* * *

Despite our best intentions to go out, the only sightseeing we did revolved around what views the numerous, massive picture windows allowed us to see. This penthouse was unreal. The walk-in closet was the size of my entire apartment. And yes, there were clothes in there for me. Countless dresses, shoes, tops, jeans and basically any other article of clothing a girl would die for lined an entire wall. I didn't bother asking him if he'd picked all this out himself. I had a sneaking suspicion he'd hired someone but would never admit it to me.

"There's a staircase in here?" I asked, widening my eyes.

"It leads up to the main sitting room. Come with me."

I followed him up and took a second to absorb my surroundings. A panoramic view of New York City encircled us. I could see everything; the Empire State Building, the new World Trade Center, Central Park, the Hudson River. All of it was amazing and breathtaking. I didn't even pay much attention to the beautiful furnishings in the room. I walked over to one of the countless windows and looked down. People scurried on the sidewalks below, rushing to some unknown destination like ants marching in a perfectly choreographed scramble.

"Do you like it here?" Alastair asked.

"It's…yeah. Wow." I tore myself away from the view and noticed him standing with his hand in his pockets. "How often do you come here?"

"Once or twice a year. Probably more now that I'm in charge of everything. Katherine and Jason used to stay here on holiday but ended up buying a smaller one a few blocks away."

"So, then, this is all yours?"

"Mostly."

Confused, I tilted my head to the side. "What do you mean?"

He moved closer to me in slow, calculating strides. "It's ours."

My jaw dropped. "*What*?"

"You're the only other person I want here. You can come and stay whenever you'd like. Here." Pulling his hand out of his pocket, he passed me a set of keys complete with the little fob needed to unlock the main doors and gain entrance to the garage.

I held them, feeling the weight in my hand. "But I don't… this is…"

He pressed his lips to mine, cutting off any further protests. The only thing stopping me from melting into a puddle was the echo of what Stephanie said last night. *Engaged? I've only known him since April. It's what, July twenty-third? It's too soon. We still have so much to…*

"Amelia Grace."

I snapped out of my own head and saw Alastair grinning at me.

"Maybe I'm wrong but when a man kisses his girlfriend he sort of hopes he has her undivided attention."

"Sorry," I said, chagrined.

"There's no need to fret about what I said to you, love. I want you to feel comfortable here. I want you to think of this place as another home. If you only want to come here with me, that's fine. But it is yours to use as you please."

"It's just…I don't want you to think you have to shower me with all this luxury to make me happy. I don't need it, Alastair. I need you."

"I know," he said quietly, cupping my cheeks. "That's one of the many reasons why I love you. I want to share this with you. I want to share everything I have with you. All of it is worthless if I don't."

My heart fluttered at how open he was being with me. "Okay, okay. Let's not get too carried away with the sentimental stuff, Holden."

"Too soppy?" he smirked.

"For someone who is a no-relationships-non-dater? Yeah."

"So my efforts at romance are falling flat? Is that what you're saying, Meyers?"

"Your efforts are just fine. Ease up on the cheese factor," I teased.

Folding his arms, he appeared thoughtful. I could see something brewing behind his pretty green eyes. He slid a finger along his lips and grinned.

"Cheese factor? I see."

In a flash I was at the mercy of his hands as they squeezed my waist. I yelped and tried unsuccessfully to gain freedom from the tickle attack. Seeing him so carefree made my heart soar. I almost forgot about the unresolved issues we still had to deal with. For the time being, I pushed those concerns aside and enjoyed this playful interlude. Breathless, I finally broke free and perched on one of the couches.

"Satisfied?" I panted.

"Almost."

The dangerous look in his eyes as he moved with precision in my direction made me weak in the knees. When he was about a foot away, he stopped.

"Stand up," he ordered softly.

I did without hesitation. He made no move to touch me or kiss me. He just stared. Not in a creepy way. He stared at me with eyes filled with wonder, adoration and gratitude. I loved seeing him so unshielded.

"You have that look," I whispered.

His mouth curved into the beautiful, shy smile I loved. "We should get ready for our fancy dinner. The reservations are for eight."

"It's only five-thirty."

"Then it should be more than enough time for you."

He's teasing me? Smart ass.

"See, now, that's too bad," I said, grinning slyly. "I was going to invite you to shower with me but you had to go and throw some snark."

Not giving him a chance to respond, I turned on my heel and went to the master bathroom. He didn't join me, which led me to believe he had something up his sleeve. After taking a long, lazy bubble bath, I scrutinized the clothes in the massive closet. Since this was a fancy dinner I chose a short, champagne colored cocktail dress with a gorgeous lace bodice. The silk hem fell just above my knees. I found a beautiful pair of Jimmy Choo heels in the same color and scurried off to the bathroom to fix my hair. I knew he preferred when I kept it down, so I let the chestnut waves fall naturally without much fuss.

A soft knock on the door startled me a bit.

"Are you ready?"

I dabbed some gloss on my lips and let him in.

Wow.

Alastair looked like he just stepped off the cover of GQ in a dark blue suit and white shirt with no tie. It was unbuttoned at the top, giving him an aura of powerful elegance that not many men could pull off. Tracing a languid gaze over my curves, he grinned.

"I'm glad you chose that dress. I had a feeling you'd look gorgeous in it."

"Good to know I didn't disappoint."

"Never," he smiled, offering his hand. "Let's go."

* * *

There haven't been many times in my life where I felt out of place. Since I'd dated a senator's son, it wasn't abnormal for me to be in the company of dignitaries and other highly ranked political types at social gatherings. I could usually turn on the charm and keep up with the conversation. As I stood next to the Mercedes SUV outside one of Manhattan's premiere French restaurants, I stared at the black Bentley with 'diplomat' plates parked in front of us. For some reason, it made me nervous.

The restaurant had been partially cordoned off due to the dinner reservations for the Italian diplomat, his fiancée and her brother. Adversely, this affected our reservations.

I watched Alastair as he spoke with the maître d'. He was professional and polite with the man but I could tell something was bugging him. His expression was stony. When he finally waved me over I flashed him the biggest smile I could muster. I wanted him to be relaxed and open, like he'd been all day.

"Everything all set, chief?" I asked, running a hand up his arm.

He nodded and led me into the dining area. Our table was against a window, tucked in the corner. From where I sat, I could see the diplomat's table. He looked to be in his mid-thirties and was seated next to a pretty blonde with a pixie haircut. I didn't want to stare for too long so I turned my attention back to Alastair.

155

He was statuesque. Confused and concerned by his change in demeanor, I reached across the small table and held his hand.

"Don't let this little snafu get to you. It all worked out. We're here and I'm hungry."

Marginally softening his expression, he handed me a menu. We studied them in silence until the server arrived to take our orders. After they'd been placed and the wine poured, I lifted my glass to make a toast.

"Thank you for inviting me to New York with you this weekend. I'm really enjoying myself."

Smiling slightly, Alastair clinked his glass to mine. His eyes flickered and danced in unison with the candle on the table. He looked amazing. If only those tiny worry lines around his eyes would go away.

"You're a little too quiet for my liking, Holden. What's going on in that head of yours?"

My heart rate kicked up as I thought back to Stephanie's proclamation. *I have to stop behaving like this. I'm being ridiculous. He's not going to propose. Stop. Obsessing.*

"I could ask you the same question, kitten. I can practically see the wheels spinning out of control in there."

"You think you're so clever, don't you?" I laughed.

"Among other things."

Oh good. He's relaxing.

"So what else do you have planned for us this weekend? Are we ever going to see the outside or do you intend to keep me occupied again?"

The stony façade melted away and was replaced with a sexy, sultry stare. "As I've told you before, my intention is to keep that look on your face permanently. If it means we sacrifice a little sightseeing, then so be it. However," he paused, brushing his thumb over my bottom lip, "your wish is my command so if you'd rather venture out into the city, we can do that."

His feather light touch scrambled my thought process. So did the low timbre of his voice wrapped in that mesmerizing English accent. How he could be so damn seductive and *successful* with it time and time again floored me. He knew it, too.

"I'm not much of a challenge for you, am I?"

"Quite the opposite. You challenge me in ways I never thought possible." His expression faltered as he withdrew into himself. Watching the transformation broke my heart.

"Hey," I whispered, touching his cheek. It took a minute but he dragged himself out of whatever thoughts he'd succumbed to and grabbed my hand, kissing the knuckles.

"Have you thought any more about coming to live with me in Glasgow?"

Our entrées arrived at that moment so I was given a small reprieve before answering. I even managed to have a bite of the butter-poached lobster. It was so tender and sweet, I had to put the fork down to savor it properly.

"Is it good?" he asked with a smug grin.

I rolled my eyes and swallowed. "Are you enjoying watching me eat?"

"Always." He started cutting into his steak. "You didn't answer my question about Glasgow."

"I want to," I answered slowly, "but I—"

"If you're worried about a job, I already told you there's a position open for an executive producer. I can get you an interview."

My curiosity muscled over my trepidations, forcing them to be quiet. "What's the show?"

"It's a news magazine program called The Archer Hour. They've overhauled most of the staff and want to take it in a new direction. From what I've heard, finding a new executive producer has been challenging."

"Why?"

"The host is a bit of a pill."

"Most television personalities are. What else is wrong with the show?"

He shrugged. "Not much, really. I reckon the whole problem is nobody wants to work with Julian Archer."

"Is he that bad?"

"I've met him a handful of times and most of our interactions revolved around him trying to get me as a guest on the program. In my eyes, he's a pain in the ass but you may see it differently."

I had another forkful of lobster and thought about this scenario. It would be a nice change to have a new job and be in charge of my own show. I highly doubted this Julian Archer fellow would be any more difficult to handle than the personalities I currently worked with. It was certainly something to consider, especially with all the drama happening at the station now.

"You're not worried that he might try to make me coerce you into being on the show because we're involved?"

"I won't let that happen. Our private life isn't a bargaining chip." His eyes hardened like marbles.

"Alright." I lifted my hands. "Just thought I'd throw it out there."

"I think you'd do brilliant work. They need someone like you. You're smart, don't take any shit from anyone and can go toe-to-toe with a big personality."

"Thank you for the ego boost, chief." I smiled and raised my wine glass.

"Send me your CV when you get back to Orlando. I'll forward it on to the hiring manager."

The reality of moving out there and living with him lifted my already good mood to new heights. Maybe this was the next logical step in our relationship. An overly ecstatic grin tugged at my mouth.

"Okay. We'll see what happens."

A huge, gorgeous smile brightened Alastair's face. The sight of him so happy was contagious. We both grinned at each other like lunatics for a couple minutes before continuing with our meals. No sooner had we finished our main course, the server presented us with the chef's special dessert of the evening, which was comprised of small fruit tarts, decadent cheesecake and assorted financiers. Each one was more delicious than the next. When I couldn't stuff another morsel into my body, I leaned back in the chair satisfied.

"I should probably pop into the bathroom and make sure the seams on this dress haven't split."

Alastair's deep, throaty laugh echoed as I walked toward the restrooms.

The cute, blonde girl from the diplomat's table was also in there reapplying some lip-gloss. She studied me out the corner of her eye as I primped in front of the mirror.

"That's a lovely color on you," she said. "Really brings out the gold in your eyes."

I was surprised to hear she had a Scottish accent.

"Oh, thank you." I smiled.

"I've never been to this restaurant before," she continued. "My fiancé thought it would be a nice place to celebrate my birthday."

"He has great taste then. Happy birthday."

"Ah, bless. Thank you, dear."

She played around with her stylish pixie cut before walking out. I dabbed a little more gloss to my lips and headed back to the table. As I rounded the corner I was shocked to see Alastair engaged in an intense conversation with Brent Garrison.

CHAPTER SIXTEEN

My feet remained frozen in place as I watched Alastair and Brent. Neither one looked pleased. Movement from the diplomat's table caught my attention. The blonde girl stood up and walked toward Brent. From where I stood I could see, clear as day, Alastair's whole body turn to stone. A sinking, sick feeling filled my stomach.

That's Brent's sister.

Not wanting to hide in the shadows like a spineless wuss, I forced my legs to move and walked over to the tense threesome.

"Lia," Brent greeted me with a smile, "how nice to see you again. Have you met my sister Olivia?"

Time slowed down to a weird, trippy pace. I felt like I was having an out of body experience. I saw myself shake Olivia's hand and say hello. She remarked that we'd just met in the bathroom. Their voices echoed through my mind, like a distant memory.

"Now that we've all said our hellos, it's time for us to get going." Alastair's icy statement snapped the world back into reality for me.

"Don't be so anti-social, Holden," Brent glowered. "We're in a public place. It's not like anything bad can happen."

For whatever reason, that statement sent a tremor of anger through Alastair. Obviously, his history with Brent was - as with everything else in his life - layered and complex. I focused my attention on Olivia. She absently twisted her engagement ring around her finger while staring wistfully at Alastair. A horrible surge of insecurity and jealousy powered through my body. *She's still in love with him.* Instinctively, I entwined my fingers with his and stood so close to him we could have been mistaken for conjoined twins.

Olivia seemed to get the hint and cast a cool glance in my direction. It took me by surprise. I shouldn't feel threatened by this girl at all. Physically, we were total opposites. She was tall, thin and blonde with no real curves to speak of. Not that I wanted to be catty or anything but it was just something I noticed. She was quite pretty though. And she had an almost ethereal aura about her.

I made myself stop all the comparisons. She was engaged. She was Alastair's past. *I'm his present and future.* Yet something in her eyes led me to believe there was still unfinished business between them.

"What are you guys doing in New York?" I asked as nonchalantly as possible.

"This is almost serendipitous isn't it? It's my sister's birthday and since she's on holiday here with Sergio I decided to fly out for the weekend." Brent turned to her and smiled. "I don't get to see my baby sister very often."

She looked at him adoringly. I could tell they had a close relationship, which explained Brent's frostiness toward Alastair.

The protective older brother. Oh boy…

"How about you, Lia? What brings you to the Big Apple?"

"Nothing special really. Just a little getaway." I smiled and squeezed Alastair's hand. He made no movement. I wasn't even sure if he was breathing.

"Ah. I've heard about Holden's little getaway weekends. I'm surprised he didn't take you to the south of France. It's one of his favorite places."

His voice dripped with acidic sarcasm. And it really pissed me off.

"I'm sure we'll get there soon enough, then," I snapped. "It's always good to see you, Brent."

Olivia looked down and seemed uncomfortable with the tone and direction of this conversation. I couldn't blame her. I wanted it to go away, too. Brent shook his head slightly and smiled at me in a way that sent shivers down my spine.

"I hope to see you again soon, Lia. I hear your friend is starting next week at Finley's. Sarah told me she's going to be working on the ad campaign for my new ultra lounge. I look forward to meeting her."

"Yeah, she's excited about it."

"You take care of yourself, love," he said with a note of concern.

"Olivia. You and your brother should come to the table. Dessert is being served. Invite your friends to join us."

I glanced over to the dark haired man with the Italian accent. He nodded pleasantly in my direction and waited.

Alastair kept his laser hot stare on Brent and answered, "Thank you for the offer but we really ought to be going."

With a small tug to my hand, he pulled me out of the tense, suffocating bubble we'd been standing in. I took one last look backward and saw Brent leading his sister to their table. Alastair had already paid the bill while I was in the restroom so we continued to the exit. I noticed Paxton exchange a knowing glance with him before we climbed into the SUV. What a weird night this had turned out to be.

Alastair kept my hand firmly clasped in his, stroking it with his thumb. I gave him a reassuring squeeze. He looked at me, his eyes worn and dim, and half-smiled. I sensed there was something big he had to tell me.

That's what this weekend was for, right? He did say I'd know everything.

Paxton dropped us off at the high-rise's main entrance, waited until we were inside and drove off to park the SUV. Riding up in the elevator with Alastair wasn't tense but it wasn't comfortable either. Apprehension seemed to seep out of his pores. When we reached the top floor, the doors opened directly into the penthouse's main foyer. We walked in silence toward the living room. There weren't any lights on in the room making the views even more breathtaking at night. I couldn't help myself and stopped by one of the windows to admire the illuminated skyline.

"You always do manage to find the beauty in any situation, don't you?" he asked quietly, placing his hand at the small of my back.

I swallowed down a healthy dose of fear and anxiety. "Don't let what happened at the restaurant ruin our night. We have all the time in the world to talk about it. I don't want you to feel pressured to let it all out now."

Nobody was more surprised by the words coming out of my mouth than me. All my instincts screamed for answers, demanding them now. I wanted to know. I had to know.

"I don't deserve you," he responded, withdrawing further into himself again. I wasn't going to let that happen. Not tonight.

"Yes you do." I cupped his chin and gently tilted his head up. "Right here, right now, in this moment and all the moments that will follow, you deserve me. I'm not going anywhere. You're sort of stuck with me."

He started to protest but I cut him off with a quick kiss.

"Whatever your scars are or whatever demons you think you have cannot tarnish the man I fell in love with. I see you, Alastair. I see your attempts to mask it all. You're a pro, I'll admit it. But I'm the only one you consistently reveal your true self to."

The muscles in his jaw tightened.

"I know you hate this," I continued, "I know it takes a lot for you to open what's in here." I touched his chest, just above his heart. It raced beneath my fingers. "I know it hurts."

He grabbed my hand and held it tightly against his chest.

"There are times I look at you and think 'this guy loves me' and it makes my heart swell so much I'm afraid it'll burst. That's how it hurts for me. You're not alone in this. Not by a long shot."

His green eyes sparked with a myriad of emotions as they

bore through me. "You make me feel so…" He stopped himself, scowling. Leveling an intense stare at me, he wet his lips. "You make me feel so wanted."

"You are wanted. In every sense of the word."

"I…when I was involved with Olivia she tried to turn what we had into a meaningful relationship. I was young. I was only twenty-four. I'd spent all of my life numbing myself from any and all emotion. I didn't want it. I didn't need it." He squeezed my hand and swallowed hard. "I used her. I used all of them just so I could feel, for a moment, like someone wanted me. I knew they were only after the name and the money. That's what made it so easy to move from one to the next. The only one who never cared was Emma. She got off on it."

Hearing her name dredged up the unpleasant memory of our meeting at the garden party. She did seem awfully proud of the fact that she had been his fuck buddy.

"I'm sorry. You don't want to hear all this."

"Don't apologize," I smiled, running my free hand through his hair. "You had to listen to my shitty history with Nathan. What's fair is fair."

Leaning his forehead to mine, he sighed. I kept stroking his hair, letting him center himself or find whatever balance he needed to continue.

"Olivia's an exhibitionist. She liked it when we recorded—" he stopped, clearly bothered by whatever the look was that had plastered itself on my face. "When I broke things off with her she threatened to use those videos against me. She sent copies to my uncle and grandfather. Needless to say, they weren't thrilled. I'd already lost favor with them by being difficult and getting into all sorts of trouble while growing up. Neither one had any patience left for my antics."

His expression hardened.

"I took matters into my own hands and paid her off to stay quiet. I had our legal department draft a nondisclosure agreement and made her sign it. If she were to ever make the videos public, she'd be sued for defamation of character and we'd go after everything her family has."

I could barely breathe I was so shocked. This was so heartless.

Shaking his head slightly, he frowned. "I use women for sex, Lia. I use them and cast them aside. It makes me feel powerful and in control and I like it. It's as though nobody can ever hurt me because I have the upper hand. Olivia tried to force something I didn't want and this is what happened. This is why Brent hates me. And he can't do a damn thing about it." His whole demeanor shifted to that awful, detached façade he'd used when we first met. He looked so cold and dispassionate.

I pulled my hand away from his chest, distraught over what he'd told me. I knew he had issues but this was too much. The blackmail was one thing. As a prominent public figure I'm sure he wasn't the only one who's had to take such drastic measures. What bothered me the most was the fact that he liked using women as objects. I'd bitten off way more than I could chew with him.

"Your feet must hurt in those shoes. Here. Sit."

He attempted to lead me to the couch but I didn't move. Completely numbed by what just transpired, I could barely look at him. "I'll just sit here."

"On the floor?"

"Yeah. I…it's so pretty with the view."

"Hang on."

He moved quickly to the couch and yanked off the cushions. Placing them on the floor in front of the window, he motioned for me to sit. Once we were seated facing one another with our knees touching, he held my hand and put it over his heart again. The gesture nearly brought me to tears.

"This is who I am. This is the man behind the mask. You have the upper hand now." Setting his jaw with determination, he looked at me. "You have the power to destroy me, Amelia."

I didn't know how to respond to that. I knew what he meant

but had no idea what he wanted to hear. The frantic beating of his heart vibrated beneath my hand. Holding his unrelenting stare, I whispered, "Ditto, love."

Releasing my hand, he slumped against the window, exhaling long and slow. I could tell he wasn't in the mood to continue with this line of conversation. In all honesty, neither was I. I was emotionally drained. Staring out at the bright lights of the city made me feel a little better. Everything seemed peaceful from so high up.

"Did you know Olivia and Brent were going to be at the restaurant tonight?" The words gushed out of my mouth and hung in the air before I could stop them.

He froze, closing his eyes briefly. I steeled myself for the response I knew was coming.

"No," he said quietly. "I knew she was in New York but had no idea they'd be at the restaurant."

"How did you know she'd be here?"

Leveling a stoic gaze at me, he remained silent for several seconds. My legs itched with the urge to walk away.

"She told me," he finally answered.

"She told you?" I snapped. "You're in touch with her?"

"No. I'm not in touch with her. She heard I was coming here for some meetings and took it upon herself to let me know she'd be in the city."

"Bullshit."

"Lia," he scowled, "you're overreacting. All she did was send me an email."

He was right about my overreacting but I was heated. This whole night had gone up in flames so quickly.

"So, is this the ex you told me about last month? The one who took all those pictures that your grandfather has?"

Alastair fortified his protective shield while keeping his eyes locked to mine. *I should stop. I'm going to make it worse if I continue asking questions.*

"Yes."

His admission stunned me. Well, not the admission so much as the ease in which he answered. I glanced out the window again, hoping the serene beauty of the illuminated city would put an end to my whirling thoughts.

"You can ask me anything, Amelia. I'll give you all the answers I can."

His tone gave me pause. When I looked back at him, he was completely hidden behind the mask. I didn't want this to continue. I wanted to be alone and gather my thoughts.

"Why is your uncle paying a tabloid reporter to spy on me?"

Christ. My mouth and brain really need to get on the same page.

Pushing out a harsh breath, Alastair grimaced. "He's not. Nathan has been lying to you the entire time."

"*What?*"

"I told you he's a con artist."

"How do you know he's been lying to me?" The panic in my voice cut through the room.

"He likes to brag about what he thinks he knows."

"What do you mean?"

A bitter smile curled his mouth, turning my stomach. "I'm not the only one who shows up unannounced to throw punches."

I clasped my stomach as a horrible, stabbing pain sliced through it. "Did he hurt you?"

Alastair's cold exterior defrosted slightly. "No, love. But he tried his hardest to hurt you."

"I don't understand. He said there was a trust account—"

"There is. It's the account we set up for Olivia. She receives an undisclosed amount each month. He discovered the account but doesn't know what it's for exactly. He made up the story about my uncle paying that reporter."

Resting my forehead against the cool glass did nothing to stop the spinning.

"Each month? I thought you said you paid her off."

He shifted uncomfortably on the cushion. "The only people who know this trust account exists are me, my grandfather, Jason, the lawyers and Olivia. Even Brent is under the impression we wrote her a check and sent her off. What she threatened to use against me could destroy my grandfather's company. We were backed into a corner."

"Not to sound flippant or anything but if it's just a sex tape how can it destroy a company?"

Alastair's fair skin turned ashy. "I can't say anything more about it." His body language and aggravated tone were enough to keep me from firing off more questions. *What did you do?* My heart longed for the simpler moments we'd shared. Hell, I'd even relive the day he told me he blamed himself for his family's death and would rather be dead himself. At least that was something I could quasi handle. This was a complete mind fuck.

"I can't…I don't…" I raked my fingers through my hair. "Jesus, Alastair, I don't know what to say. I don't even know who you are right now."

I'd peeled back too many layers. I'd seen too much of the broken, scarred man beneath the expensive clothes. Persistent, unbearable tightness squeezed my chest. I needed to get away from him. I needed to clear my head and figure out how to proceed.

My brain and heart clawed at each other, trying to convince me of what I should do next. Surrounded by the beauty of New York City and this penthouse, all I could focus on was the ugliness poisoning my mind.

"You're free to leave anytime you want." The deadness in his voice angered and saddened me.

Thick, hot tears rolled down my cheeks. I wasn't going to let him dictate this. "I'm not letting you push me away again," I bit out. "I can't be in the same room as you right now, but I'm not leaving. You don't get to control the outcome this time. I do."

I stood up and stalked toward the stairs. When I reached the closet, I kicked off my heels and went up to the roof deck. The infinity pool glistened in the moonlight. I sat at the edge and dipped my feet in the water. Leaning back, I inhaled the warm, summer night air. It did nothing to help sort through the cluttered mess that my brain had become. I tried to piece together everything that had happened over the past couple of weeks; the stalking reporter who wasn't really stalking me, Nathan's bizarre radio silence, Alastair's abrupt trip to London and anger fueled panic after I told him his uncle was paying Rachel.

And what was the cherry on top? Tonight's run in with Olivia. Jesus, there was too much to process.

I cradled my head in my hands, wishing all this would go away. I was too mentally and emotionally drained to give it any more thought. I felt like I was coming apart at the seams again.

Looking up, I noticed clouds gathering in front of the moon, blocking its light. I just sat and stared as they inevitably overpowered the moon, hiding it from view.

Nobody said our relationship was going to be a walk in the park. I wasn't willing to throw it away because he used to act like a jerk. We'd come this far and I had a sneaking suspicion we still had miles to go.

Pulling my legs out of the water, I stood up and went back down to the living room. Alastair was nowhere to be found. I ran off to the bedroom but he wasn't there either. I checked every room in the penthouse but couldn't find him. Panic grew and spread through my body. *He left. He left me here alone.*

But that's what I'd wanted, right? I wanted to get away from him. Sinking onto the mattress, I curled up into the fetal position. I wasn't the one leaving this time. He was. He'd made the decision for me again and removed himself from my life.

CHAPTER SEVENTEEN

I stared out the window at the illuminated steel playground. The city that never sleeps had company tonight. I snuggled deeper into the pillows, comforted by their softness but longing for something more. It was well past midnight and I had no idea where my boyfriend had disappeared to or if I'd ever see him again.

A shadowy reflection in the glass startled me. I sat up and turned. Alastair stood by the door with a single red rose in the palm of his hand. The long stem sat wedged between his fingers, dangling beneath. He walked toward me with great caution and sat on the edge of the bed. Still dressed in his suit from dinner, he looked beautiful and sad.

The skin on my cheek warmed from his soft touch. I was surprised to see that his impenetrable shield had dissolved. The yearning in his eyes burned with unwavering intensity.

"You left," I said hoarsely.

"I wanted to give you the space you needed. I only went for a long walk." He looked at the flower. "This is for you, if you want it."

I reached out and touched the delicate petals, running my fingers over his palm. I took the rose and laid it on the bed next to me. "Thank you."

"This day had been absolute perfection, Amelia. I'm sorry it ended so horribly. I hope that brings—"

Overcome by my fierce love for him, I climbed onto his lap and kissed his doubts and fears away, along with my own. Cupping my jaw, he hovered his lips over mine and whispered, "My Lia. Sometimes I think you're just a dream and I'll wake up. I want this to work. I want us to last. I'll do everything in my power to make sure that happens."

I let the weight of his words wash over me as he played with a strand of my hair.

"The way you make me feel," he continued, "is unlike anything I've ever experienced."

Tears burned the corners of my eyes. *Regardless of what he believes, this is the man behind the mask.* "You really are a big softie deep down, aren't you?"

His beautiful, sculpted mouth curved. "Don't tell anyone."

"Your secret is safe with me, chief," I grinned, hugging him tightly.

"You're not disgusted by me?"

I sat back with a start, confounded by his question. "No, I'm not disgusted by you. Don't be ridiculous."

He remained stoic and quiet.

"Listen, whatever you've done or however you chose to live your life in the past is just that. The past. I'm not going to sugarcoat it though. I don't like that version of you. But it doesn't diminish the way I feel about you now."

"Do you mean that?"

"Of course I do," I said, playing with his hair. "The Alastair Holden I know is playful and affectionate. You make me laugh and you frustrate me. There are some things about you that are still a mystery but underneath all this," I tugged at his designer suit jacket, "is a loving, caring, amazing man."

"I can't ever lose you," he said, his eyes blazing with need. "Ever."

"You won't."

The last thing I wanted was to engage in another draining conversation, so I kissed him. All the unpleasantness of the night floated away as we lost ourselves in each other. Sliding my hands under his suit jacket, I pushed it off his shoulders. He tossed it to the floor, keeping his eyes fused with mine. I kissed him again with unbridled passion.

"Lia," he moaned quietly.

The sounds he made always drove me crazy. I tangled my fingers in his hair and stared deep in his eyes.

"I want you," I declared. "I want all of you. Every doubt, every fear, every smile, every secret. Love me, Alastair. I need to feel you."

I sat up on my knees, pulling him up with me. We undressed each other and curled up together on the bed. He held me so close, I felt so safe. I kissed along his shoulder and up his neck.

"Look at me," he requested.

I rested my head on the pillow, leaning forward so our foreheads touched.

"I want you like this tonight. Just skin against skin, nothing more." He caressed my back, tracing his fingers up and down my spine. "This is how I feel when you're with me. Wanted. Needed. I'm loving you this way tonight, Lia. I'm loving you the way you love me."

* * *

Of course it would rain on the day we decided to go out and do some sightseeing.

"Come on,'" Alastair grinned, jogging toward the aquarium's main entrance. I sprinted behind him, trying to shield my head from the deluge.

"This is karma, you know," I said once we were safe beneath the overhang.

"For what?"

"For wasting a perfectly gorgeous day inside yesterday."

"I don't see it that way." A salacious grin spread across his face. "And I didn't hear any complaints coming from you either. Besides, it's only a little rain. This is considered a light shower in England."

"Stop it," I shoved him playfully.

Walking through the aquarium was like being transported to another world. Everything was so serene and bathed in dimly lit hues of blue. The reflection of the water from some of the tanks shimmered against the walls. I always loved coming here when I was a kid. My sister and I would spend most of our time staring at the colorful fish.

Alastair and I strolled through the exhibits. He paused by the jellyfish, placing his hands against the glass. Dozens of the dangerous beauties bobbed under the water, opening their translucent orange skin like an umbrella to move. I smiled, watching him watch the jellyfish. He looked like such a little boy. It was too precious. I snapped a quick photo of him with my phone.

"Sneaking pictures of me?"

"Maybe."

He turned to me and smiled. "I haven't been to an aquarium since primary school. I'd forgotten how awesome they are."

"Well then, let's go check out some more awesome sea life," I grinned.

"Any suggestions?"

"How do you feel about sharks and whales?"

"So long as they don't eat me, I'm okay with them."

I laughed loudly and grabbed his hand, leading him to the giant underwater tunnel. Before arriving there, we stopped to see the beluga whales through the huge windows. Two of them swam gracefully right in front of us. The mammals circled one another, almost as though they were flirting. One of them even looked like it was playing hard to get.

"She's giving him a run for his money," Alastair remarked, squeezing my hand. "Looks familiar."

I gave him a look. "Sharks are next. And I believe it's feeding time." I poked him in the stomach. "Hmm. Just squishy enough for them."

"Wow. You'd give me up for shark bait just like that?"

"Nah. It wouldn't be much of a challenge for them seeing as you can't swim."

Before he could respond, I let go of his hand and darted off to the tunnel. He caught me pretty quickly though and tickled me hard. I gasped, trying not to be too loud and cause a scene.

"I told you that smart mouth would get you in trouble every single time," he said with a wicked gleam in his eyes.

"You love it."

He lifted an eyebrow. "Fair point."

We sat on the platform edge next to the curved window and watched the sharks, turtles and other assorted marine life go about their business without a care in the world. I enjoyed watching Alastair more than anything. He took everything in with wide-eyed wonder. I could almost picture him as a little boy, before the accident, filled with curiosity and awe. It saddened me to think he'd spent most of his life closed off from all the beauty the world had to offer. At the same time, it gave me great joy to know he was moving past all of it. I didn't want to give myself too much credit for being his catalyst but I knew some of it had to do with me.

A light kiss brushed against my forehead. I looked up at him and smiled. He lifted my left hand and admired the ring he'd given me, while stroking my ring finger.

"Why do you wear this on your middle finger?"

My vision tripled. *Oh Jesus, Stephanie was right*. Pulling myself together I attempted to answer him.

"Um, I don't know. The stone is big, so, maybe…I thought it might look better there?"

"Hmm." He laced his fingers through mine.

I couldn't tame the insane pace of my beating heart. A huge fish paused in the window across from where we were sitting. If I didn't know any better, I'd say it was laughing at me as it stared with its freakishly big eye. *Look at the human jumping to conclusions and giving herself a heart attack! Haha!*

"Relax, love," Alastair whispered. "It's not happening yet."

All the activity surrounding us vanished when I looked at him. "What are you—"

He kissed me so sweetly it numbed my brain. I was completely encased in his magnetic aura and delicious scent.

"No questions, kitten. Unless I'm the one doing the asking," he smirked. "Would you like to go back to the penthouse or stay here?"

"Do I ha—"

He placed his finger on my lips to silence me. "You are only allowed to give answers."

I narrowed my eyes, waiting for him to remove his finger. These little games he liked to play could be so annoying sometimes. Charming, but annoying.

"I think we should stay here," I said when I was freed from the makeshift muzzle.

"Should we?"

"Yes." I stood up. "I hear there's a piranha tank."

He raised both eyebrows. "More flesh eating fish? I'm beginning to think you don't like me."

I grinned slyly. "Whatever would give you that impression?"

"Breaking the rules already," he said, rising to his feet. The hot, focused look in his eyes gave me a rush. He leaned closer, dipping his mouth my ear. "It's too bad there are so many people here. I would love to have my way with you against these windows."

And there go my knees.

If his goal was to take my mind off any impending engagement theories, mission accomplished. Now all I could think about was being plastered against a backdrop of live sea creatures. The same big-eyed fish swam by again, sizing me up. Snapping myself out of this lust-fueled exchange, I took a deep breath.

"You're lethal, you know that?"

His throaty laugh echoed through the tunnel. "Nah. I just know which buttons of yours to push."

"I'm not that much of a mystery, Holden. Don't flatter yourself."

"Ah, Lia," he grinned, draping an arm over my shoulders. "Come. Show me the piranha."

"I'd like to throw your ass in the tank," I muttered.

"I heard that. Put some floaties on me before you do."

Smiling, I wrapped my arm around his waist. We spent the next hour taking in all the aquarium had to offer. I loved seeing flashes of the fun-loving little boy behind his eyes. After what we'd been through last night, this was a welcome sight. He spent quite a bit of time taking pictures and reading all the informative plaques about the various animals and fish. I think his favorite might have been the sea otters. He seemed to really enjoy watching them. I saw a wistful expression cross his features a few times but for the most part, he remained open and unshielded.

"Ready to go?" he asked.

"Sure."

He'd given Paxton the day off, so we took a cab back to his place.

"Feel like going out for dinner or would you prefer takeaway?"

"I'd rather not go out if that's okay."

"Not a problem." He flashed me his megawatt smile. "What would you like?"

"You."

Still smiling, he glanced out the window then back at me. "That goes without saying."

"Well," I said, folding my arms, "Chinese I guess."

"Is that all?"

"And cupcakes."

"Anything else," he smirked.

"Can we have dinner out by the pool since it's not raining anymore?"

"Sure. Still feeling aquatic after our day out?"

I giggled. "Yeah. I'm actually going to go for a swim while you take care of all the food and stuff. Feel free to join me whenever."

Blowing him a kiss, I dashed off to the bedroom and dug my swimsuit out of the suitcase. Once changed, I went up to the roof deck. The storm clouds that had dumped rain on the city all day were breaking up, revealing a gorgeous cobalt sky. The sun still had another hour or so left to dazzle the earth.

I dipped my toe in the water. The pool was heated so I jumped in. The warmth caressed and soothed my skin. I swam several laps before pausing to drink in the view. A girl could get used to this. I was up so high I could barely hear the bustling sounds of the city. All I could see from this vantage point was the sky and buildings.

Resting my arms along the pool's edge, I laid my head back and let my mind wander. It was hard to believe how different my life was from a year ago. Hell, forget that. I couldn't believe how much my life had changed in the past six months. I don't think I'd have dared to even dream about where I was now. My life back in Orlando felt so detached from my current reality. In a way, it didn't feel like a part of me anymore.

A flurry of goose bumps rippled down my back. I smiled. *He's here.*

I pushed myself away from the edge and turned. Alastair diligently laid out the food, plates and utensils.

"Did you enjoy your swim?" he asked, fixing his emerald gaze on me.

"I did. You should join me later."

I climbed out and walked toward the table. Alastair paused and watched me. Placing my hand on my hips, I grinned.

"Enjoying the view?"

"I think green is my new favorite color."

I laughed, wrapping a towel around my waist. I'd chosen to wear a mint green bikini. It wasn't skimpy or anything but it did show off my assets.

"You're still dressed," I remarked, loading a plate with chicken and snow peas. I also nabbed a veggie spring roll and sat down.

"Am I not supposed to be?"

"Put your swimming trunks on or whatever you have. You're coming in the water with me when we finish eating."

He scowled, shaking his head. "I can't swim, Lia. I'm not going in the pool."

I nudged his foot under the table. "Relax, love. The water in that end over there only comes as high as my midsection. You'll be fine."

The sky changed from cobalt to lavender as the sun continued to set. Most of the clouds from today's rain were gone so we were treated to a rather gorgeous display of color. All talk of going in the pool ceased, which made Alastair relax greatly. I asked about what his plans were for work. He'd be in the city until Wednesday for board meetings. There was also a client dinner he had to attend on Tuesday night. I wanted to stay here with him rather than go home. The temptation do that was way too strong.

"I'll be back in Orlando before you know it," he grinned, clearing off the table. "You won't even know I'm gone."

I pouted, watching him retreat back inside. After a beat, I stood up and waded back into the pool. I probably shouldn't force him to come in with me. I'd be freaked out too if I didn't know how to swim. Then again, the water was so shallow and he was so tall, it shouldn't matter.

"This is as close as I'm getting to that pool, Lia."

The resolve in his voice rang loud and clear. I turned, about to respond, but was silenced by the sight of him. He'd changed into his swim trunks, which matched the rich color of his dark red hair perfectly. They also hugged his hips quite spectacularly. I took my time admiring his athletic physique. My eyes drifted from his toned torso all the way down to his finely sculpted calf muscles.

"I'm up here, love," he teased.

Flicking my eyes up, I grinned. "You could stand to spend a little time in the sun."

He frowned, looking down at his arms and chest. "Why?"

"It'll give a healthy glow to that pasty Britishness."

"Pasty Britishness?" His eyes narrowed.

I skimmed my hands along the water's surface, smiling. "Come in here with me."

"No."

"Please? I promise I won't let anything happen to you. It's just like getting in a bathtub."

"I don't have to swim in a bathtub," he muttered.

"You don't have to swim in here either." I waded over to the stairs. "Come here. At least try walking down the stairs."

Steeling his expression, he stalked over to the steps and sighed. "You really want me to do this?"

"I want you to do whatever makes you feel comfortable."

Shrouding himself behind the all too familiar shield, he reached for the handrail and stepped down. After a few seconds, he took another step. There were only four of them so he was already halfway to his goal.

"You're almost there, chief." I encouraged him with a smile.

"The things I do for you," he grumbled, taking the last two steps into the water. It only came up to his waist. With one hand still clasped to the handrail, he balled the other one into a fist. I knew he didn't want to show fear in front of me but I could tell he was uncomfortable. I stood close to him and placed my hands on his chest.

"See? Not so scary, is it?"

"Easy for you to say."

I held onto his fisted hand. "Come with me."

Arching a brow, he looked at me skeptically. "Stealing my phrases?"

"Yes. Come."

"Where?"

"To the edge so we can enjoy the view."

He exhaled loudly. "Fine."

Keeping his hand secured in mine, I led him the short distance to the edge. The entire area by the pool was surrounded by a high glass wall, so it wasn't like we were living dangerously or anything. Since this was an infinity pool it only gave the illusion that the water was falling over the edge of the building.

"Doing okay?"

"Yes, love."

"Just like a bathtub, right?"

He relaxed a little, chuckling. "Whatever you say."

"Come here." I leaned against the pool's wall and pulled him so he stood in front of me. Hooking my arms around his waist, I leaned close and kissed his chest. "Thank you for an amazing weekend."

"It's not over yet," he grinned, tipping my chin up. "We still have all night."

"I need my beauty sleep, Holden."

"You're beautiful enough." He put a finger on my mouth. "And don't say I'm being cheesy."

His soft lips left kisses scattered up and down my neck. I buried my hands in his hair, never wanting to let him go.

"I like being in the pool with you," he whispered on my skin before locking me in a heated kiss. "I like going to aquariums with you. And falling asleep with you. And waking up with you. And feeling you close to me everyday."

He kissed me again, slower and deeper. The subtle flexing of his hips into mine sent a pleasurable tingle through my body.

"I want all of that and more with you. Permanently."

Here it comes…

My skin warmed as his hands caressed and explored every inch of me. Any thought process I had flew out the window. Or in this case, jumped off the building.

"Live with me, Lia. Move to Glasgow. I want us to start our life together." The smooth skin of his cheek brushed against mine. "Will you come with me?"

I didn't hesitate for one second. "Yes."

CHAPTER EIGHTEEN

Operating on little to no sleep was not a talent I possessed. The two-hour catnap I took on the early flight to Orlando recharged exactly nothing. I might have even dozed off in the cab on the drive back to my apartment from the airport. My only saving grace was the continued flow of elation from my weekend in New York. The dizzying joy from Alastair's proposal kept me motivated through the morning. I was even happy to be at work.

9:32am Are you back? Are you ENGAGED?!?!?!?!

I laughed at Stephanie's text, sending her a quick response.

9:34am Yes, I'm back and no, I'm not. I have news.

9:37am OMG. Tell me everything

9:41am ;-)

9:43am >_<

9:45am LOL Call you later

10:02am Come over after work. Darren's driving me nuts

10:36am Will do

It wasn't until just before lunchtime that I noticed mostly everyone in the newsroom was on edge. Nobody was overly chatty like they usually were. They all seemed to plow through their duties without paying much attention to anything else. Tyler and Wes weren't their usual selves either. In all honesty, I couldn't be bothered with it. I was in too good a mood to let whatever workplace drama was happening get me down. I focused on my work and kept my spirits high. And then, the phone rang.

"Lia Meyers."

"Hello, Sparkle."

Crash and burn.

"Nathan," I whispered, gritting my teeth.

"You sound surprised to hear from me."

"Well, you sort of fell off the face of the earth. Where have you been?"

"Around," he answered, his tone clipped. "We need to talk."

"No we—"

"Yes, Lia, we do. Come to the house after work. There's something I have to show you."

"No. I have plans."

"Tomorrow night then. Be here at eight."

He hung up without giving me a chance to answer. I placed the phone back in its cradle and sighed. Anger coiled in the pit my stomach. Yeah, I wanted to talk to him, too. How dare he put me through all this and jeopardize my relationship with Alastair. I was pissed at him and myself.

Pushing aside my annoyance, I threw myself into my work. During some down town I searched online for any and all information about The Archer Hour and, more importantly, the host. All the articles I found said basically the same things about Julian

Archer; brash, difficult to work with and a loud mouth.

I grinned. *No different from anybody in here, that's for sure.*

"You haven't stopped smiling all day. 'Fess up. How was your weekend?"

Sydney flashed a bright smile in my direction and clasped onto the small divider between our desks.

"In a word, phenomenal," I said, leaning closer to her. "What's going on in here? Everyone looks like someone just shot their dog."

She looked around quickly and whispered, "Layoffs. Bruce has been holed up in Vincent Jennings' office all day. Apparently the bigwigs in New York are lowering the boom on all the stations. Bad year financially."

"Hmm," I responded, widening my eyes. If that were the case, giving my notice wouldn't be too much of a problem.

"Rumor has it the writers and producers are on the chopping block. I don't think you have anything to worry about though." She lowered her voice to barely above a whisper. "Louise and Jeanie might be," she made a slashing gesture across her throat.

"Oh wow," I mouthed.

Sydney nodded solemnly and went back to work. I flicked my eyes over to where Jeanie was sitting. She looked stressed. I felt bad for her. In spite of all the bickering and backstabbing, I didn't want to see anyone lose their job.

I tried not to let the general gloom in the building affect my work for the rest of the day. Once the show ended, I hopped in my car and drove to Stephanie's place. With Alastair in New York on business, I was free to drive myself to and from work. I didn't even have anyone shadowing me in an SUV. Paxton was with Alastair and I had zero clue where the other guy was. Maybe he'd gone back to England.

I parked on the street in front of the condo and rang the bell. Darren answered with a flourish and hugged me.

"Steph tells me you're on the verge of marriage. Amazing, love."

"Darren," Stephanie yelled from the living room, "leave her

alone."

Keeping an arm draped over my shoulders, he led me inside. The stark emptiness of the condo saddened me immediately. The couch was still against the wall but the television was on the floor and boxes littered every corner of the room.

"Oh my gosh," I whispered.

"Ugh, I know," Stephanie scrunched her nose. "It's like purgatory. I'm literally living out of one suitcase and ordering food every night. I can't wait to just get there so I can feel settled again."

I plopped on the couch next to her. "I still can't believe you're leaving on Friday. Are you excited?"

"Nervous. I've been in touch with Cassie all day. She sent me some mock-ups of the print campaign. It looks amazing. I just hope I don't mess it up."

"Stop fretting, lass," Darren smiled. "You're very talented and they know it. Otherwise, they wouldn't have hired you."

"Yeah, yeah I know." She turned to me. "So what do you know about this Brent Garrison guy? He emailed me this morning and wants to have lunch next week. Is he cool? A douche? What?"

Leaning into the cushions, I sighed and rubbed my eyes. "Um, he's alright, I guess. Didn't you meet him last month at the garden party?"

"Sort of. He seemed to remember me from that cocktail party we went to in Glasgow but I couldn't place him for the life of me. He knows you though."

Yep, he sure does.

"He's okay. I mean, I don't know him on a professional level. I don't really even know him on a personal level." I shrugged. "I'm sure you'll get along."

"He's handsome," she grinned.

"Anyway," I rolled my eyes, "do you guys want to go out to dinner tomorrow night? It might help if you get out of this bare bones place for a little while."

"I'm game," Stephanie answered, turning to Darren. "How about you?"

"I will never pass up dinner with pretty girls."

"Great, I'll make reservations somewhere downtown." She poked me in the side. "Enough with the small talk. What happened this weekend?"

"Uh oh, girl talk." Darren lifted an eyebrow. "Are you going to spill everything, Lia? Even the saucy bits?"

"I wasn't planning to," I said dryly.

"Oh good. I have to listen to the so-called 'ladies' in the office talk about how fit he is and what they'd do to him in the supply closet if given the chance."

My jaw must have dropped to the floor. Darren stopped talking and smiled.

"Sorry. They're very vocal about stuff like that."

"I'll put an end to that bullshit next week," Stephanie grumbled. "That's my best friend's guy they're being so crass about."

Darren and I laughed at her sour expression.

"So," she continued, eyeing me with glee. "What happened in New York?"

I launched into a semi-detailed description of my weekend. I made sure to tell them all the G-rated parts; how gorgeous the penthouse was, the nice dinner - minus the encounter with the Garrisons - and the aquarium. Stephanie looked like she was about to burst wide open. She couldn't stand it when I danced around the really good parts of a story.

"That's all fine and dandy but *what happened*?" she exclaimed.

I widened my eyes and crossed my arms. "You mean, apart from him giving me the keys to the penthouse to use as I please or him asking me to move to Glasgow?"

Stephanie's glass shattering squeal was only topped by the suffocating hug she locked me in. I thought she was going to simultaneously smother and shake me to death.

"*I knew it. I knew it*," she yelled, bouncing up and down. "When are you coming? Are you flying out with us this week? Oh my,

God. I love this."

I caught Darren staring slack jawed at Stephanie and giggled. "You okay over there, MacCourty?"

Stephanie stopped her aggressive hug-fest and squished her cheek against mine. "Do you have any idea how f-ing ecstatic I am for this girl?"

"I can guess," he said. "Just try not to kill her or break a rib in the process." He smiled at me. "I'm happy for you, Lia. Alastair is a good guy. We'll all have to go out and celebrate once you get there. Have you decided when?"

"Not yet. I still have to give my notice at work and find a mover," I paused, "and tell my parents."

"They loved him," Stephanie said, loosening her grip on me. "They'll be thrilled. Don't worry about them. You can use the movers that packed all my stuff." Her face brightened. "Have you told Dayna? She'll be so excited."

"I haven't told anyone. I just got back this morning and, you know, worked and stuff." I frowned. "There's some drama going down at the station."

"Anything bad?"

"Rumors about layoffs. It was so unpleasant to be there today. Everybody was walking around like they were on death row."

"No worries about that, lassy," Darren grinned. "You'll be long gone before anyone's made redundant."

"Oh!" Stephanie exclaimed. "Does Alastair have a job lined up for you? He does own a majority of the broadcast media there, you know."

"Does he?" I shot her a look, grinning. "He mentioned there's a news magazine program that's hiring. No, he doesn't own it, so stop with all that. I'd feel weird working for him anyway. It would look…odd."

"Whatever. This is too exciting. Now I'm not as sad to leave you."

She hugged me again, only this time like a normal person.

"I want in on all the hugging." Darren jumped on the couch

and wrapped his arms around both of us. "You two are going to be a handful for us Scottish lads. Not sure if we're ready for the American storm coming our way."

* * *

I walked into my apartment a little after ten, feeling happier than I'd been in a long time. Everything was finally clicking in my life. I had a bright future, an amazing boyfriend and the best friends on the planet. Grabbing the laptop from my dresser, I plopped on the bed and sent Dayna a quick email, telling her about my big move. I also warned her not to tell our parents until I had a chance to talk to them.

10:22pm Still awake, love?

10:23pm Yep. Just got home from Steph's

The phone rang in my hand a millisecond after I hit send.

"Eager boy," I answered, grinning.

"What can I say? I wanted to hear your voice before you fell asleep."

"You caught me just in time then. I'm exhausted."

Alastair's low chuckle rustled a few sparks in my stomach. "My timing is impeccable as usual."

"How were all your meetings? Thrilling?"

I heard a tapping sound, like he was rapping a pen against a desk. "I don't want to bore you with work, Amelia. There's something else I need to talk to you about."

The sobering edge to his tone sent me into a slight panic. *He changed his mind and doesn't want me to live with him.* I squeezed the phone, scolding myself for having such ridiculous thoughts.

"It sounds serious," I said.

"I need you to promise me something."

187

I swallowed hard. "What?"

"If Nathan tries to get in touch with you or asks you to see him before I arrive, you are to tell me immediately. Do you understand?"

All the blood in my veins chilled. "I guess."

A heavy sigh cascaded through the phone. I could almost see him running a hand through his hair. "Have you heard from him already?"

My hesitation to answer gave me away.

"I'll take your silence as a yes," he grumbled. "I don't want you speaking with him or seeing him."

"He called me at work. I didn't really think anything of it."

"Just do as I say."

I sat up straighter on the bed, confused and annoyed by what he was telling me. "Enough with the bossy crap."

"Trust me on this," he groused. "He's up to something and I'm too goddam far away to protect you. If I didn't have these bloody board meetings tomorrow I'd be there with you now."

"You're scaring me, Alastair. Stop it."

"I'm sorry, love," he whispered. "I didn't mean to do that. Scott is back from London to keep an eye on you. He should have arrived tonight. Check outside and let me know if you see the SUV. I'll feel much better once I know you're completely safe."

I went into the living room and looked out the window. Nobody was parked near my unit except for residents. "I don't see it."

"Shit," he muttered. "I'll call you back in a minute, okay?"

"Sure." I could barely speak. Overcome by an impending sense of doom, I kept a watchful eye on the parking lot for several minutes. What could Nathan possibly be up to now? A spear of light sliced through the darkness, spiking my heart rate. The loud ringing of my cell phone scared the crap out of me. *For Christ's sake, relax.*

"I see a car," I answered.

"That's Scott. I just spoke to him. He'll be there all night if you need anything. I'm having Paxton fly down first thing in the morning."

"Don't you need him?"

"No. I'm canceling my plans to attend the client dinner so I can fly back tomorrow night."

"Don't do that, Alastair. You put me ahead of your responsibilities far too often. If Paxton and Scott are both here, I'll be okay. I promise."

Now I knew he was scrubbing his face with a hand. I could hear him becoming more exasperated. "You are my number one priority, Lia. Nothing else."

I tapped my nails on the windowsill, watching the silhouetted movements inside the SUV. I didn't like feeling as though I was a caged animal again, even though I knew his intentions were pure of heart. "And you're *my* number one priority, chief. I worry that you spend too much time fretting about my safety and well-being. I'm a big girl. I can take care of myself. You need to focus on your responsibilities outside the sphere of our relationship. Nothing earth -shattering is going to happen in the next thirty-six hours. Go to your client dinner. Take care of your work. I know how to reach you if I need something."

Blood pounded in my ears as I waited for his response. I couldn't even hear him breathing anymore.

"Fair point," he finally said. "As usual."

I smiled, hearing the tension in his voice slide away. "So, in summation, Mr. Holden, you will stay in Manhattan and do your job. I'll putz around Orlando with two shadows until you get here. Agreed?"

"Ever considered a career in negotiations?"

"No," I giggled. "But I'm always stroking somebody's ego at the station so maybe that's why I've become so good at being persuasive."

"Their egos better be the only thing you're stroking."

My. God. I clutched onto the windowsill and took a second to compose myself. *Lethal.*

"Speechless again, Meyers?"

"You need a warning label. That's all I have to say."

His deep, throaty laugh filled me with warmth. I loved how it sounded, especially after hearing him so tense and worried.

"I miss you, chief."

"Ditto, love. This place feels so empty without you here. I can't wait until we're under the same roof permanently. You'll be ready to fly back with me this coming weekend, yes?"

The immediacy of his request made me nervous. Of course I was ready to be with him, I just needed more than four days to tie up all my loose ends.

"Well, I have to give my notice at work and see if the leasing office will let me sublet my apartment so I'm not charged for breaking the lease. I'll need at least a week to take care of all that, plus pack all my stuff and—"

"I'll take care of your flat. You won't have to give it up or pack anything."

"What?"

"I want to keep it. We'll need a place to stay when we visit Florida."

"Isn't that what a hotel is for?"

He laughed. "I like your flat. It's become a second home for me. I'll hire a cleaning staff to make sure it doesn't get dusty or stale smelling while we're in Glasgow. Don't you want to have a home base in the States?"

Feeling slightly dizzy, I made my back to the bedroom. "I thought the…the penthouse was going to be home base or whatever. I don't need to keep this apartment. Unless you think living together isn't going to work out."

"Lia," he growled. "Stop overthinking. I don't care where we live as long as we're together. Keeping your place in Orlando isn't an underlying exit plan. I want you to have it."

I flopped onto the bed, sighing into the mattress. My mind flew through a zillion thoughts before I sat up straight. "If you keep it, Nathan will always know where to find me."

"Fuck all," he hissed. "That bastard won't come within a hundred miles of you. I'll make sure of it."

His anger and vitriol resonated throughout my bedroom even though he was a thousand miles away. Instead of freaking me out, it made me want to know exactly what was going on. My curiosity could be quite persistent if it wanted.

"What is it that he's done, Alastair? Tell me."

"No."

"Jesus," I muttered. "You know, keeping shit from me only pisses me off."

"Don't start," he warned. "Let me handle it. He's done enough manipulating and coercing for a lifetime."

"You can't control everything."

"I can."

I bit back a salty remark, mentally and physically drained from this whole day. His stubborn streak was as impenetrable as his protective shield. Banging my head against it will get me nowhere fast.

"You win. I'm going to bed."

"Lia," he said softly, "you know I'm doing this because I love you. I want you safe. Please don't go to sleep angry with me."

Ugh, I'm too easily swayed by his soft side.

"I'm not mad. I promise. I'm just exhausted and scattered and—"

"Missing me?"

I sighed heavily, picturing his smile. "That damn charm thing."

"Stay on the phone with me until you fall asleep."

"That's a tempting thought."

"Is it?"

Grinning, I settled into the pillows. "Will you whisper sweet nothings into my ear?"

"Hmm," he hummed, sending a ripple of pleasure through me. "That would lead me to believe you think I'm romantic. I thought we'd established I was cheesy."

"Quiet," I snickered. "Just say something hot in your accent."

"Something. Hot."

"Okay, yeah, now you're cheesy *and* corny. You have a voice like velvet and a killer accent. Use them to your advantage."

His low, sexy laugh curled my toes. "I wish I were lying next to you, kitten, holding you close. Breathing in your scent. Touching you."

I pulled the pillow that still smelled like him closer to me and moaned quietly, picturing his arms securely wrapped around me. Sleep easily clouded my thoughts and took over my body. Alastair kept talking but I had no clue what he was saying. I only had a vague awareness of a stunning accent trickling through my subconscious. For a second, I thought he really was next to me.

I was on the verge of succumbing to sleep completely when I heard his silky voice whisper, "Tell me what you want, love."

"You," I mumbled into the pillow. "Always."

CHAPTER NINETEEN

"This is a good news, bad news meeting," Bruce said solemnly, pacing the conference room. I sat at the far corner of the table, flanked by Tyler and Wesley. Sydney caught my eye from across the room and shrugged. "As you know," he continued, "we've been dealing with a potential lawsuit. Thankfully, the young man at the center of all this has decided not to pursue it any further."

Vance and Cynthia applauded. The rest of the room released a collective sigh of relief.

"What changed his mind?" Vance asked.

"I think he finally realized that mistakes happen and you can't demand a million dollars just because your feelings got hurt," Jeanie grumbled.

"Not quite," Bruce interjected, annoyed. "Our legal team worked hard with his lawyers to come to an agreement. This doesn't mean we should be any less vigilant in our writing and proofing before air. We're under a microscope now with corporate. Which leads me to the bad news."

Everyone groaned.

"I had some very lengthy meetings yesterday with our vice president," he continued, rubbing his eyes. "There have been rumblings in the newsroom about layoffs. Nothing is set in stone. Don't start spreading rumors and speculating. It won't help anything. That's it. Go. Do your jobs."

Sydney cornered me in the hallway as we walked back to our shared cubicle.

"That was productive," she snickered. "What are you doing for lunch today?"

"I haven't really thought about it. Want to do a smoothie run?"

"Absolutely. We'll leave in half an hour?"

"Sounds good."

I scurried off to the main lobby before heading back to my desk. I needed to talk to Paxton. Before our impromptu good news/bad news meeting I'd been on the phone with a local jeweler about a gift I'd bought for Alastair. He'd already given me so much, I wanted to surprise him with a little something when he arrived tomorrow. I'd found a beautiful pair of platinum cufflinks at the jeweler's downtown. They were vintage-inspired, shaped like an oval. I'd requested they engrave his initials, ARH, in them. I never had enough time during my lunch break to do any personal errands so I was hoping Paxton could pick them up for me.

He looked concerned as I approached the SUV.

"Miss Meyers. Is everything alright?" he asked, stepping out of the car.

"Everything's fine," I smiled. "I have a favor to ask."

"What is it?"

"Well, I…feel free to say no if you want. I bought something for Alastair but don't have time to pick it up. Would you mind running down to Bijoux Jewelers and getting it for me?"

He leveled an amused gaze at me for several seconds. "You need me to run an errand for you?"

"Sort of, yes. Like I said, you don't have to."

He kept his imposing bodyguard/MI5 stare fixed on me. Clearly, this was a bad idea.

"You know what, never mind. I'll go tomorrow morning before coming into work."

Relaxing his stance a little, Paxton sighed. "I don't mind going for you it's just that I'm not supposed to leave or take my eyes off this building while you're here."

"I figured," I muttered. "It's not that big of a deal, really. We can go in the morning."

"I can drive you right now if you want to go."

I smiled. "I appreciate the offer but I can't. I have a ton of things to get through before we go live. Really, it's not a problem."

"Then you best not waste any more time out here and get to it, Miss Meyers," he said sternly but with a twinkle in his eyes.

"Yes, sir." I saluted him. "And you're welcome for the brief human interaction. Go back to work."

I waved goodbye and dashed across the street. My desk phone rang the second I sat down. I noticed on the caller display that it was Gus from the assignment desk. I looked up at him, confused as to why he didn't just walk over to my desk.

"What's up?"

"You have a guest waiting for you in the small conference room."

"Who?"

"Nathan Greyson."

My blood ran cold. "Why is he here?"

"He said you had a meeting scheduled with him about an interview or something."

"When did he get here?'

"Not even five minutes ago."

Son of a bitch. "Okay. Thanks." I hung up and looked over at Sydney. "I have to go take care of something. Our smoothie run might be delayed."

"No problem. Take your time."

I grumbled to myself as I walked toward the back of the newsroom. This was so like him to just show up unannounced. *I gave him the perfect distraction, too. If I hadn't been talking to Paxton, he never would have made it through the front doors.* I could see him through the windows, sitting at the table. He was in character, dressed to the nines in a double-breasted suit with his game face on. I took a deep breath and opened the door.

"Lia," he smiled, standing up. "Thank you for seeing me."

"Like I had a choice," I spat out. "What the hell do you want?"

"No need for all the hostility, Sparkle. Sit."

He motioned to the chair on his left. Several folders were spread out in front of him on the table. I sat cautiously next to him, eyeing the folders.

"What's all this?"

"Trouble."

I shot him a look, disliking the cryptic vibe he'd released into the atmosphere.

"Get to the point or leave. Your choice."

"The items in these folders could ruin your life."

Stunned, I sat up straight and stared at him. He looked smug. I wanted to slap the expression right off his face. Echoes of what Alastair told me rattled through my brain. *He's a con artist. He's lying to you.*

Composing myself, I glared at him.

"I know you lied to me about Alastair's uncle paying Rachel. I know you went to see him. You're still a sneaky bastard, Nathan."

"Is that what he told you? That I'm lying to you?" His eyes narrowed. "I'm trying to protect you, Lia."

A gravelly, bitter laugh escaped my lips. "Protect me? Are you insane? I don't believe a word you say anymore. You are doing whatever you can to get me back. It's not going to work. I don't love you. I don't want you. We're finished."

Nathan sat in silence for what felt like an eternity. The muscles in jaw tightened and bulged. His whole exterior was set in stone.

"Regardless of how you feel about me, this," he tapped the folders, "is real. This is the work of someone who holds such a grudge against your boyfriend that she is willing to destroy you. *I* stopped her, not *him*. He just rests on his fucking laurels and thinks his money will solve everything."

Not enough oxygen was getting to my brain. The room spun

violently. I honestly felt like I was being pulled in a hundred different directions. *She? What the…?* My stomach lurched in a sickening jolt. *Olivia.*

"Do you know who it is?" I barely managed to speak.

"No. All I do know is she lives in France and dated him several years ago. Obviously, it ended badly."

I pressed my hands to my temples to try and dull the throbbing. It had to be Olivia. After what he'd told me, and the way she still looked at him, this had to be her handiwork. But it didn't feel right. It didn't make sense. This could all be another lie.

"Is this what you wanted to show me tonight?"

"Yes. But you constantly have someone following you or driving you somewhere now, so it's hard to get you alone."

"I wonder why," I lashed out.

"Don't take it out on me, Lia. I'm not the bad guy here. I only have your best interests at heart."

I raked my hands through my hair. I couldn't take this anymore. My heart was racing so fast I thought it might explode.

"I can't do this here, Nathan. I'm at work. I have…I can't do this." Tremors shook every inch of my body. I didn't know what to do anymore. I didn't believe him. *I can't believe him. Nothing good will come of this if I let him manipulate me.*

"I know, sweetheart, I know. I'm sorry. I didn't want to put you through this here but I had no choice." He placed his hand over mine, making me cringe. "I care about you, Lia. Regardless of how you feel about me, that's how I feel about you. I don't want to see you get hurt. I know I have no shot at getting you back but at least let me help prevent you from making the biggest mistake of your life."

"Get out," I ordered in a hoarse whisper.

The walls felt like they were closing in on me. A familiar pain squeezed my chest, keeping it locked in a relentless grip.

"Lia don't—"

"Get. Out," I said through clenched teeth. "Now."

Confusion and hurt seized his expression. Underneath all the shitty things he'd done in our relationship, I knew he did them out some warped sense of love and loyalty. His face always read like an open book. I was too emotionally weak to fight against the remorse in his sapphire eyes. He sniffed out my fragility like a shark smelling blood in the water.

"Come to the house tonight. I know you're smart enough to give those bodyguards the slip. I want this to be over for you. I want to help."

"Leave, Nathan. I can't listen to this anymore." I stood up too fast and nearly lost consciousness. My head and the room spun rapidly, making me nauseous. Thankfully, this conference room was hardly ever used because it was tucked in the back of the newsroom. There weren't any prying eyes to see what we were doing.

"Sit down, Lia. You look like you're about to faint." I felt his hands on my waist but was too disconnected from reality to shake him off. The folders taunted me from the table. Whatever they held certainly gave all the power to Nathan. They could be empty for all I knew. This could be just another story he made up to screw with my head and my relationship. I tried to clear the muddled fog from my brain. I needed to think rationally.

In a moment of clarity, I remembered the brief meeting I'd had with Rachel.

"I met with Jameson last week. She said she's been receiving anonymous emails from someone who claimed to have something big on me. Did you know about that?"

"No. Why didn't you tell me?"

"Because I don't have to report back to you," I snapped. "Besides, you'd gone radio silent."

He leaned back in the chair, smoothing down his tie. "I needed to get away for a little while. I went down to the Keys and shut the world out. There was nothing sinister about my absence. I thought a week or so of mental recharging would help. It did until I got back this past weekend and found all this," he gestured to the folders, "waiting for me."

Confused, I pressed the heel of my hand to my temple. I wanted the never-ending pounding to stop. "So you really don't know who's behind this?"

"No," he said quietly, reaching for my hand. "We're all caught up in this mess together. You, me, Rachel. The only thing I was able to discover was that this all stems from a jealous ex."

"But how do you know that?"

"There was an email address and a note included with them. Whoever she is, she's clever. I'm willing to bet she's the one that emailed Rachel."

"Alright, wait. So you have an email address and you can't figure out who she is? Bullshit. In this day and age, and with your security team and love of stalking, you should be able to find her identity without a problem. Don't give me that look, you know I'm right."

Setting his jaw in determination, he leaned forward. "Come to the house tonight. We'll figure this out together. I don't want to see you this stressed. Ever."

"I can't tonight. I'm too—"

"Try. If not tonight, then come tomorrow. Please. Let me know and I'll be available for you."

He stood up with authority and conviction. I knew this posture. I knew that look. He would stop at nothing until he got what he wanted.

* * *

I kept all the lights off in my apartment as I stretched out on the couch. I'd canceled dinner with Stephanie and Darren because I wouldn't be able to get through it without both of them noticing I was a complete mess. My only real option was to tell Alastair. If this really had something to do with an ex, he'd know what to do. And if it didn't, he'd be with me to put an end to Nathan's harassment.

That scenario made me feel better. I wasn't about to keep anything from Alastair again. Glancing at the clock I saw it was only half past nine. I was exhausted though. I shuffled into the bedroom, grabbed my laptop and plopped on the bed. I had no clue what possessed me to do what I did next.

I typed in 'Olivia Garrison' and hit search.

Not much came up on her. There were several photos of her with the Italian diplomat and the formal announcement of their engagement. I kept scrolling through the photos until one of them made my heart come to a screeching halt. She was with Alastair. It was obviously from a long time ago but the sight of them together cut through me like a hot blade. I clicked on the picture and found an accompanying article. Scanning through it I learned that their relationship was quite serious. Or at least that was how it appeared to outsiders. They were apparently inseparable.

This particular article speculated on when they'd become engaged. I stopped reading it before I really upset myself. She was his past. That was a lifetime ago.

I scrolled back up to more recent photos of her with her fiancé. According to this article they split their time between Rome, London and New York. One of the photos showed her at a dinner in London recently. According to the caption, it was only a couple of weeks ago.

Anxiety paralyzed me.

That was the exact same weekend Alastair rushed off to London in a shroud of secrecy.

CHAPTER TWENTY

I arrived at the jeweler's Wednesday morning just as the doors were being unlocked for opening. A nicely dressed older gentleman smiled at me as I followed him inside. I told him I was there to pick up the cufflinks and gave him my name. A few minutes later, he returned from the back room and handed me a small box. I opened it, pleased at how beautiful they were.

Trotting back outside, I hopped into the waiting Mercedes SUV for Paxton to drive me to the station. I'd agreed to let him drive me to work today on the condition that he'd take me to the airport with him when Alastair's plane landed at seven. I still wasn't too sure what I was going to do about Nathan. The last thing I wanted was to dump additional stress on Alastair as he's walking off an airplane.

The mood in the newsroom was still one of gloom and doom. Nobody had too much time to dwell on it though. There was breaking news out of Tampa involving a mall shooting and we scrambled to get a crew out for live coverage.

I had a mouthful of yogurt when my cell phone rang. Swallowing, I grabbed it and smiled.

"Hey, Cinnamon," I answered cheerfully.

"Jeez, Lia, with that nickname," my little sister grumbled.

I laughed. "Sorry, Dayna. I couldn't resist. What's up?"

"What's up? You're moving here, that's what's up," she exclaimed.

"Ah, so you got my email."

"Yeah. Sorry I didn't call you right away. I've had a cold and sounded like ass."

"Feeling better?"

"Yep. So, when are you coming here? Have you told mom and dad yet? They said they had a great time visiting you and that they loved Alastair."

My sister could be just as frantic with her questions and excitement as me. Smiling, I let her continue rambling until she paused to take a breath.

"I'm not sure when I'll be there. Probably soon."

"Do you have a job lined up? Is he going to give you one at HWM?"

"Hang on." Scanning the newsroom, I stood up and went to a quiet corner in the back. Too many nosey people were around to overhear my conversation. "He said there's a position at a show called The Archer Hour. Have you heard of it?"

"Oh my gosh, yes. You'd be perfect there. Julian Archer is awesome."

I had to stifle a loud laugh. "You're the first person I've heard say that. The general consensus it that he's a pain in the ass."

"Whatever. People who think that lack a fun gene. He's great. I want to meet him once you're settled in there."

"Relax, Day. I don't even have an interview yet."

"Stop it. If Alastair has any say they'll hire you tomorrow. He's pretty influential, you know."

I snorted. "I hadn't noticed."

"So are you guys, like, super serious then? Have you talked marriage?"

"Oh Jesus, not you, too."

"What?"

"Stephanie's been on her romantic fantasy bus and won't let up on the marriage thing. She had me convinced he was going to propose last weekend."

"Did he?"

"No," I blurted. "All of you need to relax."

Dayna laughed in her girlish, lilting way. "*When* he does propose, I know some great designers in London. You'll be a gorgeous bride."

I leaned against the wall and sighed, chuckling to myself. "How's Andrew?"

"He's fine. He's in Cambridge for some lawyer thing with his firm for a few days. It's nice without him around. Much quieter."

"Dayna! You've only been married for three months. Are you sick of him already?"

"Hey, having a little 'me' time won't hurt anybody. I miss him. I'm just, you know, enjoying the peace. You'll see what I mean after you've been living with Alastair for a few months."

Out the corner of my eye I saw Sydney frantically waving me over.

"I have to go, Day. We're in the middle of some breaking news and I'm being summoned."

"Okay. Call me when you know dates and stuff. We'll take a ride up to Glasgow and visit."

We said our goodbyes and I hung up. Sydney looked panic-stricken and met me halfway.

"What's wrong?"

"I have to go. Violet fell in the playground at day care and broke her wrist."

"Oh no. Go. Don't worry about stuff here. I'll see if we can get a freelancer in to cover for you."

She hugged me tightly. "Thanks. I'll see you tomorrow."

I watched the digital clock on the rundown tease me ever so slowly as the day dragged on. *I should probably call my parents*. No sooner had the thought crossed my mind, than I pushed it away. I needed to be home when I did that. My mother would most likely keep me on the phone for hours, squeezing every last question out until I answered them to her satisfaction. I smiled, feeling wistful.

With both my sister and I living abroad, my parents would be alone here. As much as being scattered around the country and world worked for the Meyers family, I had a feeling they'd prefer it if their daughters didn't choose to live so far away.

Dayna always mentioned she'd end up in New York at some point with her career. Writing for a magazine gave her some freedom to live wherever she chose. I knew she liked London but I also knew she didn't want to stay there forever. Convincing her husband to move to the States might be challenging for her. Although I had a sneaking suspicion Andrew would go wherever Dayna wanted. He worshipped the ground she walked on.

It would be fun living closer to her. We hadn't been in the same place since we both graduated college. Dayna was only eighteen months younger than me so we were inseparable growing up. Most people thought we were twins. Our dad always said we looked like a film negative. She was fair-skinned, blonde and blue-eyed. I was the opposite with my chestnut hair, amber eyes and sun-kissed golden skin.

The thought of living closer to my sister certainly brightened my increasingly anxious mood. No matter how hard I tried, I couldn't shake the weird feeling that Alastair had jetted off to London to deal with Olivia, and not a former client as he'd told me. The nagging slivers of insecurity strengthened their grip on my thought process. They filled my head with such unpleasant scenarios that any morsels of the delicious weekend I spent in Manhattan with him were obliterated.

I'd taken a huge risk opening my heart to him. It was so fragile and broken from my disastrous relationship with Nathan. I trusted what it felt for Alastair but I couldn't deny it this moment of fear. *The heart wants what it wants.*

Sitting at work worrying about the unknown wasn't going to help matters. I took a deep breath, gave myself a mental scolding and finished out my workday.

* * *

The airplane's engine whined as it taxied to a stop about twenty yards from where Paxton parked. I stood on the tarmac, waiting impatiently. I wanted to hug Alastair so badly. Feeling his arms around me always calmed the anxiety and fear.

He appeared in the plane's doorway at the top of the stairs looking regal and handsome in dark jeans, an untucked white button down shirt and black jacket. Rays from the sun touched his stunning red hair, illuminating it in shades of copper and crimson. He saw me and flashed his beautiful, sexy grin. My pulse quickened watching him take the stairs down with fluid, determined strides.

Pausing in front of me, he brushed his thumb along my lower lip. "Hello, love."

I didn't just hug him. I jumped into his arms and held onto him for dear life. He secured me in a loving embrace, calming my furious heart and overactive mind without saying one word. His mere presence was all I needed.

"I missed you too, sweetheart," he said after a minute. "Come. We'll have a proper reunion at your flat."

Reluctantly, I let him go and climbed into the SUV. Keeping his hand entwined with my own aided in calming me down.

"You're staring at me like I've been gone for years," he remarked, kissing my knuckles. "Is everything alright?"

Such a dangerous question. A sandpapery lump forced its way up my throat. I parted my lips to take in more oxygen. Alastair's gaze morphed from confusion to downright concern.

"Talk to me, Lia. What happened?"

The floodgates opened and I blurted out everything. He listened silently, his expression hardening the more I spoke. Clenching his jaw, he looked down and inhaled.

"This happened yesterday?"

I nodded, squeezing his hand.

"He threatened you?"

"I don't know if it was a threat, exactly. He just said he has something that will ruin me."

Alastair muttered something that sounded like a profanity but I couldn't be sure. Fixing his callous stare on the back of Paxton's head, he growled, "And how was it that he managed to get into the newsroom?"

Paxton started to answer but I cut him off. "It was my fault. I'd come outside to ask him for a favor, so neither one of us had our attention focused on the building. Don't be mad at Paxton. He didn't do anything wrong."

Nodding tersely, Alastair kissed my hand again. "I'm taking you home and then I'm going to take care of Nathan."

"I'm coming with you."

"No, you're not," he said calmly.

"Alastair, I'm not arguing with you. I will not get out of this car if you take me home. He keeps telling me that you're not being totally honest and he's the one trying to protect me. I am not letting you go without me."

I steeled my expression and stared him down. The inside of the car became a breathless, wordless cavity. The low vibration of the tires rolling on pavement was the only sound. This was my mess. This was my fault. I let Nathan back in and I should be the one to put an end to it, not Alastair.

Snaking his hand behind my head, he pulled me in for a quick, passionate kiss. We both gasped when we broke our mouths apart. "Alright, love. But if he so much as looks at you the wrong way, I will handle him. Do you understand?"

Nodding, I laced my fingers with his once more. His lips curved into the beautiful shy smile I loved so much. "My Lia. My frustrating, stubborn, strong-willed gorgeous Lia. What am I going to do with you?"

I scooted as close to him as the seatbelt would allow and leaned my head back on the seat. He did the same, cradling my jaw with his free hand.

"Do you know where we're going, Alastair?"

Not breaking eye contact, he nodded. I exhaled slowly, holding his stare.

"You've gone to the house in Windermere before, haven't you? The night I told you what he'd said about your uncle?"

"Yes."

"What happened that night?"

He grimaced, shaking his head. "It doesn't matter."

"It does. Was he there?"

"Yes."

There was just enough slack left in the seatbelt for me to lean closer and kiss him. He smiled against my lips. "What was that for?"

"I've never had anyone defend my honor or whatever, like you do. I mean, yeah, I have Stephanie and my other friends and family. But this is different. I know I can handle things myself but it's nice to have someone fighting in my corner for me. If you don't already know it, I want you to know that I appreciate it. Thank you for always making me feel safe."

Pressing his forehead to mine, he squeezed his eyes shut. The inside of the car no longer felt like an empty abyss. This brief interlude managed to bring us closer despite the impending stressful situation we were embarking on. After several seconds, he opened his eyes and tucked a strand of hair behind my ear.

The SUV slowed as we approached the gated entrance to Nathan's neighborhood. I asked Alastair to lower his window so I could tell the guard the Greyson's were expecting me. He looked at Paxton and Alastair skeptically but let us pass.

Driving along the manicured street toward his family's estate brought back a slew of memories I wasn't expecting. I remembered the first time I came here. I was excited and nervous, filled with giddy anticipation at meeting Nathan's parents. Our relationship was new and filled with promise. He'd been a charming, funny guy that I'd immediately become smitten with, much like Alastair.

At their core, they were strikingly similar. But where Alastair was a genuinely compassionate person struggling with deep emotional scars, Nathan was a cold, spoiled brat who threw a fit if he didn't get his way. He used his status and privilege to bully his way through life.

The Greyson's mansion loomed in the distance like a beautiful, forbidden dream. It sat on a pristine lot overlooking the massive lake. I'd spent many summer days relaxing on their yacht when life with Nathan was still shiny and new. Shaking off the memories, I sat up straight. The pale yellow three-storey house was familiar yet scary to me now.

Paxton parked the Mercedes and opened the door for us. I climbed out cautiously, taking a moment to gather my wits. I noticed several other cars parked in the driveway. One of them was Nathan's black sports car. I'd secretly hoped he wouldn't be here. No such luck.

"Come with me," Alastair said gently, holding my hand. We strolled up the bluestone walkway to the front door. Before I rang the bell, Alastair turned me to face him. He was shielded, except for his eyes. They bore into me, filled with apprehension.

"None of that, chief," I whispered, brushing my lips to his.

I rang the bell and waited. Muffled footsteps approached the door, providing a nice rhythm for the jitters that were tormenting my body.

The door opened and much to my surprise, I saw Nathan's mother standing in the entrance hall. I think she was just as shocked to see me.

"Lia? It's so good to see you," she breathed, hugging me. She still smelled like jasmine and vanilla. I always enjoyed her taste in perfume. "Nathan didn't tell me you were stopping by. He's out by the boat." She paused, looking at Alastair. "And you are?"

"Alastair Holden," he responded without much warmth.

Recognition dawned on her face as her light gray eyes widened. "Of course. I'm sorry I didn't recognize you. You're Lia's new boyfriend. I've seen your name and photo in the business section quite a bit the past few weeks. You're in broadcast media, right? I'm Samantha Greyson. Please, come in." She moved aside and waved us in, leading us through the living room to the back patio.

"Ken is in D.C. He'll be sorry he missed you, Lia. He told me all about the Black and White Ball and how he enjoyed the interview."

I saw Alastair scowl out the corner of my eye.

"It was great seeing him, too," I said. "We always appreciate his candor." I smiled.

"Well, as I said, Nathan is out by the boat. You know the way."

I led Alastair onto the patio and scanned the backyard. The silhouette of a large luxury yacht rose out of the water. Faint light from the setting sun glistened off the glossy white exterior. I felt like someone else was controlling my legs as we walked toward the lake. They moved on their own while the rest of my body fought vigorously to turn around. I couldn't shake the bad feeling that had nestled itself in the pit of my stomach. Water lapped gently against the dock, trying to lull me into a false sense of security. The peace and quiet of the lake did nothing to assuage my fears.

I'd been on this yacht so many times I'd lost count. Most of the memories were pleasant, thankfully. I ran my eyes over the length of the vessel. It had sleek lines and curves with dark tinted windows. Emblazoned on the back in proud block letters was its clever name; Aye Candy. *Exactly what I was for him. Something to show off.*

"Lia. You brought company."

Nathan's voice echoed from the hull. I looked to my right and saw him grinning down at me. Alastair stood silently to my left, hands balled into tight fists.

"Don't be shy. Come aboard."

Taking Alastair's hand in mine, I guided him to the small door at the stern. We stepped on, then went up to the main deck. A flood of memories drowned me. I could see myself lounging on the deck chairs, soaking in the golden rays of the sun. *How lucky I believed I was*, I thought bitterly.

Nathan approached carrying two glasses filled with wine. "Welcome back, Sparkle." He smiled and passed me a glass. Alastair wrapped an arm around my waist possessively and snatched the glass from him.

"This isn't a social call," he sneered.

Nathan's eyes darkened to midnight blue as he glared at him. "You're a guest, Holden. Act like one."

"Alright, you two, enough," I said. My ex sulked and crossed his arms. "This was supposed to be just you and me, Lia. He doesn't need to be here."

"That's where you're wrong, Greyson," Alastair said in a dangerously calm tone. "I told you to stay away from her. I told you to leave her alone. And yet, here we are. This ends tonight."

Furious anger billowed around me as the two of them glared at one another. Neither one moved or appeared to have any intention of backing down. I feared the worst was about to come.

Nathan took a step towards me and was immediately cut off by Alastair. They stood nose-to-nose, shooting daggers from their eyes. Nathan was the same height as Alastair but not as athletic. I moved slowly to one of the chairs, clutching the cushion.

"I won't tell you again," Alastair growled. "Stay out of her life."

"Some boyfriend you are. You'd rather see her be humiliated in public than stop it from happening."

Alastair bared his teeth and released a quick, short breath. "There is nothing to humiliate her with, you lying bastard. Everything you've put her through this month was fabricated in your twisted mind. *You* stalked her. *You* sent her the photos. *You* wrote the emails to entice that reporter. And you made her believe *my family* was behind all of it. Why? So she'd break up with me and go running back to you? Hell will freeze over before that happens."

"You're just as cunning as I am. What are you covering up with that trust account? Who did you fuck over and have to pay off? I'm not stupid. I know what a ghost account looks like."

"That's none of your business, Nathan," I yelled.

His searing gaze burned through me. I'd never seen him so angry. "It is my business when compromising photos of you appear on my doorstep with a note threatening to go public with them if you don't drop his sorry ass."

I froze in place, unable to breathe. Nausea rolled my stomach and for a second I thought I might be sick. "What are you…?" I couldn't finish the question.

Nathan barely took three steps in my direction before Alastair put him in a chokehold against the glass doors leading to the yacht's interior rooms.

"What the fuck are you talking about?"

Nathan gasped and clawed at Alastair's hand. "Let go of me or I'll call security."

"You will tell me what you're talking about and then I'll think about letting you go."

Breathing hard, Nathan gestured to the folder on the table. Alastair flicked his incensed gaze to it as well, and then to me.

"Grab the folder but do not open it."

Too frazzled to do anything but what he asked, I picked up the folder and handed it to him. He loosened his grasp on Nathan's neck long enough to open it. His face paled immediately, sending my anxiety through the roof.

"What is it?" I asked.

He thumbed through what I assumed were photos and glared at Nathan. "Where did you get these?"

"I told you, they were dropped off anonymously. I have no idea who sent them."

"Stop lying," Alastair bellowed, throwing down the folder. Some of the photos slid out but I couldn't see them clearly. He pulled his cell phone of his pocket and dialed a number. "I need her out of here. Now. We're on the yacht in back."

Seconds later, Paxton appeared and escorted me off the boat. Alastair and Nathan were still locked in a heated conversation. I didn't want to leave him. Shaking, I stopped walking and turned around.

"We have to go, Miss Meyers."

"I can't leave him."

"We have to go." Paxton gripped my arm tightly and led me back to the SUV. The panic attack that threatened to unhinge me at work yesterday arrived with full force. I couldn't breathe. I couldn't move. I was helpless.

CHAPTER TWENTY-ONE

Stephanie opened the door and nearly threw it off the hinge.

"What's going on? Are you okay? Where's Alastair?"

I walked into her bare living room and saw Darren standing by the kitchen. His usual cheerful demeanor was clouded with worry. I didn't want to burden anybody else with this. Tears pooled in my eyes before I could get a handle on my emotions.

"Miss Tempe, I'll be back later. Please don't hesitate to call if you need anything." Paxton excused himself from the room and left.

Stephanie led me to the couch and sat down. "Is everything okay with you two?" She eyed me with caution, obviously thinking back to what happened at the estate in England.

"Yeah, we're fine. It's Nathan."

"What did that asshole do now?"

"All the pictures and…articles and…the thing with Rachel. He was behind all of it."

She smoothed down my hair in soft, mothering strokes. "Are you really so surprised? He's a master manipulator."

Darren crossed the room and sat on the floor in front of us. "Is that the ex you were telling me about, Steph?"

She nodded. "They broke up after New Year's. He clearly has issues and doesn't know how to move on."

"I'm sorry he's giving you so much trouble, love," Darren said, covering my hand with his. "Our boy will set him straight."

I shifted uncomfortably on the cushion. I wouldn't be able to relax until I had Alastair next to me and I was wrapped up in his arms. Nathan wasn't the type to resolve situations with a conversation. He preferred intimidation and loved using his security team to 'fix' problems.

"Would you like some tea, Lia? I make a pretty awesome cuppa."

Darren's question actually made me smile. "Do you even have a teapot?" I asked Stephanie.

"Nope. I have a microwave though. Darren thinks it's sacrilegious but he's been suffering through it all week."

"I'll get that ready for you straight away. How do you take it?"

"Just honey, please."

Stephanie pulled me into a warm hug. "I am so sorry this is happening. I wish there was something I could do."

"Stay up with me and wait? I have a horrible feeling he won't be back until much, much later. If at all."

"Don't think like that. And of course I'll stay up with you. Darren will, too. We can watch stupid reality shows to keep your mind occupied. How's that sound?"

"You're amazing. Have I told you that lately?" I squished her in a big hug.

When Darren finished making my tea we passed the time playing card games.

"You know what I've noticed about Americans?" Darren asked.

"Oh God, what?" Stephanie groaned.

"You're all really invested in asking others how they are all the time. Like today, I was doing some shopping and this lady just started chatting me up and the first thing she wanted to know was, how I was. I don't think she really cared how I was, she just asked me. I felt obliged to give her an answer so I made something up."

"What?" I laughed.

"Aye, I told her I had blister on my toe from all the walking. She actually started giving me names of medicines and creams to rub on it."

"That's called 'being nice.' You Scots should look into it." Stephanie teased.

"What? We're nice."

"You have your moments," she giggled.

We finished our game and spread out on the couch and floor to watch some bad reality television. Darren sat wide-eyed and slack-jawed while we watched a bunch of twenty-something mansion living girls fight with one another and throw mattresses into swimming pools.

"I bet those girls wouldn't stop to ask me how I was."

"Darren, those girls would devour you if given the chance," I laughed.

"You say that like it's a bad thing." He winked.

By the time midnight rolled around I could tell they were both exhausted. I felt bad keeping them up. After some protesting, they agreed to go to sleep only if I woke them up when I heard anything about Alastair. I curled up on the couch and snuggled under a blanket. Grabbing my phone, I sent an email to Bruce letting him know I wouldn't be coming in to work tomorrow. I made up something about having the stomach flu. It wasn't a total lie. My stomach was a mess and I would be useless at work.

I let the tears fall freely instead of stopping them. Not knowing if Alastair was okay tore me apart inside. If only I hadn't agreed to that dinner with Nathan, when I thought he really wanted to give us an interview. *If only…*

He would have tried something else. I had no doubt. Sinking further into the cushion I felt my lids become heavier and heavier. Sleep would be a welcome escape.

Soft knocking on the door woke me up. I sat up with a start, staring into the darkness. It took me a second to get my bear-ings. *I'm at Steph's.* Another soft knock startled me. Clutching the blanket around my body, I went to the window. Relief flooded through me when I saw Alastair standing on the front steps.

I opened the door and bolted into his arms, unable to stop more tears from falling.

"Inside, love," he whispered. "Come."

I hugged him fiercely for an eternity when we walked back into the living room. I didn't plan on letting him go until someone pried me off him.

"Easy, Lia, easy," he said, trying to loosen my grip.

In a panic, I pulled back and looked at him. His clothes were a mess. The shirt collar was stained red and torn.

"Oh my God," I whispered, touching his face. Dried blood marred his skin just above the right eye and at the corner of his mouth. No other bruises were visible but it didn't make me feel any better.

"What happened? Are you okay?"

"I'm fine," he reassured me. "It looks worse than it is." He smiled, wincing a bit. I ran my hands down his chest and sides. He flinched when I touched below the left ribcage.

"He hurt you," I breathed. "I'm so sorry."

"There's no need to apologize, love." He cupped my chin and kissed me softly. I knotted my fingers in his hair, holding him close. He whimpered quietly, deepening the kiss. Every stroke of his tongue and movement of his lips calmed me.

"Lia?"

I turned and saw Stephanie by the doorway. Alastair buried his nose in my hair, refusing to let me go.

"Is everything…are you alright, Alastair?" she asked.

"Yes I'm fine, Stephanie, thank you. And thank you for being here for Lia tonight. I can't tell you how much I appreciate it."

"She's like a sister to me. I'll always be there for her."

Pressing a kiss to my forehead, he broke our embrace and went to Stephanie. She saw his bruised face, frowned and looked at me. Holding both her hands, he pulled her into a gentle hug. "Thank you," he sighed.

"We both love her." She smiled at him when he released her.

"We'd both do anything for her."

Nodding, he turned back to me. "Ready to go home?"

"It's late," Stephanie interjected. "You both can stay here. I don't mind."

Alastair grinned and touched her cheek. "Much appreciated, love, but I think I've imposed on you enough for one night." He held up a hand to halt her protests. "Tell Darren we'll go out for dinner later tonight."

"Okay, fine."

I smiled and wrapped my best friend in a bear hug. "Thanks."

"You go take care of yourself and him. Call me when you wake up."

Paxton waited next to the SUV as we walked out. Not willing to be apart from Alastair for a second, I curled up on his lap in the backseat. He held me close, stroking my hair the entire ride back to my apartment. When we arrived and went inside, I made him sit on the edge of the bathtub so I could clean his face. I wet a washcloth with warm water and gently wiped the dried blood away. It broke my heart to see him like this. A pretty nasty gash looked raw and tender above his eyebrow. I rummaged through the medicine cabinet and found some Band-Aids and Neosporin.

I rubbed the antibiotic ointment on his wound and covered it with the bandage.

"That should help prevent infection," I said, kneeling in front of him. "Can I get you anything? Tea? Water? An aspirin?"

"Shower with me."

I hesitated, not really in the mood for a steamy rendezvous at the moment.

"I need to feel you close, Amelia."

The vulnerability in his voice almost shattered me on the spot. Standing up, I turned on the nozzle. Alastair slowly removed his clothes. I watched him closely, noticing a large purple and yellow bruise had bloomed on and below his left ribcage. Hatred for the man who did this coursed through my veins.

"Hey," he murmured, tipping my chin up. "It looks worse than it is."

"This never shou—"

Silencing me with a kiss, he unbuttoned my capris and pushed them down. I let him finish undressing me and climbed into the shower. A heavy sigh deflated his lungs as he stood beneath the streaming warm water. I grabbed the shower pouf, lathering it up with almond scented body wash. Starting at his shoulders, I lightly scrubbed his skin leaving behind a trail of frothy bubbles. When I reached the bruised area, I used my hand and carefully moved the soap over his damaged ribs.

While I washed him, his breathing remained quick and ragged. I attempted to catch his eye a few times but they stayed closed. I covered every inch of him with almond scented suds.

"Want me to do your back too?"

His lids popped open, revealing tormented emerald irises. The visual left me breathless. Water cascaded over his shoulders, rinsing off the soap. He bent his head back, letting the water run over his face and hair. I reached for the shampoo almost as an instinct and squeezed some into the palm of my hand. Reaching up, I slid my fingers through his hair, working the shampoo into an effervescent foam. I massaged it into his scalp as he pressed his fingers into the small of my back. Resting his forehead to mine, he sighed.

"That feels good. Thank you."

I smiled, happy that he was finally relaxing. "I've been wanting to wash your hair for awhile."

"Why?"

"Just because."

A small grin curled his lips. "Direct and to the point as usual, Meyers."

I swiped a cluster of bubbles across his nose. "Rinse."

Stepping back under the showerhead, he washed off the remaining shampoo. I admired how his muscles contracted and relaxed with each movement. It was so easy to find beauty in everything he did.

"Your turn, kitten."

The deep, sensuous sound of his voice revved up my pulse. His eyes were no longer tortured or tormented. They were dark green pools of molten lava.

"My turn for what?"

Moving closer, he skimmed the lathered pouf over my shoulders and down to my breasts. He stopped there, deliberately rubbing the mesh fabric over my nipples. The sensation made my vision double.

"Do you like that?" he asked.

I think I nodded. I was only aware of how close his mouth was to mine and feeling his heated breath on me. He continued moving the pouf lower and lower, pausing at my lower abdomen.

"Tell me where to stop." His mouth still hovered over mine so I lightly bit his lower lip, mindful of where he'd been hurt. "Hmm," he hummed. "Feisty."

Sliding his tongue into my mouth, he kissed me with reckless abandon. I shoved my hands in his hair and pulled, hard. Moaning, he parted my legs with his right knee and brushed the pouf along my hypersensitive skin. Gasping, I broke our mouths apart and leaned my head against the wall.

"Stop there?" he asked.

"Keep going," I panted.

"Like this?" Dropping the pouf, he slipped two fingers inside me and pressed the heel of his hand to my clit.

"Yes," I groaned, yanking on his hair again. Steam from the hot water swirled and billowed around us. The sweet, messy edge of oblivion took over, clearing my mind of everything. All that mattered was him; his breathing, his touch, his skin on mine.

The rhythmic way he worked my body never ceased to amaze me. My left leg started to shake violently.

"Look at me. That's it, love. Let go."

Locked in a heated stare with him, I succumbed to an orgasm so intense I held onto his shoulders for dear life. He kissed and caressed me, whispering words of affection on my skin. He still had a feral look in his eyes, which reignited my need for him.

A sly grin spread across his face. "I need to do something about this look. Come with me."

Shutting off the water, I climbed out of the shower and followed him into my bedroom. He pinned me against the wall, holding my arms over my head. I wriggled, trying free myself.

"Not this time, kitten. I want you to surrender to me completely, like you almost did in the shower."

"But I want to touch you."

"I know. I want you to touch me but this is something you need to do. You always come so close to losing yourself. So close. There's still a part of you that's afraid."

I sucked in a breath, amazed at how deeply into my soul he could see.

"I lose myself in you constantly," he continued. "It's the greatest feeling in the world. I want you to feel that. I want you to put all your trust in me. I can see you, Amelia. I can see your doubts and fears, just as you see mine. Let yourself go. Give yourself to me completely."

Warmth spread out from my core to the rest of my body, filling me with anticipation. I relaxed, nodding. Keeping my arms pinned above my head, he locked me in a heated, passionate kiss. As a reflex, I moved my hands in an attempt to touch him. He tightened his grip on me, pressing his body into mine to prevent further movement. Instead of struggling against him, I surrendered. I released all of my trepidations, fears and anxieties, focusing on only thing; how good it felt to be cherished and loved by another.

"My Lia," he breathed, lowering my arms but keeping them in a firm grip. "I love you. Always."

Wilting from his words and velvet kisses, I slumped into the wall. All my muscles became heavy and useless as love and lust danced and swirled through me. He didn't even have to restrain me anymore if he chose not to. I was immobile, completely at his mercy.

I loved the way it made me feel. He now had sole custody over my heart and soul. The gleam in his eyes told me he knew I'd submitted to him. In one fluid motion, he possessed me, sliding in without hesitation. He lifted me, hooking my legs around his hips before pressing my body to the wall. Never breaking eye contact with him, I reveled in every methodical thrust and soft moan. I saw every emotion behind his mask. He'd never looked more beautiful or vulnerable.

As the intensity of his movements increased, his grasp on my arms loosened. Letting go, he placed his hands on either side of my head, flattening his body to mine.

"Touch me," he growled. "I can't go any longer without your hands on me."

His skin warmed immediately as I slid my hands along his lower back, pausing above the curve of his backside. Panting heavily into my neck, he filled me with feverish movements and unbridled passion. Only the sounds of my back hitting the wall and his moans echoed through the room.

My mind scrambled, delving into a chaotic mess as ecstasy tore through my body. I pulled his forehead to mine, and knotted my fingers in his hair. I watched him go to the edge as he swelled inside me. I watched as his eyes shed every barrier and stared into their clear green depths. I saw everything; his love, his need, his fear, his unapologetic animalistic urge.

I climaxed without warning, his name escaping my lips in a hoarse gasp.

My body went limp in his arms. I had enough presence of mind to be grateful he held me in a pretty tight embrace.

"You're smiling," he murmured on my lips.

"I should hope so."

"Kiss me?"

I obliged, cherishing the softness of his mouth on mine. "You okay, chief?" I asked, tracing my thumb along his jaw.

He nodded, lowering my legs to the floor. They were useless at the moment, barely stronger than elastic.

"You look a bit wobbly at the knees, love," he grinned, scooping me up. I squealed in delight as he carried me to the bed. I cuddled up closely to him on the mattress, inhaling his scent. Careful not to hurt him, I lightly touched the bruise on his ribs.

"I'm so sorry this happened to you."

"Don't be. You're worth it, Lia."

"He's not," I said bitterly. "I hate that you're hurt because of him."

"Hush," he whispered, stroking my hair. "I don't want to talk about that right now. I want to feel you. Hold you. Alright?"

I sighed. "Of course. I want that, too."

We entwined our arms and legs together, holding one another close. His rapid heartbeat slowed to a more normal pace the longer we stayed in this embrace. I couldn't love him any more than I did at this moment.

"Lia?"

"Hmm?"

"Will you fly home with me this weekend?"

I kissed his chest. "I want to."

"Come with me. We'll fly back here in a few weeks to take care of the flat and whatever else you have to do."

Shaking my head, I smiled. "So you want me to just quit my job and run away with you?"

"Yes."

"Well, when you put it like that, how can I say no?"

"I'm serious, Amelia," he said, tilting my chin up. "I want you with me. The sooner, the better."

"I know, I know. I told you I'd come with you but I can't just up and leave."

"Why not?"

"I have responsibilities, Holden. I'd like to give my notice at work so I don't burn any bridges."

He regarded me with interest. I could see the cogs turning in his head. "One week. How's that? You'll fly out in one week."

"Patience isn't your strong point, is it?"

"Not when I want something," he smirked.

"You know the saying 'good things come to those who wait,' right?"

"Never was a big fan of it."

I laughed loudly, ruffling his hair. "You've waited this long for me. I don't think another week will kill you."

"Fair enough. But I have one more request."

"Jesus," I muttered. "What now?"

"Marry me."

The echo of his words floated through my bedroom. My vision went fuzzy. I just stared at him, not believing what I'd heard. He watched me, his expression growing increasingly amused by the second.

"I…are you…"

He kissed me so lovingly and gently that I turned into a useless pile of almond scented goo.

"Marry me, Lia."

I traced my thumb over his bruised eye and lip. "You know I can't ever say 'no' to you, Holden."

His brilliant smile lit up the bedroom, erasing any and all traces of the night's tension. "I know, Meyers, but that's not exactly a 'yes'."

Ruffling his hair again, I laughed. "Yes, I'll marry you." Dizzying joy filled every part of me. I'd never felt so happy or so hopeful.

"My angel," he whispered, wrapping himself around me like a vine. I nestled into the softness and warmth of his embrace and closed my eyes.

CHAPTER TWENTY-TWO

Staying home from work was one of the best decisions I'd made all week. Well, aside from saying yes to Alastair's impromptu marriage proposal. He'd gone back to the hotel to gather some clothes and finish up a few things at work. His spirits were much higher than they'd been in awhile. I'd even heard him whistling in the shower.

Since I was home, I decided to call my mother and lower the boom about moving to Scotland.

"Amelia Grace, I thought you'd fallen off the planet," she exclaimed in her chirpy voice.

"Nope. Just been doing the usual. Did you and Dad enjoy the rest of your vacation?"

She sighed. "I don't know how you people can stand living in that constant heat. Miami was an oven. Your father loved it though. He's looking into buying a small condo on the beach so we can spend the winters there. I'm assuming it's not as hot in January."

"I thought you guys liked winter. You're always sending me pictures of the snow in the backyard."

"We're too old to shovel it anymore. At least that's what your father says. I told him to hire someone but he doesn't want to."

"Well, Miami is the place to be then."

"Yes, dear," she laughed. "We'll also be close enough to bother you on the weekends."

Here we go.

"Uh, about that. I have to talk to you about something."

"Is everything okay?" Her tone sharpened.

"Everything's fine, stop panicking. Listen, Alastair and I have been talking—"

"Your father can't stop going on and on about him," she interrupted. "He thinks he's so intelligent and nice. I just wish he wasn't so shy."

"Oh my God, Ma," I said loudly. "He's not shy. He's just a little guarded, that's all."

"You have a big personality, Lia. He needs to be able to keep up with you."

I grew more exasperated by the second. "What are you talking about? He keeps up with me just fine."

"It must be because he's British. They're so reserved, you know."

"Mom, I have no idea what you're babbling about," I laughed incredulously. "Andrew is English, too. Remember? He's louder than all of us put together."

"I suppose. So what is it you wanted to tell me?"

"He asked me to move in with him and I said yes."

Silence dominated for about a minute.

"Is he buying a house in Orlando?"

"Nope."

More silence. I'd be willing to bet she was twisting the phone cord around her fingers. "So both my daughters will be living in the United Kingdom," she stated.

"Looks like it."

I knew, without question, she was nodding her head slowly and having an internal dialogue with herself.

"When are you leaving?"

"I'm not sure yet. Probably in a couple weeks."

"Tell him you both need to come up here first. Your father will want to see you and so will I."

"Okay," I grinned.

"I'm happy for you, Lia. I know this year has been rough since everything ended with Nathan. I'm glad you found someone special who adores you."

"Thanks, Mom." I heard her sniffling a little. "Listen, I should get going. I'll call you guys next week."

After we said our goodbyes I decided to go for a run. I sent Alastair a quick text letting him know I'd be at Cranes Roost Park for about an hour.

9:22am Enjoy your run, love. Let me know when you're back at the flat. x

I flirted with the idea of asking him why he wasn't sending Paxton to keep an eye on me as I drove to Altamonte Springs. I figured after what happened last night, he'd want to make sure Nathan didn't try anything. Then again, I didn't really know what happened. He hadn't told me yet so I just had to assume they'd fought and Nathan was now simmering with anger somewhere.

The park was empty except for a few women walking on the path, pushing their children in strollers. I turned up my music and ran along the edge of the lake. Running always managed to clear my head of everything and keep me more in tuned with myself.

I'd just rounded the bend when Nathan stepped in front of me, blocking my path. I skidded to a halt, startled.

"Your routines are too predictable, Lia."

His right eye was swollen and purple. I also noticed a yellowish bruise on his jaw. He crossed his arms and smirked.

"Your boyfriend likes to throw punches when nobody's looking."

"So do you," I glowered.

"I was defending myself. He came at me first."

Incensed, I ripped the earbuds out of my ears and glared at him. "What do you want? We're in a public place. If you make one move, I'll yell at the top of my lungs."

"That wouldn't be very smart. I'm only here to talk."

"We've done enough talking. All you do is speak in circles and veiled threats. I'm sick of it. This has—"

"Rachel Jameson is ready to go to print with nude photos of you. All I have to do is give her the green light."

The wind was knocked right out of me. "What are you talking about? I've never posed like that for anyone in my life."

"You like to keep your laptop in the bedroom, right?"

"Yeah. So?"

The oily smile that curved his lips sickened me. "It's not smart to leave it open without password protection. Someone could hack into it and control that little webcam at will."

I shook so violently I dropped my iPod. "Nobody uses it but me. I…"

"Tsk, tsk," he shook his head. "You're smarter than this, Lia. Think."

Thoughts raced through my shattered mind in a jumbled mess. I had no idea what he was talking about. I couldn't…*oh my God*.

"That's what you were doing in my apartment?" I blurted in horror. "That's why you snuck in." I nearly hyperventilated. "What the fuck is wrong with you?" I shouted. "Relationships end, Nathan. People move on. They don't terrorize their ex."

In a flash, he was closer, holding my arm. "You never gave me a chance to apologize. You shut me out and shacked up with the first guy who gave you a second look. You're *mine*, Lia. *I* loved you. *I* wanted you. You chose to turn your back on me."

"You pinned me to a wall and punched a hole in it inches from my face," I yelled. "There is not a strong enough apology in the world that I would accept for that. There is no future for me with a man capable of doing that. You did this to yourself by being a controlling, possessive asshole. You had me. I saw nothing but you. I did everything in my power to please you. And how did you treat me? You fucked anything in a skirt because you made it clear it was your right."

I took a breath. "You made me feel like an accessory who should be thankful that such a powerful, rich guy gave me the time of day. You didn't love me. You treated me like shit. And what did I do? I ignored it and tried like hell to *make* you love me. It's too late for that now, Nathan. I despise you. There is not one redeeming quality in you. You're a spoiled brat who doesn't know how to lose."

"I don't lose," he roared. "I never lose. Once these photos are released, I will be untouchable. Rachel doesn't know I'm the one who sent them. There's no evidence that any of it came from me."

"Alastair knows. You showed him last night."

"That prick doesn't know anything. I gave him the ones from the folder. He thinks he has the only copies." He tightened his hold on my arm. "This affects him too. You don't think there aren't any photos and video of the two of you having sex? He doesn't know about those. Break up with him or I give Rachel the go-ahead."

"Let go of me," I snapped, wrenching my arm away. "How dare you threaten him. I don't care what you want to do to me, leave him out of it."

"It's a package deal. All or nothing. Break up with him and the good people of Orlando, Glasgow, London and wherever the hell else won't be treated to your X-rated nights together. Stay with him and you'll both be humiliated."

I slapped him across the face. Hard. He looked stunned for a second, then recovered. "Never do that again."

"Fuck you."

"The power is in your hands, Lia. Your decision will affect more than one life. Think. Carefully. I'll expect to hear from you by this evening."

As soon as he was far enough away, I went under a cluster of trees and threw up. I hated him so much. I always knew he was vindictive but I never dreamed he'd go this far. The fact that he put so much effort into fabricating this sickened me.

I leaned heavily against the tree. A warm, sticky breeze coasted over my skin. For once I wished Paxton had been with me. That way I wouldn't have to figure out what to do. He'd have chased

Nathan off. Shaking my head, I sighed.

Nathan was so determined to put a wedge in my relationship nothing would have delayed him. I'd be faced with this dilemma no matter what. *Break up with Alastair? Never.*

On the flip side, I couldn't put him through another potential scandal. He already had enough trouble with Olivia threatening him all those years ago and was always so adamant about keeping me safe. There had to be a way for me to return the favor without hurting him in the process. My heart ached. Either way, I was screwed. At least if I went along with what Nathan wanted I'd eliminate the threat to go public with the photos. Alastair would understand, once I explained it all to him.

For now, breaking up with him was my only option and it killed me. I walked back to my car in a daze and drove home.

* * *

Sinking into the hot bath water relaxed me for a nanosecond. I wanted to be excited for dinner with Stephanie and Darren but couldn't muster up enough fake enthusiasm. They'd all know something was wrong the minute they looked at me. For once in my life, I wanted to be unreadable.

My cell phone rang, scaring the daylights out of me. I checked the caller ID before answering.

"Hey, Syd. What's up?"

"Just checking in to see how you were feeling. I miss you!"

"I miss you, too. Anything exciting happen there today?"

"Not really. Rachel Jameson called looking for you a few times but that's about it."

My stomach twisted in a knot. "Did she say what she wanted?"

"Something about following up with you on something y'all talked about last week. At least that's what she said. I told her you were out sick and would be back tomorrow."

"Okay, thanks."

"No problem. I hope you're feeling better. The newsroom is too boring without you."

Overwhelmed with emotion, I hung up and dropped the phone to the floor. Covering my face with my hands, I sank into the soapy water.

* * *

Trudging up the walkway to Stephanie's condo was like walking down one of those optical illusion hallways where it kept growing longer and longer. I needed to calm my anxieties. Counting to ten and taking cleansing breaths didn't help at all.

"There she is," Darren said cheerfully, escorting me inside. "You look gorgeous as usual."

An actual, genuine smile curved my mouth. Darren was such a sweetheart. I couldn't help but feel better in his presence.

"Thank you, handsome."

"Hey now," he grinned, tucking me into his side. "Where's your other half?"

"Still working. He'll meet us at the restaurant."

"That guy needs a vacation," Stephanie said as she waltzed into the room. "Oooh, you look pretty. I love that dress. Royal blue looks amazing on you."

"Thanks," I arched an eyebrow. "What's with all the compliments?"

"Just calling it like I see it. Ready to go?"

We piled into a taxi and chatted on the short drive to the restaurant. I felt completely detached from reality. As soon as we arrived at the restaurant and were seated I ordered a glass of wine.

"Oh, Lia, I sent in my first draft for the ultra lounge campaign. I forgot to show it to you. Remind me later."

"Sure. How do you think it came out?"

"It's okay for a first draft. After I emailed it I found about twenty things I would change. I'll have to wait and see what they say on Monday." Her eyes lit up. "Monday! Can you believe it?"

Seeing her so excited warmed my heart. "I can. This is going to be the start of so many great things for you."

"I know. I'm really happy. Plus, you'll be there soon. I honestly don't think life could be any better right now." She reached across the table and squeezed my hand. "I think it's all finally coming together, Lia. There's so much opportunity and possibility. It all just feels right, you know?"

I smiled and raised my glass. She was right in a way. Everything was finally coming together. I'd felt that exact way in New York. Sipping the wine, I resolved to put an end to Nathan's reign of terror and live the life I wanted with the man I loved.

"You look so serious," Darren mused, nudging my foot. "What's going on in that pretty head of yours?"

"MacCourty, if you can figure that out I'll give you a medal," Alastair responded as he approached the table. I immediately relaxed when he sat next to me and placed his hand on my leg. "Hello, love."

"My kingdom for the keys to a woman's mind," Darren joked.

"You don't want to know what goes on up here," Stephanie teased. "Ignorance is bliss."

"Is everyone ready to order?" A young man, no older than twenty, paused next to our table, pen and notepad ready. We told him what we wanted, deciding to split a few appetizers before our main courses arrived. Darren and Alastair chatted at length about their newly discovered mutual admiration for outdoor activities. I already knew Alastair played rugby occasionally on the weekends. What surprised me most was Darren's affinity for camping.

Stephanie paused mid-chew and stared at him. "Camping?"

"Yes, camping."

"Outside? In a tent? *Camping*, camping?"

"Is there another kind?" Darren laughed.

"Yeah. The kind where I'm in a hotel with running water," she countered.

"Ah, you'll change your tune. I already have something lined up for your birthday."

I thought Stephanie was going to pop a gasket. She looked panic stricken. I laughed uncontrollably.

"Darren, if you manage to get her to sleep outside you have to *promise* me you'll send pictures."

"You're supposed to be on my side, Amelia Grace," Stephanie grumbled.

"Oh, I am," I giggled. "I just think it would be hilarious to see you become one with nature."

"All the cool kids do it, Steph," Darren teased. "Broaden your horizons."

She gave him a look, rolled her eyes at me and turned to Alastair. "You've been suspiciously quiet during all this. What's your stance on camping?"

A mischievous grin played on his lips. "I prefer county fairs and aquariums."

"That doesn't help me," she complained with a smile. "You're as useless as those two." She turned to Darren and started chatting with him.

Snaking his arm around my waist, Alastair pressed a quick kiss to my temple. "You look beautiful."

"I should wear this color more often. I just got the trifecta of compliments."

He smiled, simultaneously making me melt and breaking my heart. I had to tell him about my incident at Crane's Roost Park before it was too late. I scanned his handsome face, noticing he'd removed the bandage above his eye. The wound looked like a small scratch. I impulsively reached up and touched it lightly.

"Feeling okay?" I asked.

He held my hand and kissed the palm. "Never better."

The server arrived with our main courses and all conversation halted for a couple minutes while we ate. Alastair kept his hand on my leg the entire time. I think he sensed something was off. No matter the reason, I liked feeling the comfort and warmth of his hand on me.

"When are you flying back to Glasgow, mate?" Darren asked.

"Saturday. I'm actually going to London first for a board meeting. I should be in Glasgow on Tuesday. Do you need help getting Stephanie sorted at your place?"

"My stuff doesn't arrive until next weekend. Feel free to partake in some manual labor then," she smiled.

"Tempting," he said dryly. "I might actually be back here collecting this lovely lady." He squeezed my knee and grinned.

"Shut up!" Stephanie squealed. "You're moving that soon? Why didn't you tell me?"

"We just talked about it last night," I answered. "You are literally the first to know."

She clasped her hands together and launched into a million ideas for a welcoming party. Her zest for life always added extra sparkle to any situation.

"This is going to be amazing," she gushed. "We'll combine parties. My thirtieth and your housewarming."

"Did someone buy a house?"

Every muscle in my body turned to steel upon hearing that voice. Alastair draped an arm over my shoulders protectively.

"Hope I'm not interrupting this cozy dinner," Nathan drawled. "I was at the bar and noticed you all sitting here."

Stephanie glared at him, seething under her breath. Darren watched cautiously.

"And why is it that you're here?" Alastair asked venomously.

"Enjoying dinner with some friends, *mate*. Not that it's any of your concern."

Alastair stood up slowly, adjusting his jacket. Nathan smirked, knowing nothing could happen in public.

"It's best if you go back to them, yes?"

"Take it easy, Holden." He lifted his hands in mock retreat. "It's a free country. I can say hello to whomever I want."

"Nathan," I hissed, looking up at him. "Not now."

He half smiled, smoothing down his tie. "You're right, Sparkle. I'll come by again later when there aren't so many eyes focused in this direction."

Shooting Alastair a smug look, he walked away. He'd been right about one thing. Most of the diners near our table had stopped what they were doing to catch a glimpse of the senator's son conversing with the British media mogul.

"What a jerk," Stephanie groused. "He has zero class. Zero."

My nerves didn't settle until Alastair sat next to me again. He placed his arm on my shoulders, brushing his fingers across the nape of my neck. "Are you okay, love?"

I nodded, thankful nothing escalated. "Yeah, I'm fine. Orlando's a small city. We're bound to cross paths every now and then."

"Not for much longer." He kissed my forehead before taking out his cell phone. He typed what I assumed was a text message and placed it back in his pocket.

Darren let out a low whistle. "That was a proper tense moment. You dated that guy?"

Stephanie slugged him in the arm. "Enough," she warned.

"Sorry," he winced. "Sorry, Lia."

I smiled at him sympathetically. "It's okay."

The server stopped at the table once more, asking if we wanted dessert. The general consensus was a resounding yes. The rest of our time at the restaurant passed without any further drama. Stephanie and Darren opted to take a taxi back to her condo. I went with Alastair and Paxton. Before we left, Alastair told me to wait by the car and walked off with Paxton. They appeared to engage in a strained conversation. I leaned against the SUV, wondering what on earth was going on now.

My cell phone beeped.

10:37pm Do it now or I give her the green light

CHAPTER TWENTY-THREE

I dropped the phone, covering my mouth with both hands. It broke in two on the sidewalk. *This isn't happening.*

"Lia." I heard Alastair call for me but couldn't move. His fast moving footsteps had him next to me in seconds. "What happened?"

"He…he wants me to…" I had no control over what I was saying. The streetlights turned fuzzy as a murky cloud settled around my head.

"He wants you to what?" he growled.

I looked him squarely in the eye, mesmerized by the vibrant green. "He's blackmailing me."

Anger ghosted across his face, but only for a moment. The walls were back up in no time. "That's not possible. I have everything."

"No you don't. He found me when I was jogging this morning. He has more. He sent them to Rachel and told me if I don't break up with you, he'll tell her to go public with everything."

"Paxton," he shouted. "Where is he?"

"Two blocks north. He's walking to the parking lot."

Alastair took off like a bullet shot from a pistol.

"Dammit," I seethed, running after him. I vaguely heard Paxton calling after me as I sprinted down the sidewalk. I saw Nathan walking, looking down, probably at his cell phone. A split second later, Alastair grabbed the back of his shirt and yanked him into a nearby alley.

"Shit," I panted, turning on the speed. I reached the alley in time to see Nathan get thrown against a brick wall.

"I told you to stay away from her," Alastair raged.

"Alastair, stop," I yelled, watching in horror as he balled his fist and hit Nathan right in the nose. Blood spurted everywhere.

He grabbed Nathan by his neck and held him against the wall. "Go to Paxton, Lia. You shouldn't be here."

"I will not let you fight over this. He's not worth it."

Nathan looked at me, his face covered in blood. "This is what you want for a boyfriend and lover? He's nothing but a street rat. You've seen it for yourself now."

Heavy footsteps cascaded down the alley. Paxton brushed by me and muscled Nathan to the ground, securing zip ties around his wrists. He pulled him up by one arm and shoved him against a dumpster.

"You're all going down for this," he growled. "My father is a United States senator. He has more influence and power than you, you little British shit."

"We'll see about that," Alastair smirked. "Lia, call that reporter. She may have a story after all."

"What do you mean?"

"Tell her the anonymous emails and photos are all from the great senator's son. Tell her he used them to blackmail you and humiliate you because you dumped his sorry ass. Tell her everything. Drag the Greyson name through the mud."

"You wouldn't dare," Nathan glared at me.

I thought about all the shit he'd put me through over the past two years. All the nights he made me feel worthless and all the times I ignored those feelings because I thought having his love was the most important thing in the world. Looking at him now, bloody, restrained and trapped in an alley, I felt vindicated. It was his turn to feel like a second rate citizen, even if none of this ever came to light.

A small part of me wished he'd stop behaving like such a spoiled brat. I highly doubted that would ever happen.

Not bothered by his piercing stare, I held it and smiled. "This is the kind of story we salivate over in the newsroom. Blackmail. Sex. Heartbreak. And a high-profile person at the center of it all. You did say you wanted to give me an exclusive interview that had to do with some damaging information coming to light about a prominent figure. How clairvoyant you are."

"Lia, don't."

"Why not?"

"You're not that kind of person. You don't have a malicious bone in your body."

I took a step toward Nathan and was immediately blocked by Alastair. "What are you doing, love?"

"I have to do this. Trust me." Placing my hands on his chest, I gazed into his eyes. "He's tied up. He can't touch me."

Alastair locked his jaw in determination. "I'll be there in two steps if he so much as breathes on you."

I kissed the corner of his mouth and made my way to Nathan. He may have looked beaten on the outside but I knew deep down he was miles away from surrender.

We stared at one another for what felt like ages. His sapphire eyes never left mine.

"Do you remember what you said to me on our six month anniversary when you dropped me off at my apartment?" I asked.

Caught off guard by my question, his expression faltered. "Why do you care?" he snapped.

"Do you remember?" I repeated.

"Yeah."

I lifted an eyebrow, waiting for him to continue. Sighing harshly, he grimaced.

"What is the point in this, Lia? You won. Your fucking knight of the round table will make the call if you don't."

I heard Alastair mutter a string of profanities under his breath.

"Nobody is making any phone calls just yet, Nathan," I said. "Answer my question."

Leaning his head back, he closed his eyes. When he looked at me again the harshness in his expression was gone.

"I told you how refreshing it was to date a girl who didn't care who my dad was and who was just as comfortable hanging out wearing a baseball cap at a theme park as she was dressed up for a state dinner." He paused. "I also asked how it was possible that you managed to out-sparkle every star in the sky."

Heavy silence filled the alley. I couldn't hear Alastair but I felt his intense stare burning through the back of my head.

"What changed, Nathan? Because not too long after that you turned into this…this jealous, possessive creature."

The stark contrast between Nathan's open-book demeanor and Alastair's stony façade was never more prevalent than in this moment. While my ex-boyfriend scowled and shook his head, I turned to see Alastair staring at us, expressionless.

Focusing my attention back to Nathan, I saw I wasn't going to get an answer. If anything, he looked annoyed.

"Are we done here, Sparkle?"

Narrowing my eyes, I glared at him. "Don't call me that." I turned to Alastair. "May I use your phone?"

"Yes."

Fortunately, I knew Rachel's number by heart thanks to all the times she'd called me over the past month. I waited patiently as it rang.

"Rachel Jameson."

"Hi, Rachel. It's Lia Meyers. I hope I'm not calling you too late."

"Oh. No, not at all. I heard you were sick. Are you feeling better?'

"Much better, thank you. Listen, I have a tip that you've received some compromising photos of my boyfriend and me. Is that true?"

"Uh, yeah." She sounded surprised.

"What if I were to tell you I know who sent them to you? And that this person will make an even better story than the photos?"

"You have my attention."

Nathan's face turned white as a ghost.

I smiled. "Perfect. Do you have time to talk now?"

* * *

"So you'll delete everything and make sure all traces are erased for good?" I asked, staring at the file of photos on Rachel's desktop.

"Sure."

"Do it now."

"I'm not doing anything until you tell me who's behind all of it. I've been dealing with this crap for a month. If you have a better story, I want it."

"That's not how this works, Rachel. I want to be completely certain that none of these photos will ever get out. Delete them. Empty the trash file once you've deleted them and give me any flash drives or memory sticks or whatever you might have backed them up on."

"Jesus," she muttered, deleting the files. I watched her like a hawk, making sure she didn't miss one photo. After I had the flash drives in hand –she'd backed-up on three separate drives- I held up my end of the bargain and told her to get in touch with Nathan.

"Is *he* the one who did all of this?" she asked, eyes gleaming.

"Just call him."

* * *

I climbed into the Mercedes, exhausted but satisfied. Alastair cupped his hand behind my neck and pulled me in for a kiss.

"How did it go?"

"Better than I expected. I made her delete all the files with us on it and give me any hard copies."

"Is she going to run the story about Nathan?"

"I don't know. I told her to call him. She also wants to get a comment from Senator Greyson. I feel bad dragging him into it. He was always good to me."

"I have a feeling that story will never see the light of day." He scowled.

"It's over for now. He won't do anything."

"Don't be so sure of that. People like Nathan have a long vindictive streak."

I shivered, hoping he was wrong. "Was it this stressful with Olivia?"

The muscles tightened in his jaw. "It was worse, love."

I laced my fingers with his, being mindful not to squeeze too hard. He'd bruised his hand punching Nathan. "When you're ready, you can tell me about it, you know."

We rode in silence back to Stephanie's condo.

"I dropped my cell phone in front of the restaurant. I think it broke," I said as we walked up the brick path.

"We'll get you a new one, kitten," he grinned, ringing the bell.

"There you are," Stephanie chirped when she opened the door. "I've been calling you for the past hour. Where the hell…" She paused, staring at both of us. Alastair looked like he'd just rolled out of bed thanks to the brief tussle in the alley. I must have been smiling without realizing it because she blushed and shook her head. "Never mind, lovebirds. Get your butts in here."

Alastair lifted an eyebrow and looked at me. "She thinks we had a quick shag, doesn't she?"

"Yep."

"Should we tell her?"

"Not tonight. Let her have this moment before she leaves."

"Well said, love," he smiled. "Now about that quick shag…"

"Stop it," I shoved him.

Catching me by the waist, he pressed his lips to mine. "Don't fight the inevitable."

"I wouldn't dream of it."

"Get a room, you two. I'd offer one of mine but I don't have any beds anymore," Stephanie called out from the living room.

"True that," Darren said. "My back is killing me from sleeping on the floor."

"Why don't you have an air mattress?" I asked, sitting against the wall.

"I do. It's in a box on a plane en route to Glasgow. I should have timed this better."

"What time is your flight tomorrow?" Alastair asked.

"Seven-thirty in the morning. We should land around nine, local time tomorrow night." She disappeared into the kitchen briefly, returning with a stack of paper cups and a bottle of champagne. "I know it's not very classy but I wanted us all to have a final toast in my condo."

"I'll take care of the bottle," Darren grinned, popping the cork with ease. He poured a generous amount into the cups and passed them around so we each had one.

Stephanie sat up on her knees, tears welling in her eyes. "I've lived in this place for eight years. It's seen a lot of drama and even more good times. I think it's safe to say it didn't start feeling like a home until I met this one over here." She looked at me. "We may not share any family or DNA or anything like that but you are the sister I always wanted. You've been there to make me laugh, pick me up off the bathroom floor after too many margaritas, talk me off a ledge when a boy was being stupid and just to enjoy life with. Moving to Glasgow and taking this job might be a dream come true but I dreaded the thought of leaving you. Fortunately, you have no ability to walk when you're jet lagged, so as fate would have it, you fell into this guy."

I laughed, feeling my cheeks heat up slightly.

"And now," she continued, "you're moving to Glasgow, too. I don't have to say goodbye to my best friend and that makes me the luckiest person on earth. For every memory we made here, I hope we make a million more in our new home. I love you, Lia

Meyers. Thank you for being an awesome human being and an even better friend." She raised her cup, tears streaming down her cheeks. "To what's next."

I sat up on my knees and knocked our cups together. "My turn." Her eyes widened.

"About five years ago, I was working an event at City Walk and started talking to this really cool chick with fire engine red hair."

"Oh my God," she groaned. "You remembered that?"

"Yes. It was hideous."

"You told me that, too. But only after we'd become friends."

"Can I continue?"

"Go on."

"Anyway, we hit it off once we found out we both shared a mutual love for shoes that were too expensive and shots that were too strong. Back home, I'm the older sister. I look out for Dayna and play the role of protector. But you, Stephanie Ann, took me under your wing and adopted me as *your* little sister. Granted, we're only two years apart but you took your role very seriously. Though sometimes it looked more like I was the responsible one and you were the little troublemaker."

"Cheers to that," Darren laughed.

"No comments from the peanut gallery," she warned.

I sighed, fighting back the lump forming in my throat. "It wasn't until this year that I really understood what having you in my life meant. You watched me cry, you listened to me try and rationalize something that wasn't worth saving but most importantly you always had my back. There are not enough words in the English language to thank you for all you've done. I am so happy to see you realizing your dreams. You've wanted an opportunity like this since I've known you. The thought of saying goodbye to you tore me up inside. I know it's just a plane ride away but it wouldn't have been the same. Like you said, as fate would have it, I made an ass of myself and almost knocked this guy over." I grinned at Alastair and turned back to Stephanie. "Thank *you* for being the absolute best friend and surrogate sister anyone could possibly ask for. We tore up Orlando, let's go make our mark in Glasgow." I raised my cup. "To what's next."

* * *

I finished brushing my teeth and slipped on a black and white polka dotted cotton nightdress.

"That's cute," Alastair observed as I walked into the room.

"This?"

"Yes, that. Now come here so I can take it off you."

"Bossy, much?"

I kept my eyes on him as I climbed onto the bed. He was stretched out on his back, hands tucked under his head. The purple bruise near his ribcage stood out against his fair skin. My urge to comfort him was strong. I briefly wondered if this was how he felt after Nathan bruised my arm at the Black and White Ball. Shrugging off the thought of my ex, I curled up next to the only man who mattered.

"You're very lucky to have a friend like Stephanie," he said quietly. I lifted my head, stunned to see how sad he looked.

"What's on your mind, chief?"

He sighed, caressing my back. "I've often wondered how different my life would be if I'd listened to my aunt and uncle while growing up. I was so bitter and disgusted with myself. I didn't want to be bothered with cultivating relationships. It all seemed so useless. Devoting so much time and energy into another person only to have them leave without warning…I didn't want it. They sent me to therapy but after I turned thirteen I stopped going. No doctor in the world could convince me I didn't kill my sister and parents." He gazed at me with wide eyes. "Seeing you and Stephanie tonight and hearing what you both said made me wonder how different everything could have been if I'd just opened my eyes and let someone in."

"Dwelling on your past mistakes won't change them. Learning from them will enrich you and make you see the world differently."

"That's quite poetic, love. Maybe you do have a way with words after all."

I smirked. "Smart ass."

"Cheeky."

"Numpty."

He had me pinned on my back and at the mercy of his hands within seconds. He tickled me fast and hard, not easing up even when I begged him to stop. Gasping for air, I managed to wriggle free and sat up.

"Sneaky," I panted. "No surprise for you."

His eyebrows arched. "Surprise?"

"Yeah, I bought you something but now I'm not sure I want you to have it."

"Oh, now Lia," he said, lowering his voice. The full-bodied sound sent a ripple of pleasure through me.

I slid off the bed and went to my dresser. The laptop was still sitting there. I'd unplugged it and closed it. I planned to toss it in the dumpster in the morning. Buying a new one won't break the bank too much. Reaching for the box that held his cufflinks, I smiled. I also grabbed another package that was wrapped in emerald green wrapping paper.

"Two presents?" he asked, his excitement and curiosity making him look much younger than his age.

"Yup."

"Which one should I open first?"

"Um, the little one."

He eyed me while opening the box. Looking down, he grinned. "Cufflinks?"

"Do you like them?"

"Yes, kitten, I do. I'll wear them to work tomorrow." He studied them closer. "'ARH', huh? You know you're the only one who ever uses my middle name."

"Am I, Alastair Reid?"

He scrunched his nose. "I only like it because your mouth is saying it. I never use it otherwise."

"Anyway," I rolled my eyes, "open the other box."

He picked it up and shook it.

"Don't do that." I exclaimed.

"Ah-ha, it's fragile."

"Really? That was necessary?"

His throaty laughed filled the room and made my soul soar. I loved the sound of it. He let out a small gasp after unwrapping the gift.

"I remember you said you liked it when you first came here. I thought you could put it on your desk at work or in your home office."

Tracing his fingers along the edge of the picture frame, he smiled. I watched his eyes move slowly over the photo of me from last summer at Sydney's lake house. It had been a happy moment in an otherwise tumultuous year. I can still remember giggling as I put on the ridiculously large sunhat and posed on the sailboat in my bathing suit and cover up.

"I love this picture of you. It captures your smile and spirit so perfectly. You look just like a rose in bloom."

"I, um," my lip trembled, "I can't tell you how much I appreciate all you've done for me. I know—"

Placing the frame on the nightstand, he lunged at me, kissing me with feverish intensity. Our lips glided together, seeking out the other with need, want and love. He rolled me onto the bed, taking command, greedily feeling his way down my body. I wanted him to be wild and untamed. I wanted him raw and impassioned.

Breaking our mouths apart, he captivated me with his molten stare. I was exactly where I was meant to be; caught in his magnetic sphere.

"You make me feel so loved," he whispered hoarsely.

I shoved my hands in his hair, pulling his forehead to mine.

"Marry me, Alastair."

The unguarded, shy smile I adored bloomed on his lips. "I've already asked you."

"I know. Now I'm asking you. Marry me."

He stared at me with such fervor I thought his gaze might burn through my skull. Swallowing hard, he hovered his mouth over mine. "Yes, love."

I kissed him and smiled at the same time. I was so happy I couldn't contain my joy.

"You're the best thing that's ever happened to me, Alastair Holden."

"I thought that was my line."

"I stole it."

He nuzzled into my neck, smiling against my skin. "You stole my heart, Lia." Rolling off me and onto the bed, he kept his eyes downcast. The last thing I wanted was for him to retreat behind the mask. I pressed my forehead to his, moved by the sound of his soft moan. We'd been through so much, fought through so many obstacles and still managed to find solace in each other's arms. I couldn't imagine a scenario where I wasn't with him. He was firmly embedded in my soul.

I closed my eyes, feeling protected in his arms. Sighing, he pulled me closer. We stayed this way until we both drifted to sleep.

* * *

Pre-dawn shadows stretched across the walls, spurred on by the muted light outside. Soft, measured breathing gently broke through the silent room. I propped up my head, watching Alastair sleep in peace. His youthful face, scruffy and unshaven, looked angelic. Waking up next to him was a gift I appreciated to the fullest. Seeing him this way, so vulnerable and laid bare filled me with such elation it hurt.

Heat blossomed in my stomach and spread through me. He

stirred, seeming to sense my heightened exhilaration. Even in slumber I could feel the want and need radiating off his body, mingling with my own.

"Good morning, my love," he murmured, pressing his fingers into the flesh of my lower back. Shedding off the remnants of sleep, a drowsy smile pulled at his mouth. "You're up early."

"Did I wake you?"

He left a trail of kisses along my collarbone. "Not really. Sleep can wait. I only have you for a little while before going to work."

"Take the day off."

"I wish I could." He smirked. "When you're living with me this won't be such a problem."

"We still have to go to work," I laughed.

"Logic be damned."

I studied his face, happy to see the markings from the fight were fading away.

"Lia."

"Hmm?'

"Before you fell asleep last night I wanted to tell you something."

"What is it?"

Wetting his lips, he fixed a dark stare on me. "You amaze me. I wake up every day thankful to have found you. I may not know how to show it or how to say it all the time but," he paused, considering his words, "taking a chance on you has been the smartest thing I've ever done."

"Ditto, love," I said.

"To what's next," he whispered.

The story continues in the final installment of the trilogy

Effortless

Coming Soon